I0740009

DARK ONE'S MISTRESS

Dark One's Trilogy - Book One

Aldrea Alien

Thardrandian Publications

ISBN: 0992264537
ISBN-13: 978-0992264536

www.aldreaalien.com

To Jason, my fiancé, for listening to my rants and understanding that sometimes, writing felt more important than sleep.
Love you.

CHAPTER ONE

"**C**larabelle!" Her mother's manly bellow scattered the pigeons resting atop the roofs and sent the nearby cats into hissing fits as they scampered for cover.

Clara halted on the edge of the street, her face burning as the echo continued. All around her, men and women paused in their daily business. The street gained an eerie silence. In the past, she'd heard worldlier folk boast such deathly quiet could only be heard here in Everdark.

Then someone coughed, another person sneezed, and the sounds flooded back—the hum of talk, the clink of coins. A few amongst the crowd stared at her, the young woman in question, but mostly, the irate bellowing seemed to be forgotten.

She huffed, her breath faintly misting as it passed through her lips. *Why does she have to yell like that?* She contented herself with a roll of her eyes, wishing the heat in her cheeks would fade. It wasn't as if she was some small child. She knew her duties well. Knew the streets even better.

She shuffled her burden: bread, half a wheel of cheese, a skin of goat's milk and a tiny, dog-eared book on the world beyond. The last was for herself, literally titled *The World Beyond*. Beyond what, she didn't know, but it sounded intriguing.

She knew concern hadn't driven her mother's voice. Not

concern for Clara, anyhow. She'd taken too long, pure and simple. It wasn't *her* fault the baker's son had gone missing, was it now? She'd tried her best to hasten things along, but she couldn't help his absence delaying her return. *She'll find some way to blame it on me.*

Her mother would have expected Clara to come running back too. *Oh yes, my burden is ever so light.* And if she fell and ruined everything she carried? Why, she'd be treated to one of her mother's clips over the ear.

Or worse, she could twist her ankle on the uneven stones that dared to be called a road. *Nature could've made a better surface than this.* She could've sworn she'd heard her mother saying they were repairing the roads.

Or had she meant the Road?

Her gaze lifted to the shadowy bulk of the Citadel, perched atop Mount Winding. In the morning light, she could just make out the three towers—although she'd been told there were actually six—rising like the points of a crown. On a clear night, when the people living within the Citadel's walls lit all the torches, the fortress resembled a mask with a giant, shadowy maw and horrible, glowing eyes.

Clara staggered, the ground underfoot feeling a lot softer than it should have. A yowl at her feet revealed it to be one of the braver cats. "Scat, you flea-ridden pest!" Watching the tawny animal streak off into the shadows, she heard a soft, slightly wet, thud. *Oh no.* What had she lost?

She patted the bundle. Bread, cheese... *My book!* She searched her wares again for the tiny tome, stamping her foot when she didn't immediately find it.

Her toe landed on something small and a little spongy. Wincing, she glanced down past her arms and caught sight of the dark edge of what her gut told her must be the book's spine. Further juggling of her load allowed her to see the soggy filth it had landed in. *Blast*! It had cost her a whole copper. Her mother was going to thrash her for wasting money.

"Out of the way!" a man cried, his voice cutting through the square's natural chatter. The clop of hooves and the rattle of wheels on cobblestone fast filled the sudden silence as men and women dashed to either side of the street.

Horses? Not many around here bothered with the beasts. Clara skittered towards the road edge, backing into a pole belonging to one of the many stalls lining the streets. Her burdens slid in her arms. She drew them closer, determined not to lose any more.

A black-lacquered carriage rolled by, pulled by two equally black horses and with darkly-garbed men clinging to the handholds at the back. Emblazoned on the doors, in blood red and highlighted with gold, was the Great Lord's symbol. It was meant to resemble a fire. She supposed it did, in an over-stylised fashion. Certainly more likely to be fire if it could be said to look like anything at all. Either way, it didn't stop the emblem from being a heinous thing, matching the Citadel in taste.

She shivered at the sudden coolness in the air. Without looking, she knew she wasn't the only one watching the carriage's passage. She wouldn't be surprised if all those minds were thinking the same thought. *Why is it here?* The Great Lords never came to Everdark and, although the village sat on the Citadel's doorstep, they rarely sent their servants.

Clara slunk further back into the shadow of the awning. Her mother hadn't been much older than Clara was now the last time a Great Lord had died and carriages had brought in the news of their current lord's succession.

At last, the carriage trundled out of sight, leaving only the hollow clatter of the horses' hooves on the cobbles.

A whisper crept into the crowd, growing louder with each set of ears it reached. Clara pushed her way back out into the street as the gossip neared her, her ears straining to hear their words despite all attempts to block out the noise.

"No, no. It's true, I swear," one man said to a nearby trio of villagers. "They's come for the women."

She shook her head and shuffled past the people. Street gossip, her mother often said, wasn't something one could take seriously and only a fool acted on gossip alone. But still… It *had* been several decades since the last succession. Such a sighting could grease the wheels of rumour for a week or two.

"Dead?" gasped a woman from one of the bigger groups. "Our Great Lord has been slain?"

Clara hesitated and found herself jostled closer as others pushed in to hear. Trying to get free only served in shoving her closer to the front of the crowd and further from where she needed to go. An elbow nudged her in the ribs, jigging her burden. Gritting her teeth, she clutched her wares to her chest and sought for a way home. She'd soon lose everything if she didn't win free from this press of bodies.

" 'Swat I 'eard," another man answered. Perched atop an overturned crate, he wiped a sleeve across his nose with a sickening slurp. "Came in before sunrise, that lot did. Seems the old Great Lord has gone and got 'imself killed out near Ne'ermore way."

A chorus of jeers went up, booming in her ears. Those standing behind Clara jostled her further forward. *The Great Lord has been slain*? It couldn't be true. No one had the power to kill someone as mighty as the man who ruled them. He was invincible.

The man shook his fist at the front arc of people, of which she was now one. "I bet anyone of yer a fistful o' coppers that 'is youngin'll be sniffin' round 'ere soon enough. He'll be after strong blood." He thumped his bare chest, disturbing a layer of dirt. "Could take any of 'em. Could take ye. Or ye." A finger jabbed out at the crowd, picking out would-be targets. The wizened arm swung her way. "Or *ye*."

Shaking her head, she shrank back from the man. Her foot, seeking a level patch in the street, trod on an unexpected lump in the cobblestones.

"Watch where you're stepping it!"

"Sorry," Clara mumbled as she shoved her way through

the throng. The mob thinned fast as she neared her street. The man hadn't been pointing at her. *And the Great Lord isn't dead.* Surely, if he truly *was*, it would be the town's criers who bellowed the official proclamation, not some near-toothless old man.

With the only sound to be had coming from the crowd at her back, Clara hummed to herself as she made her way home, the noise filling the silence and working towards soothing her nerves. The man was wrong. Would the carriage not have stopped if they were collecting young women? Surely the driver must have been taking a quick route to wherever it needed to be.

Absent of its usual inhabitants, the street reminded her of the first morning, some years ago now, when she'd set out alone into a fog-shrouded day. Although she could see the way ahead clearly enough today, it seemed no less surreal. The sun had yet to finish its task of warming the houses and spill down to chase the damp from the cobbles.

She passed the cobbler's shop, vacant apart from a few dusty pairs of shoes, and slowed. Peering at the grubby window, a smile came to her lips as she admired the way her skirts swung with each step. Simple brown linen. Exactly what she'd wanted. Yet it'd still taken months to convince her mother to make it.

No doubt her mother relented only because her seventeenth year loomed. Even so, it had taken weeks after the day celebrating her birth before her mother had gotten around to finishing the whole outfit. Clara let her gaze travel up. Yes, it did much to make her hair seem a less vibrant red. Reason enough to never stop wearing this dress until it fell apart.

Allowing herself a little, girlish giggle, she carried on by the shops and homes. The hushed pad of her footsteps gave way to the sounds of the village. She wiggled her toes, feeling the stones through the soles. Perhaps she could convince her mother to buy her some new shoes next year.

Hovering briefly on the corner of her vision sat the form

of a cat before it scuttled off across the eaves. Down on the road, another slinky beast swiped at a dog in passing. The mutt, scrawny and half bald from neglect, let out a whimper as it cringed under the remains of a stall.

Hearty scuffling came from the alley on her left, no doubt the product of a hungry dog. Her gaze lingered at the alleyway's dark opening. She'd heard of other places where muggers roamed the streets, assaulting people at will then being dragged off to whatever punishment awaited them.

Nothing so exciting happened in Everdark. At least, not with the same criminal. There'd be whispers of those from afar avoiding the lord's men for days before they got caught. But not here. Not for long.

The snort of a horse brought her attention back to the street ahead. Where did it come from? Naught barred her way to the corner where her home sat. Certainly no horses. Carts rarely took this route through the village since the streets were only wide enough to allow one through and there was little need of them as transport for either people or goods.

Thoughts of the black carriage invaded her mind, followed by the old man's words.

Shrugging off the chill in her spine, Clara peered around the corner. Naught to be seen except the way home. *Silly girl*. She chuckled and resettled her burden. Just a little further down this end of the road and she'd be off the streets and away from the rumours. Even if their new lord was, in truth, sniffing about for whatever reason, he wouldn't be doing it in the poorer quarters. And he'd be after women like Brenna Goodheart, the mayor's spoilt harlot of a daughter.

Yes, she'd be the sort of woman any lord would fancy. Not someone like her with a seamstress for a mother. Her boot skittered a pebble across the cobblestones. Not to say she'd any desire to be taken from family and home. Still, it would've been nice to get a peek at the inside of the Citadel. If only so she could say she'd seen it.

A hoof scraped the ground behind her, the sound akin to

the sharpening of a knife.

Clara froze, her heart thudding. Taking a deep breath, she stared at the empty road stretching ahead. She could even make out the doorway to home. *Mind your own business*, she reminded herself. She took a shaky step forward, steadfastly refusing to look behind her.

"You there!"

Unable to resist the cry, she whirled about to face them. The carriage, its black panels naught but a darker patch within the shadows, stood on the other side of the junction. One of the horses stamped a shaggy foreleg, the other bobbed its head as if in reply. How she hated the beasts. Unlike the dogs and cats she was more familiar with, horses always seemed to have a superior glint in their eyes, as if they were secretly laughing at everyone.

The driver gently pulled on the reins, stilling the creatures. He leant forward in his seat. Piggish eyes, dark like little coals, peered down at her. His lips twisted into a sneer. "She'll do."

Clara didn't fancy waiting to find out why she'd do and what for. Dumping her burden, she ran down the street, racing for the shadowed doorway leading to safety.

The clatter of hooves followed her. Black horseflesh ran alongside her, then fast pulled ahead to let the carriage trundle even with her.

She glanced at the shut doors and grimy windows of houses flanking her other side, madly searching for a closer haven. Sudden movement on the edge of her vision drew her attention back to her pursuers. She caught only the briefest flash of a horse sliding to a halt right in her path before crashing into the beast, forcing the air from her lungs.

Shaking and fighting to regain her breath, she clung to the horse's harness, the heavy strap under her touch strangely soft and firm at the same time. This couldn't be happening. Everdark had always been safe! She pushed off the barrelled body, gasping as her chest ached anew.

Hands grabbed her, their fingers digging into her arms.

They hauled her back from the horse.

A scream ripped up through her throat, exploding out her mouth to echo down the street. Her boot heels scraped against the cobbles. They lifted her clear of the road. She struggled to break free of their grip, howling her frustration when the hands stayed fast.

Tears threatened to blind her. She blinked hard, shaking her head in an attempt to free them. This might not be the iron carriage, set to take criminals to their doom, but that didn't mean she wouldn't suffer a different fate.

Her captors, strangely silent in their movements, brought her about to face the carriage. The driver still sat atop the vehicle. A third man stood near the door, holding it open in a mockery of the mayor's footmen.

Anger, writhing hot and heavy in her veins, fast over-rode her fear. She arched her back, fighting to regain possession of at least an arm. Her foot lashed out. The toe connected, eliciting a grunt from one of the men. Where was the watch? Her cries should have brought them to her aid. Why weren't they stopping this?

Clara glared up at the man holding the door, a sliver of fear stabbing her heart at the look in his eyes. So flat and dead, like a week-old fish.

They halted before the tiny steps. There, the men flanking her finally released their grip, plonking her back onto the street. One of them shoved her closer to the lacquered panels.

Not wishing to suffer being shoved inside the carriage, she ascended the steps unaided, jumping as the door slammed shut. A faint click spoke of a lock slipping into place.

Clara felt her way to one of the seats, eyes straining to see in the scant light filtering through the heavily curtained windows. The carriage lurched forward as she went to sit, upsetting her balance and slamming her into the thin suggestion of a cushion.

She leant against the wall, bracing herself in the hopes

it would help lessen the horrid swaying. Her hand rose to pull back the curtain, hesitating upon hearing the rustle of loose fabric coming from the other side of what suddenly felt like a far smaller space.

Her heart pounding anew, she peered into the gloom. Naught but a darker shape could be seen against the slate grey of the interior. The other woman scrunched further into her seat. Silent. As if fearful of being discovered.

Clara mimicked the action, hoping whatever was to become of them would not echo the horrors she'd heard about the past Great Lords. *Rumour's only gossip*, she reminded herself. *And only a fool acts on gossip*. But all rumours had a vein of truth somewhere.

She surely wished she knew what bits to believe.

Chapter Two

The carriage's swaying came to a neck-jerking halt. A dull scratching vibrated through the panel behind her. Something under her feet squeaked as the carriage rocked. Then there were more thuds and scrapes, this time at the door.

The lock clicked.

Clara straightened in her seat. It seemed far too quiet beyond the confines of the carriage for the watch to have intervened. Did it mean they'd arrived at their destination already? She could've sworn they hadn't travelled far enough to have reached the Citadel. Maybe she could use this pause to escape.

Bracing herself, she edged closer to the door and her possible freedom.

The door swung open, slamming into the carriage. Sunlight flooded the interior.

Clara threw up her hand, surprised her eyes had adjusted to the darkness after such a short time. Blinking away the afterimage, she caught a flash of flaxen hair and dark red skirts on the person sitting hunched in the opposite bench before the view became obscured by the shadow of a woman.

"And keep yer filthy hands off me, ye dogs," the new woman snarled over her shoulder before plonking herself next to the huddled form of what Clara assumed was another young woman.

The voice sounded familiar. *Penny?* Shuffling closer, Clara risked peeking out the door. One of the men paused in rubbing his jaw to glare at the carriage entrance. She grinned. If anyone would dare to punch a man nearly twice her own size, it would be Penny. She supposed such attitude came from being the youngest of six children and the rest being all boys.

Clara wished she'd had the foresight to do the same.

Again, the door shut. She held her breath, exhaling as the lock clicked. Outside, there was the discernible slap of leather on hairy horsehide. The carriage resumed its sickening sway.

"Pawh! What's with the dark?" A shadowy hand reached across the gloom and tore the curtain free. Midmorning light, made wan by the smoky glass, illuminated the trio.

Clara examined the pair sitting across from her. One she couldn't make out much more than she'd seen moments before. Of the other, there was no question. "Penny."

The shorter of the two women greeted her with a savage smile. "Got ye too, I see." Her eyes, which the muted light had made a muddy brown, narrowed. "The dogs." The full lips twisted into a sneer Clara could well picture being stamped on the face of an amazon. Her dainty fist pounded on the roof with all the grace of a blacksmith's hammer. "Are yer misbegotten scoundrels snagging every woman in Everdark?"

Beside her, the other woman flinched and scrunched further into her seat. Her head tipped forward, loose hair throwing her face further into shadow. "Don't antagonise them." Even perched on the seat and squeezed as far into the corner she could go, she still showed the obvious bulk of someone twice the size of Penny. Yet, at the same time, she somehow seemed far smaller despite the other's petite form.

Penny stared at the woman, jolted from her incredulous stupor as the carriage hopped over an uneven patch in the cobbles. "Don't upset them?" Flicking back hair barely long enough to brush her shoulders, she sneered at the panel above them. "They've no right to take us like this." She punched the roof. "Ye hearing me!" The fist slammed again, wood arching at the blow. "Ye ain't got no right to be doing this to us!"

Clara leant forward, her shoulder pressed against the wall, shivering as the cold of the metal leached through her heavy linen gown. She peered through the smoky glass at her dear town. The fronts of buildings flicked by, each layout of stone and wood panels near identical to the next. Occasionally, a group of people would appear walking along the street only to be gone in the next breath. All of them seemed as oblivious of the three women trapped within the carriage as Clara had at first been. Certainly no one seemed to have heard Penny.

She shifted her attention to the silent one of the pair. Where had she seen the flaxen-haired woman before? Her voice sounded familiar. Had she been a customer from her mother's shop? She eyed the skirts draped over the seat's edge. Heavy, dark embroidery ran around the hem. Detailed. Expensive. And, from what little she could see, they mirrored what different hands had stitched into the bodice. *Not from my mother's shop then.* The bold patterns spoke of foreign lands. They certainly didn't resemble the finer stitching she'd seen her mother put on Feast Day dresses.

The carriage rounded a corner, tilting sharply and pressing Clara against the wall. A grunt came from the other side as Penny slid into the other woman. There was more grumbling, no doubt coming straight from the short woman's mouth and likely to have gotten Clara a good thrashing if she'd repeated some of the snippets she could hear. Then the pair untangled themselves and resumed their original seats.

Outside, the weathered canvas awnings gave way to streaks of brighter shades. Their pace slowed as they trundled by a statue of a prancing stallion not much bigger than the carriage. Hadn't she been here once before? Clara peered up at the buildings, certain her mother had sent her here a few years ago to pick up a special shipment of fabric from the weaver.

Clara searched for the building, disappointed she couldn't pick it out from amongst the wall of polished wooden doors and windows. Maybe she'd been wrong. In a place as big as Everdark, things were bound to repeat themselves when it came to looks.

The square and its statue slipped beyond sight as they rolled on. They were slowing even further. At this speed, the carriage resumed its nauseating sway, bumping over the cobbles and gradually coming to a halt. A street, and its scant handful of people, dominated much of the window's view. The rest showed the stone archway of a private garden, still cloaked in morning shadow. Indistinct blobs moved within, fast becoming clearer as they neared the entrance.

With her nose scrunched against the glass, she made out the form of a young woman, dressed in a simple gown of blue and silver. A pair of the lord's men flanked her, one leaning closer to the woman as they headed towards the carriage. The woman inclined her head.

Clara wouldn't easily forget the face peaking out under the tumble of brown hair. No one just forgot *Caring Katharina*. Not after the first meeting. She was the youngest daughter to one of the councillors and could, more often than not, be found wandering the poorer parts, always feeding beggars and tending to injured animals.

Four men sporting the livery of the watch rounded the bend in the street, meeting the trio as Katharina and her escort stepped out of the walled garden and onto the road.

Clara held her breath as there was a brief exchange of words. One of the watch, a captain to judge by the knotwork adorning his cuffs and shoulders, waved his hand about. He seemed quite heated. His voice, the words muffled beyond understanding, carried a heavy layer of disapproval. Had word of their abduction reached the watch? Would they be freed after all? If only she could see his face and be certain.

The taller of the two lord's men stepped closer. He laid a hand on the watchman's forearm, stilling the man with a chilling suddenness. Giving his companion no more than a twitch of the head, the pair continued escorting the woman to the carriage.

"Why doesn't the watch stop them?" she murmured, her breath fogging the glass. It had only been a touch and the man seemed unharmed, yet none of the watch appeared willing to go near the carriage. Did they not know what the carriage harboured?

"Interfere with our lord's men?" The flaxen-haired woman scrunched further back into her seat. "They wouldn't dare!"

Beside her, Penny frowned, her generous lips narrowing as she gave a terse nod.

Clara flinched at the reminder. She'd hoped that maybe, just this once, help would be at hand when she needed it. She should've known better to hope for rescue from the watch. *Not from* them. How many times had she been told there was naught to fear from the lord's men? *They do only as the Great Lord commands*, she reminded herself. Not even their own wishes were to be filled. If only her lessons had included the obvious question of why. Memory recalled all too clearly how asking had been greeted by an uncomfortable, and knowing, look before she was hastened off on some errand. *Only as the Great Lord commands.*

So what did *he* want with them?

The door opened. Katharina stepped in without pause to seat herself next to Clara. Adjusting her skirts as the growing group was once more shut in, she glanced at the rest of them. A smile plumped her cheeks, echoing in her the creasing around her eyes. "Greetings fellow travellers."

"Travellers?" Penny snorted, her arms folding across the ample curves that defined her bosom. "More like captives."

Katharina's full lips pursed. Without seeing her eyes, Clara knew the woman's gaze must have shifted to the door. Little doubt she hadn't heard it lock. "A simple misunderstanding, I'm sure." She barely moved as the carriage trundled off again.

Penny's brown eyes widened until Clara was sure they would pop from her skull. "Misunderstanding?" she shrieked. Her fists slammed into the padded seat on either side of her. "Those scoundrels bundled us in here as if we were wayward sheep and yer saying it's a damn mistake?" Her fingers had uncurled to clutch the cushion's edge, her arms shaking as her knuckles went white. "Somehow, I doubt there was *any* misunderstanding."

"But there simply must be." Katharina waved a hand at the wall behind her. "The lord, may he live a long and fruitful life, sent a handful of men to the council at dawn. Amongst the messages given was a decree to relinquish one highborn lady into his care to become his mistress." Her head bowed, a curtain of hair falling forward to shroud her face. "I chose to accept this burden."

If this woman *was* to become the Great Lord's mistress—and she seemed a rather poor choice for their mighty lord, but then Clara knew not what sort of woman he'd demanded be brought to him—then for what earthly reason were the rest of them being dragged along?

Clara tried hard to swallow the lump in her throat. Were they to become servants? *Surely not.* The lord would have plenty amongst his people and, in any case, what foolishness it would be to grab people off the streets and press them into a service they'd not been trained to do. Penny would certainly *not* have been her first choice as anyone's servant.

"Ye chose?" Penny's lips twisted into a snarl. "*Chosen*, more like."

"Better her," came a mumble from the dark corner holding the flaxen-haired woman.

Clara flinched at the words. Her mother would've dealt her several good lashes for voicing such an opinion. The Great Lords were not cruel men. Not anymore. The old one, in the time of her grandparents, had reputedly invaded the surrounding kingdoms no more than a mere handful of times. Purely for appearance sake, at least, according to the rumours of old men. They certainly hadn't taken any land beyond the moors surrounding Endlight, which had been centuries ago. Try as she might, she could only recall the army moving once. Roughly three months ago. How many of them would be returning now they'd a new lord?

Katharina showed no sign of having heard either woman. She'd twisted to squarely face the window. "Why are we slowing? We can't be anywhere near the city gates." She waved a hand at the window as a fountain came into view. The middle of which bore four rearing horses carved from a whitish stone, the ears level with the nearby roofs.

The carriage trundled around the fountain. Clara, catching a golden glint, leant closer. Down near the waterline, blossoming from the fountain's centre, sat a school of metal fish, some partly submerged. Each one, with water spouting from their mouths, seemed to be in a constant state of leaping away from the crushing hooves of the statues.

The picturesque backdrop of buildings beyond passed by until they came to a stop outside the many-columned, gaudy front of the village hall. A handful of equally garishly-dressed men stood on the steps before the massive structure. The village council. She'd always envisioned them as being elderly, yet some of the men appeared to be in their late thirties; no older than her father before his death.

Brenna stood beside the men, robed in the exact shade of red rumour said to be favoured by the old lord's son. Between the dress and the noonday sunlight, her porcelain skin took on a sickly hue. She crossed her arms in disgust as one of the men pointed towards the carriage.

"Another passenger," Clara mused aloud. First Katharina and now Brenna appeared to be heading for the Citadel. How many mistresses had their new Great Lord truly requested?

"Another?" the flaxen-haired woman blurted. "But this carriage can't hold any more people."

She peered about the interior of their trundling prison.

Although the vehicle had more than enough space to comfortably seat its four passengers, Clara guessed it could easily fit another two people with little trouble. More if they were as small as Penny.

The lock clicked. The hinges issued a faint, ever more familiar, squeak as the door swung open to reveal Brenna's glowering face. She stood beside the bobbing door, hands on her hips and a stern defiance in her eyes. "Forget it!" she snapped over her shoulder at the men. "I'm *not* getting in there."

Frowning, the closest man pushed her until she took a halting step forward, heels clacking on the cobblestones.

She spun to face him. "Keep your hands off me, you filthy peasant." A jerk of the head disturbed the fine array of curls in her black hair. "*I* am to be the next Countess of Endlight. I will *not* stand being treated like some copper-bit whore." Brenna leant forward, her hands balling into fists. "Not even by the *lord's* men."

Over the woman's shoulder, she saw the man's face, which had hardly been forgiving in the first place, harden further. Such an expression on any other man and she would've said he was angered, but it there lacked a certain fire in his eyes to give the emotion its proper heat. If anything, his gaze was deader than those of the men who'd captured her.

Brenna must have seen it too for she faltered before him, her shoulders slumping as she faced the carriage door. She glared at the interior, her gaze flicking to each of those who were to be her travelling companions, the generous pout fast twisting into a sneer.

Clara felt herself fidgeting under the icy stare before she could stop. Her mother used to give her such a look before hurrying off to get the thin belt. From the corner of her eye, she could see the flaxen-haired woman shrink further into the seat.

Unshielded hostility glittered in her dark eyes. The rosy lips parted. "Move."

The word, delivered in a near hush, was a whip cracking across her bare skin. Clara shuffled closer to the wall then, seeing the gaze had not lifted, squeezed herself between Penny and the other woman.

"Peasants," Brenna muttered. "Give 'em a whiff of higher living and suddenly they think they're somehow nobler than their betters." She stepped into the carriage, shoving Katharina further along the seat. "I swear." Her eyes lifted to reward Clara and the two women flanking her with another cool glare. "The world would be *better* off without them."

Clara rolled her eyes. Just who did she think made the clothes she wore or cooked the food she ate? The woman had probably never set foot in a kitchen, never mind a place of labour.

To her left, she felt Penny stiffen. Her thoughts snapped to the recent memory of the nameless man nursing his injured jaw. Clara clamped a hand down on the smaller woman's arm, her heart jumping as the limb twitched. "I wouldn't," she whispered out the corner of her mouth. If Penny decided to hit Brenna, then she'd certainly break the woman's dainty nose, and Brenna would make sure a suitable punishment was delivered in return. *Flogged to within an inch of her life, no doubt.* She wouldn't be surprised if Brenna ensured all of them were chastised, just in case they got the same ideas.

"We are less than those we mock," Katharina murmured.

A less-than-delicate snort erupted from Brenna's nose. "I'd expect such syrup from *you*." With eyes shadowed by more than dark powder, she slowly faced the woman, her gaze flicking up to bore into the brown-haired head. "And you're a fine one to talk of being less." Her petite nose wrinkled. "You've everything a lady could desire and yet, for some reason only the Goddess herself can even begin to fathom, you prefer wallowing in the mud with all these filthy peasants." She ran a considering eye over Penny, her lip curling. "Small wonder they think of themselves as our equals." Her gaze slid over Clara to peer at the woman huddled in the corner. "Although, *this* one seems to comprehend her status perfectly well. You two could learn a lot from her on proper behaviour around your betters."

"Yer not betta'!" Penny muttered and Clara fancied she heard the woman's teeth grinding off several layers of enamel. "Fancy clothes and trinkets don't make ye betta' than no one. Not as if it all belongs to ye, is it? In fact, if it weren't for yer pop's coin, ye'd just be another flamin' tart."

A cold silence crept into a space that suddenly seemed a lot smaller. *She should've kept her mouth shut.* Clara hunched her shoulders, waiting for the backlash. She'd seen Brenna's temper in full force before and, if anything was to incite such outrage, it would be this.

"What was that awful noise?" Brenna put the tip of a finger in her ear and made a show of wriggling it about. "Is *that* what you call talking?"

Still held down by Clara's firm grip, Penny leant across the space, raising her other hand before she could be stopped. The snap of her dainty fingers connecting with the pale cheeks cracked through the carriage. "Ye want me to break yer pretty, little jaw as well?" Balling her hand, she waved it under Brenna's nose. "One hit s'all it'd take me, then we'll see how well *ye* talk."

Brenna's hand froze in rubbing at the steadily reddening cheek. Only her dark eyes dared to move as she tracked the fist. The rosy lips moved wordlessly before shutting, anger continuing to glitter in her eyes.

The carriage bounced, briefly lifting Clara free from her seat. Out of the corner of her eye, she caught the thick planks of a gate. Her gaze snapped from monitoring the two women to stare out the window. Wood gave way to stone set in large and imposing chunks. *The western gatehouse.* It must be. Pressing her back into the thin padding behind her, she watched as the final piece of the gatehouse slipped by, vaguely aware the others were mimicking her. *We've left the village.* No hope of a rescue now.

The crack of a whip split through the gentle rumble of wheels on cobble, a whinny fast following. The carriage rocked and bounced up the road. The speed did little to the field of grass that was their only view. Green and uniformly short, it stretched from the edge of the walls to the bare foot of the mountain without even a single bush in sight. To the east and on either side, miles of open land lay between Everdark and the nearest forest.

Clara's vision blurred, the brightness of outside blending with the gloom of the carriage. She wiped the tears away. What would her mother think of hearing her daughter had cried like a two-month babe? Clara sniffed back the beginning of a sob, her tears renewing their silent flow. How unlikely was it that anyone would know what had happened, let alone what she'd done? No matter what transpired in the Citadel, she'd a sinking feeling she'd never hear her mother's voice again, never mind the acidic retorts that had become so familiar. Nothing to be sure of anymore.

Only the Citadel. And their waiting lord.

Chapter Three

Mount Winding. Named so because of the swirling way it rose, as if the Goddess had failed to smooth out all the little whirls in the great cake of the world. Or where the demons had broken into this land. The reason given seemed to depend on who Clara asked.

From the humble streets of her home, the mountain had been little more than an impressive silhouette. On the Road, the barren and scarred land had bordered on the depressive. Now, standing on what had once been the mountain's peak, staring down at the kingdom stretched before her, a strange transcendent feeling welled in her breast.

Looking squat and dismal, Clara's beloved Everdark sat in the shadows at the mountain's foot. Beyond the surrounding forest lay the haphazard patchwork of farms, pockmarked with villages and more woodland. Through it all ran the Murkwater, meandering as far as she could see only to be lost in the forests bordering, and sometimes encroaching on, the steppes of their southern neighbours.

The world beyond. Awe of a different sort crept up from deep within her chest as she tracked the increasingly-jagged horizon. To the west, barely visible in the haze brought on by distance, stood five towers. *The mighty Pillars of Endlight.* She'd heard of how imposing they were and their impenetrable defences. At a distance, they appeared to be as massive as the tales said. And yet, they would've been dwarfed by the behemoth looming behind her.

The gates to the infamous Citadel lay open like a great yawning mouth with portcullis teeth, its tips glinting near the upper rim. Although it was still early enough to be afternoon, dim lights flickered from within.

A shadow appeared in the opening, faint at first, but fast solidifying into the outline of a man.

Clara took a step back, wishing the option of climbing back into the nearby carriage was available. Bumping into one of her captors, she staggered a few steps towards the opening as the man shoved her.

The light shifted and the outline revealed itself to be the hunched form of an old man adorned in a ragged assortment of clothes. His head, bearing the crumpled remains of a suede cap that had to be decades out of fashion now, lifted as he neared. "Ah, the lord's requested young women." He took a hobbling step back and beckoned them onwards with a wave of his hand. "Come, come. Your rooms await you."

Brenna let forth with a gasp and strode up to plant herself, her arms akimbo, before the man. Taller than he, even without the man's stoop, she towered over him. "Old man," she snapped. "I demand to speak with your master over this injustice. Take me to him at once."

"Dear lady." He offered her a low bow. "I regret to inform you our most esteemed lord and master has not yet returned." Straightening as much as his back seemed able, he resumed his shuffle towards the gates. "Rest assured you shall all have your chance to speak with him in the morning."

A man's hand clasped Clara's upper arm, the fingers firm and surprisingly gentle. She was guided through the gateway and into the courtyard, the others following in a similar manner. Jerking around as the rattle of chain reached her ears from behind, she could do naught but watch as the portcullis dropped to the ground and the gates, twin slabs of steel-bound wood, swung shut.

To her right, the flaxen-haired woman whimpered.

"Do not be concerned," the old man said. "It is a mere safety precaution. Done only to ensure those who aren't welcomed do not get in."

And those who want to leave cannot get out. Clara's gaze lifted to the wall above the barred entrance, marking the archers and crossbowmen lining the parapets. How many more would be there to guard the entrances once the lord arrived?

Everyone knew their Great Lord had enemies. The neighbouring lands were ever eager to be rid of what they perceived as a threat. And once, nearing three decades ago, their kingdom had been a threat. Now the borders were said to be endlessly patrolled. Bastions like the Pillars of Endlight barred the way through the more obvious routes for an army. Nothing could possibly push this far in to attack.

Yet the old Great Lord had been slain. *At Ne'ermore.* Why, after coming a hairsbreadth from conquering the city and the kingdom it governed, had their lord risked entering the same place he'd been pushed back from? Clara wished she'd lingered for once to hear the rest of the old man's rambling. *And miss being snatched up like some waif.* Of course, she would've gotten a lashing from her mother for being late instead. At least her punishment would've been over by now.

"This way, dear ladies."

She fell into step beside Katharina as their little group followed the old man into the Citadel's main entranceway. Lanterns glowed along the corridor, tiny flames lending a tender warmth to the otherwise pressing chill of the stone. Their light illuminated a vast array of tapestries and banners, some of the latter looking suspiciously like emblems of fallen enemies, with those nearest the doorway fighting, and losing, their battle against time and age.

The hall stopped at the foot of a stairway. Clara halted on the first step, her gaze following the red and black carpet up to the next landing. There the stairs split into four miniature, but no less grand, versions of the staircase...

She tipped her head back, continuing to track the steps. Another landing sat high above them. Without seeing it, she knew there was, at least, a fifth flight of stairs. And, no doubt, there was a sixth hidden from sight somewhere. It stood to reason six towers would require just as many stairways. She doubted they'd been placed there purely for appearance's sake.

The old man clapped his hands twice. It echoed up the stairs to be accompanied by the rapid tap of feet running across bare stone. Five men materialized from around the base of the stairs to silently stand before the old man. They seemed to be older than those who'd brought the women here, certainly less thuggish in form, yet they bore the same dead look in their eyes.

"These men will escort each of you to your prepared quarters." Now he stood in the well-lit room, she could see even this old servant had the same odd tinge to his face. "And I must ask you to not try leaving your rooms."

"Is it because we *should not* leave," Penny said, "or *cannot?*"

"Regrettably, I am afraid that, for your own safety, it must be cannot for now." He waved a hand about. "The Citadel has a great many rooms, some have been unused for years, and we wouldn't want any of you to go missing." With the click of his fingers, which sent the men to stand by their sides, the old man shuffled off into the shadow of the main stairway.

"Miss," said the man closest to her, "if you would come with me."

Clara tore her gaze from the shadows to give her guide a nod. The uneasy twinge in her gut returned as she followed him up the main stairs, then to the smaller flight on her left. A few glances over her shoulder revealed the other women taking similar treks up the other stairways. The idea of being separated from them was enough to make her stomach churn. As much as she would've loathed the company, she wasn't keen on being alone either. Who knew what they could do with them then?

The minutes seemed to lengthen on to eternity as they climbed, encased in the yellow glow of the candlelight. The stairs she'd first thought were so short had doubled back on themselves a number of times, with each landing leading to yet another level, before leading off into a small room and beginning what seemed to be a long, spiralling ascent. Was she being led to one of the towers?

Her guide silently walked up the steps before her, silhouetted by the light. How fast could he turn to stop her if she fled? Clara glanced behind her where the stairs vanished further down into darkness with each step.

"What is to become of us?" She'd a sick feeling she already knew what one of them was destined for. *A new mistress for the new lord.* Were they all to be pressed into such a service? Surely he'd no need of a harem anymore than he required extra servants.

The man paused on another narrow landing. More stairs led up and into gloom beyond the candlelight's reach. "That, miss, is for our lord to decide," he said before resuming his steady pace up the steps.

Clara envied her light-footed guide. Being used to the more-or-less flat streets of Everdark, she could feel her legs beginning their wobbly objection to this unusual punishment, aching more and more with each step. If the Citadel did have a number of unoccupied rooms, then why put them in towers? And, seeing they were already perched atop a mountain, how tall did these towers need to be?

"Not much further, miss."

Puffing, she glanced up at the shadows ahead. Naught to be seen but more stone. Another step and then, as if called into being by the man's words, a door came into sight around the curve of the wall. She slowly followed him, muttering to herself as her guide trotted up the last few steps.

"Your evening meal shall be along presently," the man said. "Until then, please feel free to make yourself comfortable." He bowed, the door swinging inwards at a gentle push. Ruddy light flowed out into the tower, bringing with it the musty warmth of an unused space that had only recently been aired.

She entered the room ahead of her guide, barely taking a couple of steps from the threshold before the door slammed shut. Clara spun, grabbing the handle and fighting to turn it when she heard the lock click. Pressing an ear to the wood panel, she listened for any hint of what would follow. No sound came through. *Stupid girl.* Her fist thumped the door, letting out a muffled thud. She should've predicted this. *Stupid, stupid girl.*

Flattening her back against the door, she peered around the room. Dwindling afternoon sunlight shone through a trio of floor-to-ceiling windows facing the west. The glass, still covered in patches of grime, allowed streaks of light to fall across the room. Nothing suspicious lurked in the shadows.

Clara squished her face against the window and peered at the roof below. It had to be no more than a story lower. She used to clamber down such heights on a regular basis during her childhood. Surely she still could now. Her fingers caressed the latch. The metal gave a faint screech as it moved. If she could just open the pane wide enough to get out, she could escape this room. But to where?

Her brow twitched, squeaking on the glass. The longer she stared at the roof, the more certain she became of its steep pitch. One mistake could send her plummeting over the edge. There had to be another, less dangerous, way out.

A small bed sat against the wall to her left, its bedding smooth and the drapes pulled back. On the far side hung a mirror, the silver backing near opaque with age. A table stood under it, on top of which sat a candlestick, its metal bands glinting in the light as she rounded the bed end.

She picked up the candlestick and, removing the unlit candle, bounced it in her hand. The smoothed wood felt hard and solid. It might, just, be heavy enough.

Someone rapped on the door. "Miss?"

Scurrying across the room, Clara pressed herself against the wall beside the door.

Another, harder, knock came. "I would come back another time, miss, but I've been instructed to serve you the evening meal now." The rattle of a key in the lock followed, then the creak of the door handle.

She stiffened. The door slowly swung into the room. The unmistakable jingle of crockery filled the silence. Lifting the candlestick high, Clara waited for the man to step into view.

"Miss?" A head, the hair just beginning to show the signs of balding, stuck out from behind the wooden panel.

She struck with all the force she had, sending the man to the floor before he'd the chance to fully enter the room. The platter he'd been holding fell with a clang. Plates smashed as they connected with stone, their contents spilling onto the rugs.

Clara dropped the candlestick. Picking up her skirts, she hurdled the chaos she'd created and ran. Down the spiralling steps, one hand on the inner wall to keep her steady. A brief pause on the first landing, then out through the door and into the empty corridor.

The carpet muffled her steps, she rushed by closed doors and vacant halls in her search for the main passage down. One corridor appeared more used, and therefore more promising, than the others. She took it, finding a short flight of stairs at the end to take her to the next level.

Onwards she went, racing down another level to creep along a third as the halls resonated with the sounds of life. It could take hours for her to make her way to the entrance like this. How long did she have before they noticed the absence of one servant? Would they have opened the gates by then? When *did* they open the gates?

Clara slowed as the last question buzzed through her mind. She could run through these halls all night and avoid every person within, but it would all be for naught if she couldn't get outside. *Out into the dark.* Down the unfamiliar road and back to those who hadn't stopped this. *They'll send me back.*

Maybe this was a sign she should leave Everdark. Wandering aimlessly through the world beyond her village didn't sound at all bad, especially given the alternative.

The heavy tramp of boots echoed through hall, preceding the wan glow of candlelight coming from around the corner ahead. Clara halted in the middle of the corridor. She needed to hide. But where? Going back would take too long.

The hall was pocked with closed doors. No sound came from the rooms they shut off. Could she hide in one and wait? She fled to the nearest doorway. The handle twisted at the softest of jiggles and she hastened inside, gently pushing the door shut behind her.

She listened for the man's passage, the muffled thump of the unseen seeker's steps paling as a steely hiss issued from within the room. Fear of what stood behind her put a lump in her throat, choking off any thoughts of crying out.

"Don't move."

Clara halted in the act of turning to face the sound. Only now did she note the warm light flickering in the hearth, its smoky aroma adding to the soapy smell in the air.

"Step away from the door. That's it. Now turn around. Slowly."

She did as the deep voice commanded, fast flattening herself against the wall as the blade of a sword came into sight. It was held steady before her, the tip glittering in the candlelight. Her gaze travelled down the sword's sharp length to the man on the other end.

Dark eyes blazed with barely restrained fury as they regarded her from under a wet mop of black hair. "Who are you?" he asked, his teeth clenched and his lips barely moving. "Who sent you? What are you doing here?"

"No one sent me anywhere. I—" Her eyes snapped back to stare at the sword's lethal point as it twitched. "I was brought here against my will."

"You?" The sword lowered, its tip brushing against the

rug. One dark brow rose, the glint in his eyes intensifying as his gaze slowly ran over her once more. "They picked *you* to be my mistress?"

This is our new Great Lord? No longer faced with the weapon, she risked a glance at her surroundings. Little furnished the room—a table and stool in one corner, a chair sat by the fireplace and a couple of rugs littered the floor. Two doors sat in the far walls, one shut and the other open enough to allow entry to the amber glow of candlelight.

Her gaze returned to the man before her, her cheeks warming upon realising he wore naught but a towel around his waist. The light played upon his bare shoulders, seeming to delight in giving his wet skin a faint shimmer and glistening through the dark hair on his chest as much as it glittered on the sword's blade.

A sharp knocked rattled the door. Clara jumped, stifling a shriek with her hands.

"My lord?" The door opened. In the dim light shining through the crack, she saw the glint of an eye. "Ah, master." The gap widened and the old man stepped through to offer the younger one a low bow. "You found her. We feared we'd lost one of them."

"*One* of them?" The Great Lord's gaze jerked from her to bear down on the man. "How *many* have you acquired?"

The old man cringed. "Five, master."

"Sirius," the word hissed out between his teeth, his voice without heat. "I only asked for *one*." His brows lowered, merging in the middle. "In fact, I do believe I *ordered* it." A faint sneer pulled at his lips. "I thought *one* was the number even a drooling imbecile could count to!"

"Forgive me, master, the change in your order was my doing." The suede cap seemed to tumble off his head and into his wrinkled hands, where the fingers deftly wrung it into a tube. "But you have kept to yourself for many years. Your visits here ever fleeting. None of us were certain enough of your tastes in women to pick one." He waved a hand in Clara's direction, the cap flapping back into its more-or-less original shape before returning to cover the balding head. "You may take as many as you desire, of course, those you do not wish to keep shall be disposed of in whatever manner you like."

"You're giving me a choice?"

Clara stiffened, painfully aware of the heat in her face as the Great Lord's gaze ran over her once again.

Running his fingers through his hair, sending droplets of water onto the bare stone with a hushed splat, he sighed. "Very well. Gather them in the audience chamber at first light."

There would be a choice? No one had mentioned the Great Lord choosing between them. "B—"

Sirius' hand, far stronger than she would've thought for a man of his advanced years, latched onto her wrist. She opened her mouth again, gasping as the pressure increased.

"But of course, master." Sirius bowed, dragging her down with him. "You must be weary." He stepped back, pulling Clara along with him and opening the door in the same motion. "I shall return this errant young woman to her quarters at once."

Again came the silencing pressure on her wrist, this time before any thought of voicing her opinion bubbled to the surface. Gritting her teeth, she glanced over her shoulder to find their new Great Lord still staring at them, even as Sirius pulled the door shut.

Clara quietly allowed herself to be guided back up the corridor. He'd asked for one woman and they gave him five. *A choice.* She stumbled as the old man muttered and prodded her to move faster. *Goddess, please don't let him pick me.*

CHAPTER FOUR

*C*lara rubbed furiously at her arms in an attempt to stave off the cold seeping through her heavy linen dress, the action mimicked by the other women around her. Morning had come fast to her little tower prison—certainly quicker than she would've liked—but it had yet to warm the cavernous audience chamber. The stone here still clung to the ancient coldness of the mountain. Not even the fires illuminating the room made enough of a difference.

Framed by the amber light of torches and candles, the Great Lord lounged at the far end of the room on a throne the old stories said had been carved from a single chunk of black marble. It shone against its backing of muted red and grey stone, adding vibrancy to the crimson cushions attached to its back. More pillows lay scattered about the dais. Clara didn't wish to think any further on their presence. Perhaps the lord's men truly had thought their new master would've preferred to be attended by several women.

The man himself sat dressed in plain, black leather. The sword he'd threatened her with last night stood bare at his side and the only concession towards colour he seemed to have made was a simple, deep red sash around his waist. Distance could've warped much, but she couldn't help thinking his face bore the polite expression of the profoundly bored.

Before him stood Brenna, planted firmly at the head of

the carpet running up from the door to the throne. She'd insisted, quite loudly, on herself being the first to confront their new lord. No one had cared to stand in her way. "I am to become the Countess of Endlight." The words, spoken far louder than rest of her great speech, rang out across the room.

Clara had given up counting just how many times the woman had stated the same fact over the short time they'd been forced to share each other's company. What did she care if the woman was being married off? *Arranged.* How appalling to have someone else deciding who, and when, you'd be wedded. She'd rather be allowed to make up her own mind on such matters.

"My future husband is expected to arrive within the month. As such, I demand you return me to the village at once."

The sword flickered in the torchlight as he twirled the hilt in his hand, its tip grinding into the stone. "Endlight?" A faint chuckle filled the room. "I didn't realise Farris had gone senile already." The Great Lord leant back in his seat. "He's more than welcome to you, *Countess*."

Brenna jerked backwards, perhaps catching the hint of ice in his voice. She gave him a low curtsy and hastily made her way through the open doorway at their backs.

Sirius hobbled his way over to stand before them. "You," he said, grabbing Penny by her upper arm and leading her closer. "This one, master, has shown much spirit." He pushed her further ahead with a rough shove. "Tell our most esteemed lord and master your name."

"Ye be sure to keep yer hands off me, ye dog," she snarled over her shoulder. Stepping closer to the steps, she offered the man upon the throne a bow. "I be Penny Tanner, my lord." She straightened with a jerk, her hands flew up to sit on her hips. "And I'd rather be damned than let ye lock me in this cold hole of yers and be yer stinking whore." Her fist waved in the air between them. "*And* if ye try to lay one hand on me, I'll feed ye yer balls!"

Clara held her breath, expecting the man to explode in rage. She took a step back, vaguely aware of the other two doing the same. Speaking as she did to a mere councillor's daughter—even one who was to become a countess—was one thing, but to do so to the Great Lord himself? Men had died for lesser reasons. *Goddess, protect her soul.*

He leant forward, his hands coming to rest on the sword hilt. Rich laughter filled the room. "Oh, she does indeed have spirit, Sirius." He sat back in his seat, amusement still playing on his lips. "But the humble flame is rather different to a raging inferno." One hand lifted to flick Penny her dismissal and the short woman stamped out the door. "I've no desire to be burnt."

"Of course not, master." Sirius' arm swung wildly behind him, latching onto the flaxen-haired woman's wrist. Naught but a quick glance was given to who he had seized before he dragged her forward with more haste, and roughness, than he'd done with Penny. "Perhaps his exalted one shall find *this* young lady more suitable?" He prodded her back, pushing her a step towards the throne. "Your name, girl."

"L-Lillian," she squeaked.

Silence enveloped the room. The air grew thick with it, clogging Clara's ears until she could hear only the swift beat of her heart.

"No." The word pierced the quiet, neatly slicing it in two.

Lillian's booted feet shuffled on the carpet, the susurration they caused leisurely circled the room. "I-I assure you, m-my lord, i-it is."

He sighed, massaging his temples with a single hand. The other shook as it gripped the sword hilt. "Sirius, have you brought me any worthwhile women?"

The old man cringed, half-ducking behind Lillian and looking for all the world like a dwarf standing beside a giant. "Master, please do reconsider." One hand pushed the cowering woman forward, whilst the other stroked the wisps of hair dangling at her waist. "She is docile, sturdy and... Ah, has good, wide hips."

Lillian jumped as the man place his hands upon her waist.

Does he describe a woman or a cow? Clara frowned. Was there any difference when it came to the whims of nobility? *What do wide hips have to do with it?* The question meandered its way up from the treacherous depths of her mind, hitting her cheeks in a flash of warmth. *They don't marry.* A well-known fact. She supposed their heirs had to come from somewhere. *Please,* please, *Goddess. Not me.* She'd even less desire to bear his child than she did in becoming his mistress.

"My decision stands. Send the girl back to her family."

Lillian collapsed onto the dark red carpet with a squeak. "T-thank you, my lord. Thank you."

The Great Lord grimaced. "Just leave."

She scrambled to her feet. "O-of course, my lord." Taking a step back, she bowed as her foot touched the ground. "Thank you." The words kept spilling from her mouth as she continued to walk backwards, bowing with each step.

Drawing level with the last two of their group, Lillian spun and fled through the doors. No one appeared to stop her.

"I wouldn't think about trying to follow, miss."

Clara stopped watching the woman leave and stared at the old man. *I'm next?* She'd a vague awareness of Katharina opting to stand behind her when they'd first arrived. The woman hadn't moved since. *Dear Goddess, no. I can't be next.*

Having no desire to be dragged before the steps like the last two, she brushed off Sirius' attempt to grab her. Staring straight ahead, she mimicked Lillian in taking a step back. The room had one exit. No one guarded it. The old man wouldn't be able to catch her if she ran.

The subtle groan of well-oiled hinges rumbled through the room. A boom followed quick on its heels. The torches hanging over their heads shook in the breeze of the doors' passage.

She gawped at the massive twin doors, suddenly feeling colder than she'd been moments earlier. No one stood near the thick panels on this side. No one could've pulled them shut from the outside either.

She'd heard rumours of how the Great Lords were also great sorcerers, using their magic to hold back the kingdom's invaders. But her mother had always said rumour was only gossip in another coat. *And sometimes gossip spreads because of its truth.*

"Come." The Great Lord's voice lashed across the room as cold, and as fast, as a serpent.

Clara took an involuntary step towards the dais, her leg moving by some unseen force. Another, less jerky, stride swiftly followed heedless of her wishes to stay put. Then another and another, until she stood at the foot of the stairs, her gaze steadfastly refusing to lift from the first block of stone. Fully illuminated by the torches, the stone adopted a faint yellow hue.

Now whatever held her fast had positioned her where she didn't want to be, it suddenly let go. She staggered forward, righting herself before she could topple. If he thought she could be made to kneel, she was happy to prove him wrong.

A barely audible intake of breath came from the man sitting atop the throne. "It *was* you I saw last night." He descended the steps in a sure-footed clatter of boots, his darkly-clad form dancing on the edge of her vision. "I wasn't certain with the low light, but your hair... It's so *red*." He circled her, his boot heels tapping out a slow, measured beat. "Like—"

"I know," she muttered, cutting him off before he could spout whatever syrupy dribble he'd conjured to flatter her. Did he think no one had ever remarked on its colour before? "It's as red as the darkest of roses," Clara said, quickly rattling off the insipid words men had used in the past. "Like a rich autumn's sunset, or—"

"Blood." He halted before her. One hand held tight to his

sword hilt whilst the other twitched as if it longed to reach out and touch her. "It's as rich and as dark as freshly-spilt blood."

Blood? Despite it being the most accurate comparison, if not as poetic, not a single person had ever tried likening her hair to blood. *And fresh blood at that.* Her scalp itched. She wound a tress about her fingers, half expecting it to feel slick.

"Master," Sirius said. "There is one other young—"

The Great Lord cut the old man off with a wave of the hand. "No need." His eyes travelled down Clara's body, mirroring the look he'd given her last night. "I've made my choice."

"As you wish, master." A muffled cough cracked the silence. "Ah, master? The door. If you don't mind..."

"Hmm?" The Great Lord's head moved, slowly as if reluctant to tear his eyes from her face even for a moment. "What of the door? Oh, of course."

The subtle creak of hinges vibrated through the room once again. Clara glanced over her shoulder to see the old man leading Katharina away. *It should've been me.* She should've obeyed her first instinct and not have allowed the woman to stand behind her.

"Tell me, dear lady, what is your name?"

"Clara—" Jaw clicking shut on the rest, she hastily bobbed. "My lord." Sure she'd erred in the first curtsy, she gave him another, taking pains to make it more measured and not show her true feelings. Inside, she couldn't help but seethe. How foolish and thoughtless she was to let anything slip out without considering the ramifications. Even having him know her name could be used against her. *Stupid.* Her mother was always telling her to hold her tongue. Surely she wouldn't be in this quandary if she'd kept her mouth shut and mimicked Lillian's meekness.

"There's no need for you to do that." Clasping her hands, he coaxed her to stand straight. "I don't require my mistress to show such submissiveness."

Surprised to find herself clinging to his hand so tightly, Clara fought to release her grip, his calloused skin scraping against her palms. "As you wish, my lord."

He chuckled, the sound setting her heart to racing. "Also, you may call me Lucias."

Her lips squashed together in an effort to stay silent, she couldn't stop the name rolling around in her mind and she did not at all like the supple way it warmed her thoughts. He wasn't some pretty fop. She certainly couldn't label him as being ugly either. Quite handsome in a way. This close, she could see his eyes were not the black she'd first believed them to be, but a rich brown. *Maybe being his mistress wouldn't be too bad.* What did she have to go back to? Home had become little more than a life of drudgery for her screeching mother and she could quite happily let such an aspect go.

She shook her head. *But what about freedom?* she sharply reminded herself. He would keep her here forever if she gave in now. "My lord?"

A spark of displeasure flashed across his face. His lips twisted sourly. "Perhaps in time then," he murmured, seemingly to himself. "Come... Clara." Lucias proffered his arm. "Allow me the privilege of showing you around your new home."

Placing her hand in the crook of his elbow, she gave another bob, trying to mimic the timid curtsy Lillian had made. Would he let her go if she proved herself to be as meek as the fair-haired woman? "If it does please you to do so, my lord." The briefest of glances up at him revealed a flicker of distaste warping his features.

They walked through the halls, passing by the doors she and rest of the women had originally been led through. Sunlight warmed the stone underfoot. It seeped into her clothes, contrasting with the shade on her left side and making her shiver. Her gaze lingered on the empty courtyard lying beyond the unguarded doorway. She caught a glimpse of the black-lacquered carriage trundling through the open gates before it dipped out of sight.

Clara released his arm and, gathering up a fistful of skirt, ran out into the courtyard. Her feet slapped against the cobbles, each step jarring her to the bone. Ahead, the gates remained open. *Faster*! her mind screamed. She stumbled on an uneven stone, righting herself with a hop, her heart pounding with the fear she wouldn't make it.

She passed through the gap, her legs wobbling as the strain caught up with her victory. *Can't stop. Not yet.* Never mind no cries for her *to* halt had come from behind. No one shouted a warning from above, although she felt them watching her. Any moment now and they could rain arrows down on her. Her shoulders prickled with anticipation.

Onwards she pushed, flogging herself down the Road. The carriage would be well ahead of her by now. She'd never catch them on foot, which suited her fine. She wasn't planning on returning to Everdark. There was a whole world out there just waiting for her to explore it.

Veering towards the rising sun, she dashed off the Road. A discarded cobble rolled under her foot. Clara fought to stay upright, wincing as her ankle twisted. She hobbled a few steps, her eyes watering. A few choice curses grumbled through her lips. *Ignore the burning.* It was no worse than any number of times she'd acquired the exact same injury whilst walking the village's shoddy streets.

An errant tussock, pinned under her other foot, wrapped over her boot. Shuffling along the ground to free herself, she'd almost gotten the toe free when her ankle gave, dropping her face-first onto grass still wet with dew. Rolling unto her back, intent on appraising her throbbing ankle, she slowly became aware of beginning the cold and subtle glide downhill. Her speed increasing with the incline.

Clara scrabbled at the ground, tearing up fistfuls of grass and dirt as she tumbled and slid down the mountainside. One tuft held long enough to slow her down. Another brought her to a stop. She clung to the fragile strands, carefully trying to get her legs under her.

The blades released with a sudden and loud rip, throwing her into a clump of bushes waiting on the slope below.

Hurling the underhanded grass to the ground, she glared up at the towers. Her fingers ached and her knees, no doubt scraped, stung. She wouldn't have felt less sore if someone had whipped her. Granted there'd be more bleeding, but not by much. *It's all* his *fault*! If only he'd let her be, as he'd done with the others. She didn't want to be *anyone's* mistress, let alone his.

Branches snagged on her hair and clothes as she struggled to free herself. Gritting her teeth, she plucked at them, snapping off what she couldn't remove to be dealt with later. In any case, Katharina was a far better fit for such a life than her. If he'd just deigned to look at the woman instead of stopping at Clara, he would've seen it too.

The steady thud of hooves marching along hard ground reached her over the muted rustle and creaking of branches. Halting all movement, she waited for the sound to fade, hoping the plainness of her skirts would blend with the bushes.

"Quite the tumble you took there." The owner to the smug voice soon came into view as Lucias nudged the horse to stand before her. He leant forward, an arm resting on the black beast's neck. "Are you whole?"

Clara glared up at the man. Whilst she'd been attempting to flee, he'd come after her on horseback. And, judging by the sweat-free coat of the animal, quite calmly. *The nerve.*

"Here, let me help you."

As she reached for his extended arm, the idea of hauling him from his seat and into the bushes flashed through her mind. He didn't appear to be well balanced, but the horse... The way it eyed her didn't match the docile look of the beasts back in the village.

The rustle of twigs pulled her attention back from the animal. She hadn't as much as touched his fingers and yet she could clearly feel herself being lifted free of the branches. What was holding her?

Her stomach quivering, Clara dared to glance down. She hung in the air with naught to halt her fall. Although, as faint as it felt, she fancied sensing a tendril of something—she daren't think too long on exactly what it was—coiling around her body.

Pulled free of the bush, she could only glower at him as he draped her before the saddle. Even with him near enough to physically keep her in place, he seemed intent on using his magic to hold her fast.

The horse came around at his command. The base of the animal's thick neck moved with an oily grace. She tried to wriggle off.

Her foot twitched in response. What did she care if it meant risking being trampled? Her left hand, pressed hard against the front of the saddle, moved and got caught between leather and horseflesh. Was it not preferable to the sort of imprisonment Lucias offered? Her other foot jerked, the toe of her boot kicking the beast who merely continued its stately pace.

The muted thud of the horse's steps became the clatter of shod hooves. She lifted her head, sweat breaking out on her brow. Through the tangle of her hair, she spied the dark walls of the Citadel gateway, then the gates themselves. Her gaze dropped to the cobbles and the play of shadows as the horse carried on.

"Ah, master," came the wheedling note of Sirius' voice. "You caught her."

The horse halted. Lucias remained quiet.

"Men!" Sirius' voice bounced off the stone. "The gate!"

Clara caught the scuffle of feet scurrying about the courtyard like giant rats and the subtle creak spoke of the gates swinging shut. There would be no escape today. She would have to bide her time and wait for the right moment.

Whenever such a moment may be, one thing was certain. They would *not* catch her next time.

Chapter Five

The aroma of roasted beef and lamb wafted up from the table. Swallowing, Clara struggled to keep her focus on the far wall. The scent mingled idly with the fresh bread sitting before her—the golden crust promising to be crisp—and the lesser, vaguely soapy, perfume emanating from her skin.

On the edge of her vision, she spied Lucias shuffling in his chair. The squeak of leather on leather filled the room, masking the rumble in her stomach. He sat at the head of the table with her sitting just to his left. As far as she could make out, they were alone.

"Clara," he breathed. "I do wish you would eat." The glint of light on metal spoke of him picking up the carving knife. No such implement had been gifted to her, just a fork so blunt and fat it might as well have been a spoon. Anything sharp appeared to have been carefully placed out of her reach.

There was the soft squish of a blade slicing through meat.

Her gaze flicked down to the food-laden table, her mouth watering at the sight of the pinkish flesh being placed on the plate in front of her, before returning to stare at the wall. "I'm not hungry, my lord." It would've been easier to refuse if the bare stone could offer up something to look at beyond its dark surface.

Lucias set the knife down with a sigh. "It has been two days." The words came softly, as if he spoke to a spooked cat. His chair creaked as he leant forward. "You must know by now I will not negate my decision."

She did. He'd been most adamant about it. "I still believe Katharina would've been a better choice, my lord."

"Perhaps she would, although I have my doubts." With his elbows resting on the table, he steepled his fingers. "It is *you* which... intrigues me. Thrice you have tried to escape and thrice you've failed to get much further than the main stairway." His dark eyes glittered in the candlelight. "Yet you continue to defy me."

She snapped her head back around to stare at the wall. "And I shall do so until my dying breath, my lord." Her last attempt had been somewhat spontaneous. To test out the loyalties of his men. She hadn't expected it to be undying.

"Do you not worry I will force you?"

Coldness washed over her. He could. No doubt as easily as he had lifted her onto the horse. Easier in fact, seeing there would be no lifting involved. Her gaze dropped to her lap. He wouldn't even need to resort to his magic. *Just his own hands.* And the power they had at their command. "Then why don't you?"

Lucias chuckled mirthlessly. "My father learnt the folly of force. And paid for it with his life."

Slain at Ne'ermore. No one here would tell her why. *He* likely could, but she couldn't bring herself to ask him lest he mistake her curiosity for her something else.

With his left hand—it was always the left he used, although he seemed to handle the sword at his hip with the other hand readily enough—he filled her goblet. "At least drink something, I promise there is nothing more within than apple juice."

She itched to take up the cup and drain it of the sweetness it held. *Juice.* Not wine like he drank. *No attempts to get me drunk then?* Already, there were beads of water forming on the metal. She licked her lips and stayed her hand.

Her stomach gave another tiny rumble. She'd been surviving on cups of water for the last two days. "I'm not—"

He snatched the goblet off the table, the cloudy juice sloshing over the rim, and downed the liquid in one gulp. "Nothing more than juice," he snarled, wiping the back of a hand across his mouth. "Do you not see it now? Can you not believe I don't seek to harm you? It's the furthest thing from my mind."

"Then please, my lord, let me go."

"Go?" he roared.

Clara flinched. She closed her eyes, her fingers deftly entwining themselves into her skirts, and braced herself for the slap that would surely follow. Her cheek tingled in anticipation. She risked a peek when nothing came.

The goblet flew down the table, rebounding off the wood and hitting the floor with a dreadful clang. "Go?" The word growled through his teeth. His eyes seemed to glow with an inner fire. They sparkled with a pale silvery-blue glow, the subtle colour of his eyes lost to the dark inferno of his rage.

She shrank into the chair.

A flicker of pain darted across his face. "Do not look at me so!" His fist slammed onto the table. Plates bounced, cutlery rattled, wine slopped out of the pitcher beside him. "I will *not* have you fear me." He pushed himself from the table, his chair skidding across the stone floor, to stand and pace the room's length. "How can I prove I mean you no harm?" He halted before her, distanced only by a slab of wood and the wealth of silverware it bore. "What must I do to win your trust, Clara? Tell me."

Let me go. She shook her head. It would be foolish to repeat such a request. "There is naught you can do to make me willing to stay, my lord." She would *not* yield to him. She *would* find a way to be free. "Force me if you must sate your desire, but I will never wish to stay. And you will never have me trust you."

"Sate?" His laughter rang out, icy and mirthless. "Is that what you think this is about?" He shook his head, further messing his hair. "I would not have sent them out, would not have kept you here for so long, for even a *night* of empty pleasure." He leant on the table, his veins bulging along his forearms. "If I wanted *that*, I'd have paid for it and would've had far less trouble, too." Those dark intense eyes grew wild with hunger as he stared at her. "What I want," he grated from behind clenched teeth. "What I *need*, is a son. An heir to take my place when I have passed on."

An heir? So he did want her here to bear him a child. She'd thought his desire for a babe was the reason, but hoped it wouldn't be true. No wonder his head servant had preferred Lillian with her docile manner and wide hips.

"You—" She moistened her lips, wishing she still had the goblet of juice at hand. "You have no children?" Surely he would not have kept to himself over the years. The way he looked at her, both unnerving and enticing, spoke of a man who knew exactly what to do with a woman once she was within reach.

One corner of his mouth lifted in a sneer. "Despite the rumours the other kingdoms like to spread about us, I am no savage. I do not rut with every woman I come across." His gaze dropped to the table. "Able as I am, I, unlike my father, would prefer being able to trust someone before letting them share my bed."

Surprised to find she'd been clutching her skirts tightly to herself, she forced her hands to smooth the wrinkled linen. "I find that hard to believe, my lord."

One brow lifted. His lips parted, the ghost of a laugh passing through them. "Ah Clara," he breathed. A hand ran through his hair, drawing the wayward strands from his face. "If we had but known each other well before my father's demise..." Candlelight shimmered in his eyes as he glanced up at her, a soft smile tweaking one side of his mouth. "I was a different man then. Certainly harder to anger."

Clara bit her tongue and let her gaze run along the tapestries adorning the far wall in an effort to remain silent.

Lucias straightened. "I understand there's a lot you need to adjust to before you can accept your new position. I can, and shall, wait for a time to let you come to me on your own. On this, you have my word." Turning his back to her, he marched towards the door, his boot heels clicking against the stone. "Do keep in mind my patience is not eternal. I cannot risk being the last of my line forever. Not without endangering the kingdom and her people."

"The kingdom will survive." Maybe not as it once had, but its people would carry on the same as always no matter who ruled them. It wasn't as if the Great Lords were deeply involved in the day-to-day running of the land they ruled. How many would even notice his absence?

Lucias halted, his hand gripping the door handle. "Will it?" Still holding onto the handle, he twisted to face her. "Tell me, have you ever feared walking the streets of your village?"

Her chin rose, pride for her beloved Everdark swelling in her chest. "Not until your men came and kidnapped me." Even on the darkest nights, the streets were the safest to be found for miles.

He waved the taunt aside. "And of the roads between? They were also safe for the common man to travel?"

"Of course they are." Everyone knew it to be so. When not invading lands or pushing back any invaders who dared to attack, the army spent its time tracking down those few who broke the law. *Then they come here.* Locked in an iron box to meet their punishment.

"Well there you have it. None of this protection will continue without one of my blood to carry on."

She bit her lip and frowned. *The Great Lord's rule is absolute.* But surely a kingdom's existence didn't hinge on something as flimsy as the life of its ruler. Cities couldn't crumble in an instant and the land wouldn't fall into chaos just because there was no one to take up the mantle of Great Lord. *Then why does he sound so sure?* It couldn't be true. Could it? "Then why did your father go to Ne'ermore?

Why take the risk?" Yes, Lucias' father had an heir, but it seemed foolish to willingly head into danger.

The door squeaked as he leant against it. "For love, of course." Folding his arms across his chest, he shrugged. "What other reason could possibly be good enough to risk one's life?"

Walking the land of their enemies would've been dangerous enough, but to try and enter the city... Well, the old lord *must* have realised how slim his chances of survival would be. He'd have known the likelihood of returning. "Surely for him to step even one foot into Ne'ermore was suicidal." Clara peered at Lucias, trying to decipher his emotions. Such a thing must have occurred to him too. His face was too guarded. She wished he would come back to the table, it'd been easier to eke out his feelings then.

He waved a hand about in vague circles. "Well, perhaps not if he'd actually made it into Ne'ermore. My father was attacked whilst traversing the nearby land. It's all hills around there, leagues of it, perfect ambush territory." A jerk of the head flipped the hair from his face. "It's why the city's never been taken. They've built it on the highest hill they could find. Whole place looks like a stairway to the clouds, but you can't march an army up to the gates without them knowing well beforehand."

"And your father... You think they saw him?" Saw him and undeniably thought themselves favoured by the Goddess to be given such an opportunity.

His lips, already thinned with repressed anger, twisted. "I doubt it. The fool took only a three-man escort, along with my mother." He shook his head. "Although, I suppose he wouldn't have been any better off with an army at his back."

Clara bit her lip again. An army wouldn't have stopped his death? "How *did* he die?" She held her breath, expecting him to relate of how an assassin had slipped into his tent at night.

"On the head of an axe wielded some blood-thirsty barbarian who was likely already on his way here to deal to my father anyway." Again his hand combed through the dark mess of his hair. "Or so she tells me."

"Who?"

"My mother." His boot scuffed against the floor. "At her behest, one man was kept alive to send word to me of my father's death." He grimaced. "Not that I needed it. My family have a way of knowing when our predecessors have passed on and I met the messenger on my way back from the eastern border."

"Your mother?" she blurted, unable to believe what she'd heard. "What sort of mother would do such a thing?" Even her own mother, a woman as unforgiving as stone, wouldn't have been so cruel. She'd loved her father, cared for him as he had wasted away and, although she hadn't hesitated in beating Clara, her mother never did it for something undeserved.

Sighing, he walked back to the table and proceeded to pace its length. "She was—" Lucias halted and scrubbed at his chin. "Still is, I suppose... a lady of the Raven Household, foremost in the Ebony Court at Ne'ermore. My father had her abducted within the first few days of the siege there." He eyed her, a brow lifting. "You've heard of this time?"

Clara nodded. Everyone had heard of the Ne'ermore Siege. It'd been the last time their lord had dared to invade the surrounding kingdoms.

"Well, when they finally managed to push him out of the kingdom, she got dragged along with him." Lucias plucked an apple from the bowl as he passed, tossing it from hand to hand. "Naturally her people came after her, but..." He shook his head, giving a dry chuckle. "Their strength has always been in those mighty fortresses. Such skills are useless without several feet of stone between their men and an enemy."

She was kidnapped. Undoubtedly with even less of a desire to linger here than Clara, yet the woman had still given her captor a son. *Through force?* No one mentioned where exactly the Great Lords got their women. Foolish to think they'd all been willing to serve. *I have to get out of here.* She frowned down at her plate. But how could she possibly hope to escape when an army hadn't been enough to free her predecessor?

Clara poked her fork at the meat he'd piled onto the silver dish, watching the juice pool around the bottom slice. Death would be the easiest way to end her captivity. Her stomach cramped as she went to push her plate away. *There is no escape through starving to death.* To die was to give up. A concession of her being too weak, too much his lesser, to fight back.

She stabbed the beef, lifting a generous chunk free to gnaw at it like a starving mutt. Tender, it succumbed in one bite. Rolling the morsel around her mouth, she savoured the taste after two days of living on water. She'd not eaten meat since her father had fallen ill and even then the cuts he'd brought home had tasted nowhere near as good as what she ate now. Swallowing, she took another bite.

Movement across the table drew her gaze. Lucias was smiling at her like she was some pup who had, after much training, at last obeyed a command.

She'd rather die than let him touch her, but far better to have him fall instead. To be free once again, for that alone she would fight him until the last drop of strength had been wrung from her soul.

CHAPTER SIX

*C*lara descended the steps. The clash of metal on metal echoed from somewhere in the halls below. She clutched her skirts, quietly delighting in the silk against her fingers. Her mother rarely let her touch such fine cloth; now it swathed her from neck to toe—or at least from chest to toe. The silk was dyed blacker than ink with highlights of red as richly dark as her hair.

She'd caught a glimpse of herself in the mirror. Her guardians, having finished dressing and grooming her to what she assumed must be the standards of a Great Lord's mistress, had then all but dragged her from the room. She resembled a walking, bleeding shadow. Even her hair, carefully teased and bound into two buns, was now framed by the dark points of a collar. Like an oversized crown or the velvet crest of a black dragon.

Slipping a finger beneath the soft leather strap they'd fastened around her neck, she eased it forward enough to soothe the tortured skin lying beneath. *I'll throttle whoever came up with this design.* She hadn't minded the fussing over her. It had bordered on pampering. *This*, however, had to be the most foolish means of anchoring such a heavy netting of wire and fabric that she'd ever come across. It tugged at her throat with each step, digging deep whenever she tried to turn her head.

"This way, mistress." Clara's guide, having already

reached the bottom of the stairs, beckoned her onwards. With her wrinkled hand shaking, the woman indicated a passageway Clara hadn't been led down before. The metallic clash, louder now, came from one such hall.

Clara hadn't expected to see women here. Something in the way people spoke about the Citadel's servants always suggested men. True, the women she'd seen were advanced enough in their years to be grandmothers—she wouldn't have been surprised if the eldest had claimed to have great-grandchildren—but they were women nonetheless.

Like the other servants she'd met, they had the same flat look in their eyes. She'd listened to their soft voices as they spoke amongst themselves, about trivial matters and seldom with any feeling. It reminded her of the cheap travelling theatre she'd seen some years ago. There'd been no spirit behind their voices. The lines they'd rehearsed were just... words.

Would she end up like those women? Like the one she now followed through the unfamiliar corridors? Hard to imagine what could be capable of draining someone of all emotion.

The metallic racket ahead grew closer and sharper, punctuated by the grunting of men and an occasional hiss.

She hesitated as the hallway walls on one side gave way to a set of carved pillars. Sunlight lit up a floor bereft of the black and red carpet under her feet. Silhouettes flit back and forth along the worn stone as if in some intricate dance, the delicate way the shadowy lines of swords brushed each other at odds with the clang of metal on metal. One of the lines dipped to hit the greyish shoulder and a yelp came from within the yard.

"Oh come now," Lucias said as the other's silhouette knelt at his lord's feet. "Get up! It's only a flesh wound."

Clara drew level with the first pillar. The smell of sun-warmed air and dust reached her on the faint, curling breeze. The area before her stood open to the sky and was ringed by thick benches and wooden figures. At one end of the grounds stood a handful of men. They seemed to hover on the edge of shadows gifted by the building, waiting to spring forth at a word.

Another man, the lord's stricken sparring partner, knelt in the middle of the yard. Blood flowed from a wide gash in his upper arm, running over reddened fingers and continuing on to drip off his elbow onto the dry earth. He lifted his head to stare up at Lucias. "But, my lord, it's to the bone."

"Oh?" Lucias paused in wiping the blade of his sword. "S'pose you should give it a minute or two then." He waved the man away to an empty bench. "Next."

One of the men separated from the group. He ran out into the sunlight with a jump to stand before his lord.

The first sparring partner scurried off to one side, collapsing onto one of the benches. His wound still bled, although no longer as heavily. No one else seemed to be at all concerned with his health. Was no one going to assist the man? He'd bleed to death without proper attention.

Hitching up her skirts, she strode out into the sun-drenched square. She couldn't call herself the daughter of a seamstress and not have been able to sew. Since the age of ten, her mother had insisted she learn. Granted this was flesh and not fabric, but the principles of needle and thread were largely the same. She even knew where some of the necessary equipment still lay, but first she needed to stop the bleeding.

Lucias stiffened as her slipper touched the grounds. He swung to face her, his boot heel grinding in the dirt. His gaze swept up over her, then lowered to eye her gown.

Clara felt the onset of a blush bearing down on her. She did her best to stifle the warmth to no avail. "My lord?" She bobbed the briefest of curtsies, her eyes flicking towards the wounded man. The arm appeared to be bleeding even less than it had when he first sat down. "Do you not think he requires attention?"

Lucias spun to follow her gaze, his boots scuffing up dust, and laughed. Pleasant and rich, it nevertheless seemed to chill the air around her. Why did he shake his head so?

"But... he'll die," she said.

"Not here he won't. Come." Lucias beckoned the man over.

Blood still streaked his arm, near black as the sun's heat baked it dry. Above, where there should have been a gaping wound, was naught but skin. Frowning, Clara brushed a finger over the heavily scarred arm. Another scar sat there, silvery pink as if close to the end of healing. *How can it be*? She'd seen a wound marring this limb. It *had* been there.

Gasping, she watched the scar change colour, adopting the more flesh-toned hue of the others criss-crossing his skin. *Magic*. Lucias controlled the doors by it. Had bound her using the same method. Now, after ruthlessly striking them in the first place, he healed his men? And, if the previous marks were anything to be judged by, not for the first time.

"See?" Lucias clamped a hand on the man's shoulder. "Being in the training ground ensures he's perfectly fine. Go." This last word was directed at the man as his lord propelled him towards the shadows. "Sit back down. And be sure to drink something."

Clara watched the man obey the order without a word. *They're like walking dummies to him*. Better than an inert lump of wood, but just as replaceable if they happened to become... worn out. Was there nothing beyond his power?

"Now then." Brushing the hair back from his face, he once more focused his appraising gaze on her gown before turning to the old woman who'd led her here. "Gettie, do explain to me what possessed you to dress her like *this*?"

It *was* a nice gown, if not exactly to *her* tastes. The ruffles and lace on her skirts and sleeves felt overdone and the neckline dipped a little bit too far into what her mother would consider as unseemly. The women had even given her a shift to match the low cut, leaving her shoulders the barest they'd ever been outside of a washtub.

She had to admit the effect would've been better, if the Goddess had chosen to give her Brenna's fuller figure. Even Penny, with her short stature, had more than enough in the chest region to give her a decent cleavage. Clara's apparent lack in the area seemed to have bothered the women for they'd offered her the choice of several corsets—some garish in design and others decades out of fashion—to accentuate her curves and give a little boost to her modest bosom. She'd refused. As it was, they had laced the bodice tighter than she'd have preferred.

The old woman shuffled out into the training grounds. "I do not understand, my lord. You requested she be garbed to suit her status."

"Yes, but just look at it. Look at what you've done to her." He sheathed his sword, his free hand waving in Clara's direction. "I believe I specifically requested it to be *tasteful*. Does she look at all elegant to you?"

Not elegant? *I bet you wouldn't say the same about Brenna*. Then again, the buxom tart would've allowed herself to be tumbled into his bed at the first instance.

Gettie wrung her hands. Her mouth moved silently and her head jerked from side-to-side as she tracked his pacing steps.

"And what were you thinking with the colour? You've completely paled her skin."

Those watery blue eyes stared at him, incomprehension creasing Gettie's face. "But black and red are my lord's favourite colours." She waved her hand over his attire. For the moment, his chest was bare, yet he still favoured the black leather pants and dark red sash. "They are the realm's colours." Gettie's indicated her own two-toned garb that covered all but her head and hands. Clara would've preferred a similar garment.

Lucias halted. "Fair enough. But they do not suit her." A weary sigh slipped through his lips. "Do tell me, though, what is the logic behind the collar?"

"It is what your father—" The woman fell silent as he

rounded on her.

"I care not for what my father would've done or wanted! Stop comparing me to *him*! I am not him!" Shaking, he ran his fingers through the sweaty mass of his hair. "I'm *not* him." His gaze fastened onto Clara as if he were suddenly aware of her presence. "Take it off."

Putting a finger on the buckle at her throat, Clara paused. His glare spoke of waning patience with the world and all those in it. Perhaps, just this once, she should be completely sure of the orders he gave. "Take what off, my lord?"

"The collar," he snapped, giving her a covetous glance over his shoulder. "Although if you feel inclined to remove anything else, you are free to do so."

Clara unbuckled the slim strap. Her neck tingled as the weight lifted. "You can have *this*." She flung the collar at his feet. "You'll get naught else from me." Remove more, indeed. Why she felt exposed enough standing before him and there were two distinct layers between her and the air, three if she included the bloomers hidden beneath her skirts. Any less and she might as well *be* naked. *Here. Before the servant woman and the lord's men.* Her face warmed at the image.

Something flickered across his dark eyes. Bittersweet. Haunted. "You tried to escape again last night. Four times in the last five days. Does it not tire you to always fail?"

She smiled to herself. Not even a full week had passed since her kidnapping, yet each attempt got her out of every room they'd locked her in. "I warned you I wouldn't stay here willingly." Although he kept the gate to freedom closed, he could not stop her seeking another way out. She *would* find it.

"It surprised me to hear how easy it has been to catch you. As it did learning your technique, which is weak at best, has not shown any sign of progressing." He strode towards the waiting men, seizing the bucket one of them held. Water slopped over the edge to hit the ground with a dull hiss. His hand dipped, drawing the liquid to his face.

Clara waited for him to finish, her mouth suddenly dry. It was the heat. Had to be. The sun sat directly above them and the walls cut off all wind. When had she last had anything to drink? Must have been an hour or two now. She would *not* ask for a drink.

I'm weak? She'd fought full-grown men. *Easy*? How dare he think her effortless to contain. Her struggling against their hold had continued until they'd been left with little choice but to release her. One had even been brought to his knees by a calculated blow.

"My men were given strict orders not to hurt you." Flicking water from his fingers, he faced her once again. "Yet you still could not best them."

"Then I shall endeavour to improve my efforts." She hadn't been trying to make it *easy* for them.

"Indeed. Your fighting can only be described as amateurish and pathetic. If these walls are ever breeched, I've little doubt those who seek to kill me will have no qualms in also harming you. I mean to make certain you can defend yourself should the need arise."

"Defend," she echoed. "Like with a knife?" Escape would be far easier if she were allowed access to some weaponry. Given a blade, she could be free within the hour.

Lucias shook his head. "Unarmed combat only." One corner of his mouth lifted for a brief moment. "Even if I trusted you with something as simple as a dagger, you'd need more training than I've time to give." Waving the men back, he beckoned her forward.

"Surely you do not expect me to fight in *this*." Her dress barely let her walk freely.

A black brow rose. His lips twitched with the shadow of a smirk. "You're wearing undergarments, are you not?"

She folded her arms over her breasts, steadfastly attempting to ignore the panels of the gown digging into her flesh. Did he imagine her parading about in naught but petticoats? "What lies under my skirts is none of your concern."

"I wouldn't agree there." He chuckled, the sound heating

her cheeks. "In fact, I am *very* interested in what's under your skirts." His gaze, bright with amusement, ran over her, fanning the warmth across her face. "Perhaps it is for the better if you learn within the strictures you shall be living with. Now come at me. I promise I won't hurt you."

He wouldn't hurt her, would he? *Well, I'm making no such promise.* If she couldn't do permanent damage here, then she could at least deter him. Do it well enough, then perhaps he'd amend his decision to keep her. She swung, her fist aiming for his face.

Jerking out of the way, Lucias caught her arm. "No, no, no. You don't want your thumb *there.*" Cupping her hand, he prised open her fist, unfurling the thumb from beneath the protective cocoon of her fingers. "Not unless you're looking to break it." He manipulated her digits, tucking the thumb against the bottom curl of her fingers. "There." Stepping back, he spread his arms wide. "Care to try again?"

She frowned down at her hand, clenching it until the ragged, bitten ends of her fingernails dug into her palm. Maybe knocking him unconscious would allow her access to the gates... and freedom.

Her gaze lifted to take in the handful of men quietly flanking their lord. What steps would they take if she *did* knock him out? She swung up, aiming slightly lower in imitation of the fighting on the streets. Hit his chin and he'd go down. She'd seen so many successful attempts done. It had to work.

Once again, Lucias dodged her blow. "Better." Grabbing her by the shoulders, he swung them around. "Now put a little more force behind it." Grinning, he stepped back. "Also... Try not to overreach so much."

Clara rushed at him, thumping at his chest and stomach with equal force.

He took most of her punches, grunting as they landed, only moving to deflect whatever blows she aimed higher or lower than his torso. "So easy." His arms wrapped around her, drawing them closer together. The musky scent of dry-ing sweat clogged her nose. "One could believe you *want* to be caught."

She pushed against him, wriggling to get free of his grip. Nothing gave. She might as well have been trying to shove down a wall.

"I wonder…" He pulled her closer, crushing her to his chest. Cupping her chin, he tilted her head back. "What else will you allow?" His eyes, dark enough in the noon light to be called black, lightened a shade towards brown as his head shadowed her face. "A kiss?" His lips neared hers, parting to let his hot breath caress her skin.

Shivering, she stopped trying to fight him. If he wanted to take her now, she'd no say in the matter. Nothing she did would be enough to keep him away. Her fingers brushed the hilt of his sword. *Given a blade…* Her knee came up. His hold on her loosened and the sword came free.

She scurried back from him, gripping the weapon tightly in both hands. The blade glittered in the light. It was heavier than she'd imagined. She could lift it. Barely.

"And what shall you do now?" Lucias asked, all trace of humour evaporating. He straightened, his hand pressed to his lower gut. Her aim had been off. "Run me through if you think it wise, I'll still heal." He gestured with his other hand. Behind him, the men drew their weapons. "By then, *they* will have subdued you."

"You won't always be in the training grounds." She'd entered his chambers before, unwittingly yes, but she could do it again. Preferably whilst he slept and not surrounded by his men. "And I'll *never* stop trying to escape this place." *Given a blade…* "I could kill you. Anytime." She could. As easy as any other man. Easier even. No one would know she'd done it until the next morning. She could be far from here by then.

His eyes narrowed. The sword wobbled in her hands, slipping from her grip to float across the space. "No, you won't." He returned the weapon to its sheath, the hiss of its passage deafening.

Clara ground her teeth together, fiercely resisting the urge to scream as it came bubbling from deep inside. "You don't think I've the stomach for it?" The air around her hardened, pinning her arms to her sides. More magic. Dear Goddess, why did he bother with this pretence of courteousness when he'd such power at hand?

Lucias stood before her, his left hand holding tightly onto his sword hilt. "Oh, you've the stomach alright." The unseen restraints released an arm. He took up her hand before she'd a chance to move and gently kissed the back of it. "Just not the heart."

<h1 style="text-align:center">CHAPTER SEVEN</h1>

Rough stone scraped across Clara's knuckles, mindlessly grating off a layer of skin. Cursing under her breath, she jerked her hand back to suck at the barked flesh. Chips of stone and dirt coated her lips. She spat them out.

This *had* to be the way. She'd walked it several times to be sure. Walls couldn't move on their own. Especially not in the dingy old servants' passages. It'd be no help to anybody at all to let them get lost down here. Why, a person could wander for hours before they were found, maybe even days. *With naught but the cold stone around you.*

She reached out, her hand slapping against the brickwork. Could someone have bricked it over whilst she'd been locked in her chambers for the last three days? It wouldn't matter. If this route was blocked, she'd find another way.

Her fingers danced along the stone, feeling for the mortar between the bricks. Hard to tell between something being fresh and wet or merely old and damp. Squinting, she peered into the darkness, hoping to see anything different.

It wasn't moonless-sky dark, which at least had a lighter edge to the skyline. This was the sort of blackness the night could only dream of being. The kind where you weren't quite sure if the hand you knew you'd just waved before your face had *actually* been there. This was a place where you were wise to bring a reliable lantern and a dozen or so matches to boot.

Above came the mournful groan of the main gate opening.

Of course, she'd gone right at the *previous* junction. This was the *left* turn. How could she have let herself get a step behind? One wrong turn now and she'd miss her chance.

Putting her back to the wall, she marched off into the dark, steadily counting her steps as she went... *ten... eleven.* Up the second flight of stairs she came to, then another left at the top and onwards until the last barrier to freedom stood before her. Naught but a simple, wooden door.

Clara peered through a knothole. People with torches bustled about, tending to their business in the eerie single-mindedness she'd come to expect from servants of the Great Lord. *Not far now.* She pushed open the door, the hinges giving a tiny peep of protest. The sound was all too easily lost in the clatter outside.

Little shivers of glee tickled down her spine. Too easy to catch, was she? The entrance sat just to her right, likely still open and a few sprinting strides away. Nothing stood between her and it.

She slipped out into the courtyard, pressing one shoulder to the wall. *Keep to the shadows,* she chanted. *Walk like you belong.* No one ever bothered anyone who seemed as if they were meant to be there. With her new, high-necked gown, she should resemble a servant from afar.

In the middle of the yard stood a carriage. A hideous boxy thing, bound with metal in too many places to be carrying anything nice. *An iron wagon.* She'd never seen one before, but she'd heard of them a great many times. *Be good or face the iron wagon.* Clara shivered at the memory. The priests, the guards, her parents... From before the first time she'd been old enough to walk the streets alone to just a few months back, she would always hear that warning.

The doors opened, the carriage rattling as the heavy panels swung freely. Clara paused, unable to tear her gaze from the dark shapes within. *Criminals.* The law said if you weren't good, then you must be bad. And all bad men met their end here.

"Come on! Come on!" a man bellowed, thrusting his torch into the wagon. "Step out or be dragged out, your choice." He laughed, the dreadful sound echoing in the silence. "Be the last one you'll ever get."

One by one, the three men left the dubious safety of the iron-bound box. *They look so normal.* She never would've picked them as criminals. Maybe the scrawny one, but only because of the guilty way he shuffled. Why one even bore a striking resemblance to—

"Tommy?" she breathed. *It can't be.* No reason it should be. Nevertheless, there was no mistaking the lanky form with its mop of dark hair. She could recall his face just as easily as the countless times he'd cheerfully helped her and then been on his way to whatever alley he slept in. *What's he doing here?* There wasn't a chance he'd done something wrong. Surely this was a mistake.

Clara pulled her gaze from the wagon and its men. Before her lay the open maw of freedom. Darkness ruled the land beyond. The moon had risen, although it had become close to turning into a dark circle over the week, leaving the sky to be dusted in sweeping arcs of stars. Such a sight beckoned her forth. No one would notice her departure. Not until the morning. She could be on the road to Ne'ermore by then. There, behind those impenetrable walls, she would at last be safe.

"Onwards lads!" the driver bellowed. "That's it, step lively to your doom!"

She glanced back. The men had gone. The only thing marking their passage was the creak of a door not quite shut. *I should help him.* Tommy would be fine without her, wouldn't he? They'd see he didn't belong here. He wasn't like the other two. *Only bad men come here.* Tommy wasn't even aware of being a man. He'd been nine for the past ten years.

"Curse it all," she snarled. She couldn't leave it up to

those monsters. What would they care if he'd done anything or not? If you arrived in the iron wagon, you must be bad and if you're bad, you must be punished. The crime was no longer important.

Keeping to the shadows, Clara snuck over to the last door she'd seen move. She'd never dared this entrance. The panel gave to a cautious prod and she peeked through the gap.

Footsteps echoed from somewhere deep below, growing fainter with each stride. Down the stairs she crept, her slippered feet softly tapping on each bare step. Torches lined the stairway, turning it into a coiling patchwork of light and dark. This had to be the dungeon. A place like this would be remiss not to have one.

The end corner peeked around the curve. No one appeared to be coming back up. She could sneak in, hide in some dark corner or behind something and then it would just be a matter of waiting for the right moment to free Tommy.

"No, please. I'm innocent, I tell you! Goddess, please help me!"

Foreign words, resonant and a little bit guttural, coiled up the steps to greet her. A flash of silvery-blue light brushed the stone at the foot of the stairwell.

"N—"

Abrupt silence unfurled before her, winding its icy fingers about her neck.

Despite the heat of the torches, she shivered. *Dear Goddess, give me strength for what I must do.* What were they doing to those men? At least it hadn't sounded like Tommy. *What if he's next?* Three men had exited the iron wagon, how many had they gone through already? Would there still be time to stop them?

Clara scurried down the last few steps to halt as the final curve fell away and the dungeon lay open before her. A relatively bare space to what she'd expected; more akin to a tomb than a prison. Where were the chains and cells? And why... Why were there no prisoners?

Tommy crouched near the bottom of the steps. Beside him stood the wagon driver, along with two others wearing the red and black garb of the lord's men. Their attention seemed focused on one of the criminals as more guards dragged him out into the middle of the room, silently passing the kneeling figure of the third man who'd left the wagon. The man drew himself upright and stepped back from—

Clara clapped her hands over her mouth, smothering a gasp. Standing in the middle of the dungeon, surrounded by an array of circles and glyphs drawn onto the floor, was Lucias.

The guards shoved their prisoner onto his knees before their lord. Still not uttering a word, the man tilted his head up. On the steps, with his arms wrapped over his own head and a soft moan issuing from within his self-made cocoon, Tommy rocked back and forth.

She bit her lip. With the men fixated on their lord, it shouldn't be too difficult getting close enough to the boy without alerting the guards either side of him. Crouching, she took another step closer, freezing as one of the men shifted from one leg to the other.

Out in the middle of the room, Lucias placed his hand on the man's upraised head and spoke. Words she couldn't understand, uttered in the same resonating, guttural tone as before, spilt from his lips. The air crackled, lifting the hairs on her neck and arms. At the pair's feet, the lines encircling them shimmered, the glyphs flaring in a bright, silvery-blue burst before fading.

Clara squinted. The light continued to blaze around the kneeling man. It arced from him in great ghostly flames, then dimmed to a faint corona only to spurt anew.

Still talking in the strange language, Lucias removed his hand from the man's head. The glow rose with his fingers. It pulsed to some unheard beat, taking the form of an upright man before crushing down to a palm-sized ball. Then, with a flick of his wrist, the light vanished. "Stand," Lucias commanded, his voice hollow. "Return to the others."

The kneeling man obeyed. Moving stiffly, he halted by the guards who bent down to haul Tommy to his feet.

Crying out, the boy struggled. He lashed out with foot and fist, too wild in his flailing for his blows to connect with much force.

"No!" Clara staggered down the last of the steps after them, stopping as they all faced her. The men, both criminal and guard, watched her with their flat eyes. Just like the men who'd kidnapped her, and the old women who attended her during the day. Lifeless. *The light.* What had it been? *What has he done*? What could he possibly *take* from them?

"How did you—" Lucias scrubbed at his face, dragging his fingers back through his hair. "I am ceasing to find your attempts at escape amusing," he snarled. His head snapping around, he glared at the nearby men as if they were responsible. "See she is returned to her quarters and make sure there are at *least* two of you guarding her door." His gaze dropped to Tommy whilst the lad was forced to his knees before him.

No. A hand clapped onto her shoulder, pulling her backwards. She shrugged it off and raced across the room before they could stop her. "Leave him be!" Collapsing at Tommy's side, she wrapped an arm around the boy's shoulders, briefly aware how her hand barely made the final curve.

It was always hard to remember he wasn't a small boy. For some reason his form tended to shrink in her mind, although common agreement on the streets made him two years older than she. "It's okay, Tommy." She smoothed his hair, steadfastly ignoring the urge to then wipe her hand clean on the folds of her skirts.

"Clara." Like a frightened child half his age, he snuggled against her, pillowing his head on her shoulder.

Lucias glared down at her, his heavy brows furrowing. The light had taken over his eyes, turning them into silvery-blue orbs. All around them, the circles glowed and pulsed.

"Release him at once!" he demanded, his voice taking on the guttural note.

Tommy wriggled in her arms. Whimpering, he buried his face into her armpit. Clara sorely wished she could do the same.

"Please, my lord, I beg you, don't harm him." Her grip on the lad tightened. "Tommy's never done a thing to anyone."

His expression did not falter. If anything, it hardened. "He must have done *some* thing to end up here."

"Does he look to you as if he's capable of any sort of crime?" Minor theft, maybe. Who would care if he took the food no one else would want to eat? No one had been bothered by him taking such items before. Not enough to warrant a trip in the iron wagon. *Poor boy must've been scared half to death.* And by the look in the two criminals' eyes, Lucias planned to take Tommy closer still. She shrank back. What *had* he done to them?

Lucias sneered. "Looks have nothing to do with it."

Although a small part of her agreed, Clara shook her head. "I know him." She'd witnessed a horse kick out at the boy, sending him flying across the street and into an alley. Tommy had emerged with several fresh cuts and scrapes. He'd then hobbled up to the horse, patted it and *apologised* to the beast. "He wouldn't hurt anyone." She doubted he'd even the capacity to dislike, never mind hate.

"Those who come here have already been found guilty. I cannot release him."

Clara no longer knew whether she or Tommy shook more. "Then give him to me. To be my servant." Someone who could aid her in escaping without alerting Lucias.

One brow twitched up. His face darkened, the silver-blue light in his eyes increasing as his gaze flicked from her to Tommy. "What would you want with a page? You're unlikely to have any errands which my men cannot handle."

I could make some. A letter to her mother would be precedence. Having him discover the way out would be better. "Please."

Lucias hesitated, seeming to mull over her request. "No." He stepped closer, towering over them. "I cannot let him wander these halls with him still in full possession of his soul."

His soul? Was that what Lucias had taken from those men? She'd never have thought their lifeless gaze was because of their missing soul. She swallowed the bile rising in her throat. "Let me have him as my personal servant and I-I swear I..." Taking a deep breath, she let the words out in a rush, "I'll stop trying to escape."

"You—" The silvery-blue light in his eyes vanished in a blink, allowing them to regain their original dark colouring. "You'll *what?*"

"I'll stop trying to escape," she repeated, her voice little more than a whisper. Trapped here and the only one who'd care, let alone help, would be a young man who thought of himself as a boy. Her chest tightened at the thought. "I swear it."

Lucias frowned. "You'll stay in exchange for the lad to keep his soul? And with the understanding that, *should* you decide to try escaping, I shall resume his punishment, for regardless of whether you think he's in the wrong or not, his fate has already been decided."

She nodded. A tear escaped down her cheek to fall on Tommy's shoulder. She'd been so close! *I could be halfway down the mountainside by now.* But no, they'd taken him. And why? She wished she knew. Whoever had thought it a good idea to be rid of him, had also taken her last chance at freedom.

The glow emanating from the circles died. A handful of torches dotted the room. Their light, so common after the unworldly shimmer, sparkled off the elegant curves of pale stone set into the grey slabs of the floor.

"Deal." Lucias marched over to where his men, and the newly-recruited criminals, still waited at the foot of the stairs. "Take the lad with the others," he said to one of the guards, "and have him adequately enrobed. Gettie will know with what. But no armour." He glanced over his shoulder at Clara and Tommy. "And make it known he is *not* to be given any weapons." His voice echoed behind him as he trotted up the steps.

The man Lucias had spoken to bowed. "As you command, master." He swung around to face Clara and Tommy, his eyes bearing a familiar flatness. The soul that powered him stolen.

Master. She hadn't given any thought towards the word when Sirius had first used it to address his lord. It was a common enough saying in Everdark to be dismissed. Now she could all too readily hear the intonation. Master of their lives. Of their *souls*. What did he do with the souls once he had them? Did he use it to power his magic?

And what of her? *My patience is not eternal.* His words. Would he take her soul too if she kept refusing his company? Her stomach quivered. The trembling fast spread outwards, robbing her of any strength.

The men tore Tommy from her grasp. Clara couldn't stop them. She couldn't stop anyone. Least of all Lucias.

CHAPTER EIGHT

*S*he stared at the painting before her without truly seeing it. Somewhere on the outer rim of her thoughts came the vague awareness it was a woman, dressed in a black gown or a colour close to it.

Someone cleared their throat. A dark shape hovered on the edge of her sight. "I hear your page has returned from his errand." The figure took on the more recognisable, yet no less ominous, form of Lucias.

She nodded. Yesterday, as Tommy's first task, she'd given him a letter for her mother. The boy had gone off with, at Lucias' insistence, a couple of armed men for his protection. This morning, he had returned with a response.

Of all the people to miss her presence, Clara thought it would've been her mother. But no, not Marian Weaver. She'd mourn her husband's passing until her death, yet couldn't care less if her daughter, her only child, was trapped with their lord. Not having Clara there to take up needless space and money seemed to have been her only concern. On top of it, she'd the nerve to ask if the Great Lord wouldn't mind *compensating* her for the loss of Clara's abilities.

On the edge of her vision, she saw him lean against the railing behind them. "I'm sorry. It must've come as quite a shock."

Clara shrugged. He couldn't be blamed for her mother's

callousness. Why, her mother had revealed in the letter that she'd been meaning to match Clara with the cobbler on Main Street. *Arranged without even a mention of it to me.* The widower was twice her age, with children nearly as old as she and no doubt looking for another wife to add to his brood.

She could imagine her father coming up with such a ridiculous idea. *He* would've at least listened to her when it came to preference, but her own mother? *She'd planned to hand me over next month.* Her teeth ground together. She refused to be disposed of like chattel.

Lucias let out a soft, considering hum. "I've done as you've asked with the boy. Are we back to you not speaking to me now?" There was an edge to the words. Cool enough to slip its iciness into her gut.

She shivered despite herself.

He cleared his throat. "I fully believe you shall keep your word and have even given you leave to walk the Citadel unescorted as proof of my trust in you." True, the hallways and rooms may have been hers to wander whenever she felt like it, but he hadn't granted her access to the gates. One foot into the courtyard and she could feel his men watching her every movement. "What else can I possibly do to redeem myself in your eyes?"

You could set me free. She spun to face him. "You steal men's souls." Bad men, granted, but surely no one could do something so heinous as to deserve that as punishment. "Why would you even need them?"

Silence filled the room. Her question echoed up to the ceiling several floors above.

His shoulders hunching, Lucias stared at the floor before them. Here, the natural bleakness of rock had been given a touch of colour by way of a narrow rug running the curved length of the landing. Like most of the decor, it was a dark red.

Then at last, he sighed. "It wasn't my idea, if that's what you mean to imply. This..." He sneered. "This *gift* has been passed down through my family, from father to son, for... I make it *eleven* successions now."

Eleven successions. *Hundreds of years.* They'd been stealing the souls of the kingdom for *hundreds* of years. "But... why?" What use could they be?

"I've little idea what my ancestors aimed for. We seldom get the chance to meet our grandfathers but, according to my father, my *grandfather* preferred using the power to punish those who deserved it. My father followed in his footsteps." His head drooped, his unbound hair obscuring his face. "And so must I."

"You could just stop."

"You sound like my mother. She'd no perception of this land's life either." His head tilted, sending a ripple across the unkempt locks "Tell me: if I stop, what would we do with the criminals who would've been brought here?" The glint of his eye came through a break in the curtain of hair. "They'd still be around, you know. A crime doesn't just go away because it's no longer punished." He tucked the hair behind an ear. "And we no longer have prisons big enough to house much beyond a dozen or so men. I suppose you could hang them all, but it'd be a waste of a perfectly good resource. Is it not better for the kingdom if they serve to protect what they once tried to destroy?"

She shook her head. "They've been given no choice."

The soft, contemptuous gasp of a laugh escaped his lips. With his hands clasped behind him, he left her side. "I can relate," he murmured, the words all but lost over the thud of his boot heels against the blood-red rug.

Clara trotted after him. "*You*? You've more choice than anyone here." More than her. Certainly more than the men he commanded. "How can you possibly understand?"

He rounded on her. "*I've* more choice than most? We are under constant threat of war and the presence of our army is the only thing stopping invasion."

Even living at the heart of the kingdom, she well knew the volatility of the relations with their neighbours. "What does it have to do with taking—?"

"Who do you think makes up the main force?" His shoulders shook. The dark eyes glittered with repressed anger. "Would you rather free men, *good* men, be pressed into service and die whilst the murderers and thieves of the land grow fat?"

Her mouth worked silently whilst her mind struggled to find an answer. Of course it wouldn't be better for honest men to fall in place of the corrupt, but to willingly drive those who'd no choice in the matter to their deaths seemed just as wrong.

"It was my grandfather's idea." A hand, seemingly of its own accord, flicked towards a painting. It held a man garbed in black and red, his face lined in a permanent frown. "Or may have been my great-grandfather's, I forget exactly." Again the hand twitched. She daren't let her gaze wander to the wall. "No free man has been conscripted for decades. What would've been soldier's wages have been used to better the kingdom instead. And, more importantly, those who would've destroyed the land would instead fight for the freedom of others."

And die without ever knowing such freedom again. "You could change it."

"It has been this way for over six *hundred* years. Since our reign first began, we've had numerous kingdoms attempt invasion, but they've never won. Despite their best efforts, we've *never* been conquered." He shrugged. "It works. Quite well, in fact. In light of such evidence, I'd be a fool to change it."

Clara frowned. Had she imagined the catch in his voice? The subtle twang of an old wish one has long known would go unfulfilled. Taking people's souls, especially those of criminals, couldn't be pleasant.

Their idle wandering had taken them to the foot of the stairs leading up to the northern wing. The paintings had aged with each frame. *Eleven successions.* Apart from the newest one hanging at the head of the stairs to the lower floors, all of the portraits depicted men. She couldn't recall seeing Lucias amongst them. *Eleven pictures.* Her gaze fell on the wall's last painting. Was this the face of the man who'd started it all? He certainly didn't look congenial, but hardly threatening either.

"Lord Kerwin the... Vanquisher."

She glanced over her shoulder at Lucias. The name sounded familiar. *It couldn't be.* "The first Great Lord?" This atrocity went all the way back to the founding of the kingdom? Surely she hadn't heard right. Someone would've found out by now. Everyone would know.

Lucias bobbed his head. "He was indeed. And aptly named as it so happens."

Clara peered at the portrait. *Vanquisher?* The wizened face spoke more of an old scholar than some mighty warrior. Certainly at odds with the image the old stories used to conjure. But then, a sorcerer would have other means at his disposal than brute force. "How exactly did he vanquish his foes?"

"It's said he originally designed the *gift* to only be used for his enemies, the rival nobles of the land, and their more... meddlesome underlings. Then he would have them order the attack on the outlying settlements." He paced the narrow section between the wall and the railing. "This was back before a true kingdom had been forged, you understand. There were many enemies then. The land had long been divided into little, squabbling estates and they fought over practically everything."

She nodded. Her knowledge of the kingdom's past may not have been as good as his, but she knew there'd been much fighting at the beginning. "What happened in the end?" He'd died, obviously.

But there was much about what she'd been taught that she was beginning to doubt. Distinguishing which parts were real and which were false didn't seem quite so easy anymore. Especially when she couldn't be certain of which facts to trust. What had been glossed over to shield the common people?

"He was, I believe, slain by his own son. He grew a little bit... Well, unhinged at end."

Unhinged. With all those men blindly obeying his will. How bad could it get with such power at his command? Feeling cold, she put her back to the painting. "In what way exactly?"

He grimaced. "I've been told he tried to take his son's soul. I'm surprised you don't know this."

"Criminals leave, they don't come back." At least, not the same. "Most believe they're either killed or imprisoned." It's all her parents had ever said. They were, in a way, right about the latter. They'd been trapped within their own bodies. Owning the same memories, moving the same way, just unable to act as they wished. When it came to why most of them came here, she supposed it was a good thing. "If you can take anyone's soul, my lord, then why haven't you tried to take mine?"

One side of his mouth twitched upwards. "I did wonder when the thought would cross your mind." A hand ran through his hair, painstakingly combing the strands back from his face. "Simply put, a soulless body cannot create or carry life." He held up a finger, stilling her before she could even think to speak. "I require a woman who can conceive my heir, not another servant."

"Then you might want to start looking for another woman." She'd rather death took her than be forced into either service.

He smiled. At least, his lips curved. Sadness haunted their corners. "I hope it does not come to such measures. I've precious little time."

"You're not ill." She eyed him. Several words came to mind. Ill was definitely not one of them.

A chuckle shook his shoulders. "If only it were something so mundane." Wordlessly, he walked down the hall, returning to stand before the sole painting of the woman. "I wonder if you recall my mention of the messenger who brought word of my father's death."

She nodded, her gaze flicking to the portrait, appraising it properly for the first time. Unlike Clara's gaudy attire, the woman's dark gown was trimmed and embroided with what she swore was gold thread. Although the lady lounged upon the throne—the same one in the room below, Clara was certain of it—there seemed to be a subtle majesty about the way she held herself.

Clara bent to peer at the small, brass plaque on the frame. *Lenora of the Raven Household*. Was this his mother? She supposed he bore a certain resemblance to the woman. In the nose certainly. It was a powerful nose. Fit for any nobleman. A pity it had found itself on the face of a noble-woman instead. And there was the dark hair; glossy, like the wings of her family's namesake.

"There was more in her message than the simple affir-mation of my father's death. She knows I didn't need it. She sent a… I suppose you could call it a threat. The man who'd killed my father shall be sent after me. She's quite certain he'll defeat me just as easily."

"But she's your mother." Any defeat, especially one at the hands of this barbarian, could only mean Lucias' death. *What would they do with me?* Clara cringed as the thought bubbled up. Perhaps they would let her leave. She was, after all, his prisoner. "She brought you into this world."

"*That* she most certainly did. Although you can hardly say the choice was hers and, technically, she's still consid-ered an enemy of the kingdom. She never stopped fighting." Lucias shrugged, turning his back on the painting. "Whereas I'm my father's son in enough ways for her to jus-tify having me killed off. No doubt she sees it as a service to her kingdom to ensure my death and allow the land—" He took up her hands. "—*our* land to grow defenceless."

The kingdom. Always did he speak as if his death would cause the earth to shake. Clara leant close. "Do you think me a fool?" One hand slipped free of his grasp. "No mother would order the death of her own son."

The brief huff of a sound seemingly caught between a sigh and a sob hung in the air. "Oh, to have such innocence." Those dark eyes peered into hers. An old sadness lingered in their depths. His lips curved, mirroring the emotion. "It must be nice to have an uncomplicated outlook on these matters." Softly patting her enclosed fingers, he released her other hand. "Keep your illusions if you must. I am aware it's not the norm, but I assure you it *is* the truth."

She backed away, uncertainty gnawing at her. Perhaps his mother *did* plan to kill him. *And me.* The woman would be all too aware of the reason behind Clara's imprisonment. She had to be gone by the time his mother arrived, whenever she did. But how? She'd given her word she would not leave and if she went back on it, then Tommy would lose his soul. "Will your mother not have me killed if I'm found to be pregnant?"

"Naturally, I would send you away before then. Somewhere safe to raise our child in peace."

Away. Far from here, where no one would know who she was, let alone find her. She'd be free to do whatever she wished. Go wherever she wanted. "Then do it. Send me away."

A chuckle curved his lips further and gave a glimpse of a row of perfectly whole teeth. "You would need to conceive first." He leant closer, a hungry glint appearing in his eyes. "And in order for it to happen we would need to..."

Clara took another step back.

"Ah." The sad smile returned. "I didn't think so." He swung around to descend the stairs, his hand on the sword hilt tipping the sheathed blade upwards. "I've no doubt my mother will seek to strike as soon as she is able. There are dozens of men on guard in all the pathways joining our kingdoms and many more between here and the border to warn of this barbarian's passage." Lucias halted at the midway platform. "You've until the moon completes one cycle to choose how you will come to me or, regretfully, I shall have to decide what to do with you."

She watched him go until she stood alone except for the cold eyes of men who were long dead. Madmen. Murderers of a sort. Certainly thieves of the ultimate treasure. Yet they'd cobbled a kingdom from their madness, had made a land that depended on the continuation of this dark magic to protect it.

She couldn't aid in this wickedness. *I have to get out of here*. And, because it didn't feel right to leave him trapped in this madness, she'd take Tommy with her.

CHAPTER NINE

*T*he Citadel's halls seemed endless. Whenever she wandered them, there would always be a new corridor she hadn't walked down or another set of rooms she'd not yet explored. All of them uniform in their oppressing air and, once she'd reached the upper levels, devoid of anything but the presence of rats.

This time, her feet had led her into the northern section. Her slippers padded down the carpet, each step deliberate and soft.

Like in the Citadel's main rooms, the dust here had been wiped free. No cobwebs adorned the ceilings and the windows on her left allowed a generous stream of sunlight to pour in. It heated the hall, the warm air inviting her to stay a little longer.

She could see why Lucias had chosen to reside in this region of the Citadel. Fortunately, he would be down in the training grounds at this hour. It seemed he could often be found practicing his swordplay, although from what she'd seen, she couldn't understand how he could possibly improve it.

"…the alterations?"

Clara halted midstep. *Lucias*? But he wasn't meant to be here. His voice, a mere whisper in the pressing silence, had emanated from somewhere behind her.

She spun. No one else walked the hall.

"They have been done as per your request, my lord."

Gettie. She frowned at the last door she'd passed by. Creeping up, she peered through the crack, her eye fast watering as she struggled to decipher what she saw. There was a blob that might be a table. Atop which sat a lit candle. Behind it, the wall.

She prodded the door. It swung inwards a little. Enough to ease her eyes, but not showing more of the room. Perhaps this was the wrong door.

"Master," Sirius said, his voice alarmingly loud. "If I may speak bluntly." There was a pause. Lucias must have given his assent for the man continued, "I do not see why you're going to such extreme lengths just to get the girl pregnant. I certainly wouldn't be pandering to her."

"I'm sure if I desire the advice of a murdering rapist on how to handle young women, you shall be the first man I seek out."

A shadow moved against the wall. Now her eyes knew what to look for, she could spot the decidedly human shape. Was it just the three of them within the room?

"My apologies, master," Sirius said. "I merely suggested you'd get a better result using your father's method and seeking redemption aft—"

"Because it worked so well for him. Oh, wait. He's dead. By my mother's order, if not by her hands."

"And yet, my lord, here you are," Gettie said. "If you continue at this rate, you cannot be certain the girl has conceived *and* send her away before your father's murderer arrives."

The creak of wood filled the silence. Did he consider her words in earnest? Clara pressed her face closer. Would speak his answer? What would it be?

The old man grunted. "Master, forgive my impertinence, but you should've heeded my recommendation and chosen the fair-haired one. Even the obnoxious brat would've been in your bed many times by now."

"I don't desire some simpering cow, Sirius. Nor do I feel

inclined to steal old Farris' future wife. He's welcome to her. They should be well matched."

Someone near the door shuffled their feet.

Clara held her breath. Creeping back from the door, she waited. The noise stopped. She exhaled, softly lest they heard her.

"There are plenty of women who would accept payment for carrying my lord's child." Gettie again. The woman used softer words, but no less pleading for her lord to change his mind.

What a thing to be suggesting. *Just the thing I need to be free.* Although she couldn't imagine what sort of woman would accept payment in lieu of their child. Would they have mother and babe separated at birth? *Would they do it to me?*

She shook her head, scattering the idle thought. What did she care? She was not planning on letting him get close enough for such questions to matter.

"No! I've told you I do not want my son to come in such a way."

"My lord." The woman paused, the intake of her breath audible. "I do believe what you *are* wanting you simply cannot hope to possess."

A chill silence seeped into the air. Clara cringed. Unable to see them, she could still picture the two servants doing the same.

"Gettie, you forget your place. I am your master, you will show me due respect and you will hold your tongue."

"I apologise most profusely, my lord, but—"

"I said silence!"

Something hit the door, which snapped shut and pinched the tip of Clara's nose. She stepped back, biting her lip to keep from crying out and rubbed furiously the offended organ.

The wood groaned, the door pushed against its frame until, with the hinges screeching, it won free of its confines, flying across the hallway to shatter against the opposite wall.

Gettie sat in the remains, blood dripping from a cut in her temple. She lifted her head, her face frozen not in fear, but a calm mockery that spoke of acceptance of whatever would follow. Like the men Lucias sparred with, the old woman couldn't help but obey her lord.

"I—" Lucias strode over to the stricken woman. Gripping her wiry arms, he helped the old servant to her feet. "Gettie, I'm sorry, I didn't me—" He stiffened. His gaze lifted to stare at Clara, recognition slowly moulding his face into one of despair. With a snarl that rattled the candles in their holders, he stormed off down the hall.

Clara watched him leave, waiting until he was well out of sight before turning her attention back to the injured woman.

Giving the cut a closer inspection, it seemed worse than she'd first thought. Quite deep in fact, although not as severe as the cut the man had suffered whilst sparring with Lucias. *Of course.* The training grounds could mend a wound like this in seconds. "Come on, we'll get you down to the training grounds and—"

"No, mistress, that'll be where he's headed."

She frowned. Surely even he wouldn't deny the woman a brief moment to take advantage of the healing magic. Then again, she hadn't thought him capable of striking someone as old as Gettie either. *He hadn't meant to.* Even so, perhaps it would be best not to aggravate matters and give him some time to calm down. "I'll need some thread."

"That won't be necessary, my lady."

"Yes, it will be." Clara grasped the woman's arm, firmly guiding her down the hall. "Now tell me where I can find some thread."

The woman peered up at her, those blue eyes narrowing slightly as if trying to dig out an answer. Then Gettie's shoulders slumped, her manner suddenly as old and as frail as she first appeared. "My quarters are not far." She waved a hand at the hallway stretched out before them. "This way."

Clara guided the woman to her rooms, leaving the airy halls and padding on through the darker corridors, lit by the occasional torch. Windows appeared once again to grace the wall as they rounded the last corner. A few had been opened to let the warm breeze in and a hollow thwacking noise drifted on the wind.

Lured by the sound, Clara peered through the next window as they walked by. The training grounds took up much of the view below. A haze, part heat and part dust, rose from the baked earth. Lucias stood in the middle of the sun-drenched ground.

Men encircled him. Silent. Blades at the ready. Clara halted, grasping the window ledge.

The men lunged.

Her heart thudding, she watched Lucias parry one man's attack. Then, faking a thrust at a second man, he booted a third in the gut. *So fluid.* Graceful. It put her in mind of a sleek tomcat. She couldn't bring herself to look away.

"In here, mistress."

Tearing her gaze from the fighting men, she followed the woman into the room. There were no windows here. Candle ends, giving off the only light to be had, burned in shallow bowls atop an old table. Beside them sat a chair. A basket, full of various odds and ends, nestled in the threadbare cushions.

Gettie rummaged through the basket, fast producing both needle and thread. Although the wound must at least sting, she calmly held the needle in the low flame of a candle and motioned Clara towards a footstool hidden in the shadow of the table.

Clara dragged it from the darkness, surprised such a small piece of furniture could have so much weight. Placing the stool before the woman, she waited for Gettie to slowly lower herself and perch on the edge of the stool.

With threaded needle in hand, Clara began the task of sewing up the cut marring the wrinkled forehead. A thin film had congealed over the wound. It bled anew as the needle pricked the surface. Wincing, she dug further into the woman's scalp, slowly drawing the gap closed.

Gettie endured the shaky prodding in silence. Clara frowned as she fumbled with the last few stitches and tied the end. Had the roles been reversed, she'd have either passed out or would still be screaming. The woman hadn't seemed at all bothered by the wound either. Was this the soullessness at work? Surely they must feel something, for the man in the training grounds had cried out after being struck.

Carefully placing the needle on the table, she peered at Gettie in much the same fashion as the woman had done to her. "Will you be fine like this? I'm sure I can make a bandage." She eyed the bits and pieces of fabric in the basket. A few strips seemed as if they may possess some length to be of use.

"I will be well enough. Once he's had time to wind down, I shall draw upon the grounds' healing power."

Wind down? The way she spoke... This couldn't have been the first time he'd reacted so strongly. "Is he always so..."

"Odd?" The woman smiled. It was a familiar smile. One that brought to mind little children and their grannies. "It's the souls, mistress."

Clara paused in picking up the needle. "The souls?" So they *did* do something to him. She knew a man couldn't rip the essence of another from their body without suffering some sort of backlash.

"He tries so hard to keep it all inside, mistress. It's why he spends so much time in the training grounds." She shook her head, suddenly wincing and gingerly fingering the wound. "Quite foolish, if you ask me. The truth of it is, in the end, they all go a bit wonky in the old brainpan."

Clara's stomach did a little flip. Stripping the needle of the spare thread, she jabbed the sharp tip into a pin-encrusted cushion. "You don't say." Mad? All of them. She thought back to the portrait of Kerwin, the kingdom's first Great Lord. *He'd tried to steal his son's soul.* But his son had fought back. *Killed him.* He'd been strong enough to resist.

What would Lucias be capable of when the madness set in? *I barely know what he's capable of now.* She only had to look at the woman's temple to see what could happen to a person when he *didn't* mean to hurt them. *Imagine if he had.* She shuddered. And if she continued to refuse to give him the heir he so desperately wanted? Would he come to consider her as useful to him as a blind falcon?

"It's a shame things have to be this way," Gettie continued, seemingly oblivious to Clara's silence. "I used to know him as a wee boy. Such a solemn lad back then. Hard to get out much in the way of any sort of emotion from him, truth be told. I think he'd an inkling of what his fate would be years before they told him."

Clara frowned. *How old is he*? She didn't know. Early thirties would be her guess. Certainly no more than mid-thirties, although he might sit on the cusp of forty. He never said much about himself beyond the reason behind her presence. Even then, she'd a feeling he was leaving something out. She'd thought it the dark business of stealing souls, but the sensation hadn't vanished.

There was something else he didn't want her to know. Too many secrets he kept from her. "Gettie, how long have you been here?"

"Oh it's been *years*, mistress. Wouldn't have been much older than you when they brought me in."

An iciness settled in her gut, slowly drilling its way through to her spine. The woman had been a prisoner for decades. Gettie would've started walking these halls in the time of Lucias' grandfather. She'd practically be old enough to *be* his grandmother. "I thought they only took in criminals." She eyed Gettie as the old woman nodded. Hard to think of her committing any sort of crime. "What did you do?"

"Ah, yes. You are young. Don't suppose you've heard of

the old tale about the Gutter of Neardim, hmm?"

Gutter? *Gutting Gettie.* The story had circulated around the older children when she'd been quite young. It had vanished from the streets ages ago. This woman was *that* Gettie?

Clara shook her head. It couldn't be right. Gutting Gettie had been a cold-hearted murderer. A monster who preyed on innocent men, ripping them open. This woman didn't look like a killer.

"Of course, I was good with the old knife back then. Still am, I suppose."

"Back in the room," she said, trying to shunt back the image of the woman doing the exact thing that had coined her name, "you mentioned Lucias wanting something he couldn't have."

Gettie's eyes glittered with the candlelight. "Were you eavesdropping, dear girl?"

Warmth seeped into her cheeks. "He was so loud, how could I not hear?" Feeling her face growing hotter still, she stood and strode over to the door. The racket of the training grounds drifted up to greet her. The thud of bodies hitting the dirt and, every so often, the dreadful clang of steel meeting steel. "Is that why he's always down there? Because of the souls?"

"He swears... How did he put it? Ah yes, prolonged strenuous activity, of any sort, helps him regain his old, less volatile, temper."

Clara crossed the hall, stepping into the window's warm pool of sunlight.

Lucias still battled the same men, or at least others who were remarkably similar. He charged at the group like a madman, the sword he always had at his side swinging to evade their blows whilst striking some of his own. No longer did the image of a sleek tomcat invade her mind. It had become a rabid lion.

One of the larger men knocked the sword from his lord's grasp, sending it flying to one side and into the shadows.

Two others lunged for him. One tackled Lucias about his waist, bearing him to the ground where the second landed on top of them. Others joined in only to fall back to a boot or fist as their lord fought to regain his footing.

Although Lucias swayed on his feet, she caught the telltale signs he'd been hit before. Blood covered the dirt at their feet in large, dark patches. His shirt had gone, likely removed before the sparring had commenced, but his back and shoulders told of where fresh wounds had healed over.

His mother needn't bother sending her pet barbarian. He would kill himself soon enough without their help. What he needed was to take up another, less dangerous, activity. But what else could cool his temper as fast as this? What would tire him out quicker still? *Prolonged strenuous activity.* Her face blazed anew at the thought, its heat slinking down her neck.

Clara plucked at the dress' high collar. *She* would not become his new pacifying tool. "Gettie?" she called over her shoulder, unable to look away from the swaying man who tried to fight even as he fell. "What *is* it he can't have?"

"Only what his mother wouldn't give and his father tried to offer, but could not." A squeak of a door hinge spoke of the woman's passage.

What did she mean by that? Clara spun, further questions surfacing. The hall before her stood bare.

Chapter Ten

er toe bashed against the edge of another step. Clara jumped, catching herself before she could stumble and do something as silly as twist an ankle. Climbing up here purely because Lucias had requested her to was stupid enough without adding to it.

She wasn't even sure *where* they were. Near the base of a tower by the feel of it. Although those steps weren't the only winding stairs in the Citadel. She could've been anywhere in this accursed place. Alone. *With Lucias.*

With her palm pressed flat to the cool stone of the stairway wall, she fingered the blindfold and gave serious thought to stripping the coarse linen from her face. *I gave my word I wouldn't.* She would've labelled it as yet another foolish choice, just above her promise to stay in exchange for Tommy keeping his soul.

Since her abduction nigh on twelve days ago, she couldn't come up with a reason not to trust Lucias' word. As far as she could determine, he hadn't once lied to her. Although he needed her solely for producing an heir, he'd been honest about it and hadn't tried to so much as kiss her after the failed attempt in the training grounds. His actions, on the other hand, well they just puzzled her.

Her foot tapped against the stone, the toe of her slipper lightly brushing another step. At least, she hoped it was a step. Ahead, muffled by the fabric pulled tight over her ears, came the soft squeak of a hinge.

What *was* this thing he wanted to show her anyway? He'd refused to answer beyond two words. *A surprise.* It could be anything. He could be leading her to anywhere. *His bedchamber?*

She shuffled on the spot. Tommy stood at the foot of the stairs. They weren't high, not from what steps she'd counted. A story or two. Tommy might hear if she screamed. There'd be naught he could do except get himself killed.

A finger not belonging to her brushed her forehead, the nail chill against her skin. Clara flinched, not daring to pull back lest she made a deadly misstep. The blindfold lifted. She blinked in the dim light.

Lucias stood before her, a mere silhouette against the brightly lit doorway. His hands took up hers and he gently guided her towards the door. The promise of light and space beckoned her forth. Shrugging him off, she stepped into the room beyond and froze.

Candlelight glittered against mirrors and polished metal. Clara flung up a hand and, her eyes watering, peered through the narrow gap between her fingers. *A bedroom.* What else could the shimmering curtain at the far end hide but a bed? Why bring her all the way up here to show her this? Was it *his* bed? Did he think her already cowed?

Her eyes having finally adjusted to the light, she took another, more cynical, look about the space. *No.* He'd never slept here. The room's decor didn't hold to his preferred motif of red and black, swapping gold for the former. And surely his chamber would have less lace.

"Do you like it?" he whispered, his breath hot on her ear.

Stiffening, she lurched into the middle of the room. Two large screens sectioned off a corner. Someone hadn't chosen just embroidery or mosaics on the panels, but opted to lavish them with both. Then they'd put gilt over the frames. Over most of the furniture, in fact. None of the other rooms bore this much ornamentation. And there was the lace... The same person had put lace on everything they could. Did he mean for her to *stay* in this temple to gaudiness?

"You... *don't* like it, do you?"

"It's a bit much." Curtains covered the left wall. They billowed in the centre, parting to briefly allow a sliver of natural light into the room. It didn't improve the look. Who would choose to live like this? "Can I not stay where I am now?" She eyed the way out. No doubt the door bore a sturdy lock to which he'd have the only key.

"Traditionally, the mistress sleeps here when not in her lord's bed." He grimaced as if suddenly aware of what he'd said. "I can have it redecorated to suit you. Anything you want." Lucias fumbled with something in his hand. "Here." He pressed the cold, hard object into her palm, closing her fingers over it. "I-I swear, there's no copy. Use it however you wish."

She opened her fist. A key, barely the length of a finger, glittered in the candlelight. *No copy*? Did he actually expect her to believe him? She'd only his word it fitted the lock at all. "You led me all the way up here to show me my new prison?" She would not be staying here. She'd rather death claimed her than be forced into another cage. However spacious and tacky that cage might be.

"I don't intend it to be such, although you can lock yourself in if you wish. What I came to show you is behind there." He waved a hand at the curtains. They slid apart at the flick of his wrist and the sharp snap of his fingers.

Like many of the rooms holding such luxury, windows made up much of the wall. Here, most of the view was barred by large leaves ribbed in green and yellow. A glass-panelled door stood in the centre, already open and letting in the cool breeze.

She stepped through the doorway and into the area beyond. Sunlight warmed her face, tempered by the wind. An earthy scent hung in the air along with an aroma that reminded her of the flower sellers in mid-spring. Breathing deeply, she pushed her way through the overhanging leaves, halting as the garden opened out before her.

Large flowerbeds took up much of the balcony, giving way to a row of small bushes. Bees busied themselves amongst the petals, each little buzz working towards a solid hum. Sunlight bathed them, its warmth a welcoming sensation after the chill climb.

Clara walked along the garden's edge, halting as her gaze settled on a metal fence running high above the otherwise low castle wall. Even here, amongst what beauty nature had to offer, she was to be reminded of her imprisonment. A cage would still be a cage even if she possessed the only key.

"My mother's legacy to this place." Lucias halted beside her, his hands clasped at his back. "I can have it removed, if you wish. Although the netting below will remain."

She peered over the edge. A large, awning-like net spanned the drop. She couldn't see a way to climb down to it, safely or otherwise. No doubt the netting was strong enough to keep a person from splatting onto the rooftops or the walkway beyond. "Your mother tried to kill herself?" She glanced at him over her shoulder.

He inclined his head. "When she was pregnant with me. My father had been walking the path below at the time. He put up the net and she tried again."

Kill yourself to destroy the heir. Her stomach twisted at the thought. How long had the old Great Lord held Lenora to make her so determined? "She didn't attempt any other means?"

"She tried. But, like you when you first arrived, she was not let near the sharper implements."

Clara winced at the memory. Although they checked each knife and fork before letting her leave the dining hall, at least they now allowed her to cut her own food. "There are other ways." Her gaze wandered to the windows and the curtains hanging on the other side. Given enough time alone, she could strangle herself with them. "I'm surprised she didn't try killing you sooner." Surely a babe would've been easier to slay than a fully-grown man.

His silence drew her back to stare at him.

Those dark eyes watched her, their sadness mirrored in the quirk of his lips. "I was removed from her side at birth. Nursed by so many servants I cannot recall all their faces." His lips curved further, the smile self-mocking. "My mother wasn't permitted in the same room as me until my fifth year and even then, not without an armed escort at my side." With one hand on his bet, his thumb hitched behind the dark leather and the other hand gripping his sword hilt, he put his back to the fence to stroll about the garden. "S'ppose it's about as far-fetched to you as my mother seeking to kill me."

She glanced at the netting. The ropes seemed new, but their anchors bore the rain-worn mark of age. "Some things are looking a little more plausible." If it was possible his mother had been imprisoned here and kept from killing herself, then who was she to say it wasn't likely the same woman would attempt to do away with her unwanted son? "Your father must've cared a great deal to ensure your safety."

Lucias halted by a raised flowerbed. "My father?" He shook his head. "I was something he needed to have. He cared more about what I was than who I am." Sighing, he sat on the high stone edging. "At his word, I was ushered off to the outposts as soon as I could lift a sword, only to return for one month of every year to live within these walls and learn of the family's *gift*." He eyed the garden as if held more than vegetation and insects. "By the end of the month, I would always look forward to my next posting. Even the dangerous ones."

"Then why stay here?" If she could get him to leave this place to an area less simple for him to enclose, then perhaps she and Tommy would be able to escape.

"This is where the Great Lord lives. It's where he's always lived. Where else would I go?"

"Surely there must be somewhere which makes you feel more at home." Would it be too much to hope there was also a young woman missing his presence? He must have had *some* small measure of womanly interaction during his time amongst the guards. The way he stared at her spoke of knowledge she did not yet possess. It scared her. And yet, it also bore an alluring edge, which frightened her even more. How long would it take before she could no longer ignore its pull and gave in?

He shrugged. "I've never stayed in one place long enough to know the city much less the people, with the exception of Endlight but..." Even with his head lowered, she could feel his gaze on her, peering covetously through the mop of black hair. "In any case, out there, amongst the guards not under my father's command, many a man's dealings with women end in the exchange of coin. I was probably about the same age as you when the local guards at Port Dank took me to a certain house along the wharf."

She squirmed, her cheeks warming despite herself. "I don't wish to—"

"It was quite the eye-opener."

Clara frowned down at the tiled floor, her face now fully ablaze. "I'm certain it was," she mumbled. She should've known, should've expected it. "Then why didn't you choose one of them to carry your heir? They would've been more suited than I in a-ac-cepting y-your..." The heat in her cheeks grew, taking her voice with it.

His gentle smile returned in force, amusement crackling in his eyes. "Why would I?" A chuckle escaped the small gap between his lips. "Apart from the necessary waiting required to ensure it is indeed *my* child, there is quite a difference between spending an hour, or a night, in their company and suffering it for nine months."

"So then you intend to do as they did to you and separate mother and child at birth."

Lucias leant forward, his lips brushing against the forefingers steepled before him. Those dark eyes stared at her. Intense. Hungry. "No," he sighed. His shoulders drooped, his hands falling to dangle between his knees. "That is to say, I had hoped you'd opt to stay." One brow lifted. "You know, I've the power to give you everything you desire."

"It'll do you no good, my lord. All I desire is to go home."

"Why?" he blurted, leaping to his feet with such speed that she jumped. "Your mother has made it plain she doesn't want you back. You have no other family to take you in."

"Because, like this place is for you, it is *my* home."

He stared at her, his mouth agape. "Fair enough. I cannot condemn what I am also guilty of." He finger-combed the hair back from his face. "I swear if I'd the time to spare in courting, I never would've..." His arm fell to his side. A sigh puffed out his nose. "If you wish to return home after you've conceived, I will not stop you. I probably won't be in any position to argue the point, if I'm to be realistic. All I ask in return is for you to give me a..." The entreaty trailed off as she silently backed away. "Again, you look at me with fear in your eyes," he snarled, following her passage across the garden. "Clarabelle, ple—"

"Do not speak that name to me!" How she hated the way it sounded coming from his lips. Like she was some farmer's cherished cow. "Clara will suffice."

He halted, his brows lifting incredulously. How many people would dare speak to him in such a manner? Anger flared in his eyes, briefly twitching across his face.

She trembled under his gaze. Would he attempt to take her here like he'd threatened to do come the new moon? Perhaps force her down amongst the flowers and empty his seed into her own section of fertile ground. Had he not promised her a month to decide? *A full passing of the moon.* She hadn't even been here half the time.

The door wasn't far, although he stood between her and it. She clenched her fists, prepared to fight her way free if she must. The key bit into her palm. "This room," she snapped, "it is mine?" Clara held her breath, both waiting for and dreading the answer. What if it was no? She didn't want to think on it.

Frowning, Lucias gave a curt nod.

Crossing her arms, she gathered her strength. "Then you have overstayed your welcome."

Those dark eyes, harder than stone, glared at her. So intense, she thought his gaze could drill its way into her mind. "It appears I have." With one hand clutching his sword hilt, he strode across the garden in silence, his boot heels tapping his fury into the tiles and halting in the doorway. "I... I'm sorry," he said, the words barely decipherable as he spoke into the bedchamber. "It was not my intention to upset you. You have been here but a short time and I understand you are not yet ready to accept your fate."

Her fate? This was *not* her destiny. She wasn't sure what the Goddess had planned for her, but it wasn't *this*. "Gettie's right," she spat, aiming to strike the one place she knew she could. "What you want, you simply cannot hope to possess."

He stiffened as if she'd run him through. The look he shot her bordered on pained, then he inclined his head, nodding gently. "I shall relieve you of my presence this evening. Good day, Miss Weaver."

Feeling sick at having spoken the way she had, she watched him leave in guilty silence. The hum of bees and birdsong gradually invaded the quiet, both sounding far too cheerful for her liking.

CHAPTER ELEVEN

$\mathcal{T}$he room had a subtle warmth about it, adding the cosy air of home to the dim glow of the candles, their ruddy light turning the gilding brassy.

With the key firmly stuck in the lock, she pressed her back again the door. Solid wood. Not enough to stop the determined. Even the lock wouldn't keep the more resolute out. No escape from this place. No secret passages to aid her in times of danger. At least, none she was aware of. She could hardly ask Lucias and expect a believable answer.

True to his word, he'd left her in peace this evening. Clara hadn't expected the dining room to be utterly devoid of life when she'd entered. Her meal, so rich in looks, had lacked the flavour it'd borne in the past week. *Twelve days.* Strange to think it had been so short a time. She could've sworn she'd spent months under this roof.

And, for the first time since she'd been kidnapped, she felt alone. Tommy sat at the bottom of the stairway, the closest he'd been for any extended time, and she still couldn't shake the feeling. Odd it hadn't struck her before. Not even when they'd shut her away against her will and left her utterly by herself with no explanation of why she was there.

Could she actually be missing Lucias' company?

Clara shuddered. It couldn't be right. She was just stunned by *not* having to listen to his soft, almost rational, voice. *Yes, that's it.* Being free of his captivating gaze and the way it raked over her every time they were together would make anyone feel strange.

An unusually square glow came from behind the screens cutting off the far corner. Was there a door along the wall? Frowning, she crept up to the black screen. The door stood open. Steamy warmth wafted in from the room beyond, bringing with it the scent of soap. A smile tugged at her lips.

Peering at the furniture, she struggled to decipher the dark shapes in the gloom. One shadowy bulk seemed to be mirroring the candle sitting upon the black surface. Closer inspection revealed what she'd first thought had been a simple desk was actually a dressing table, complete with brushes, hair clips and perfume bottles. And like the furniture, they were either gilded or crafted from a similar dark wood as the furniture.

Clara picked up the least gaudy hair clip of the bunch and squinted at the mirror. Although the single candle showed up in the silvered surface readily enough, the light it threw wasn't strong. She could make out the unflattering, pale oval of her face, but little beyond. Grumbling, she padded over to the bed and took up the candelabra sitting on the little table.

Something to her left hissed, the sound soft and drawn out like meat being slowly lowered into boiling water.

Clara swung with the trio of candles thrust before her, their flames sputtering in the breeze. She jerked her arm back as the velvet darkness of the bed curtains rose to greet her. The hissing, just loud enough to be noticeable above her own harsh breathing, emanated from behind it. She eyed the curtain. The heavy fabric encircled the bed. A lot of things could hide behind it.

She reached out to pull the curtain aside, her hand stopping short of touching it. *Get a hold of yourself.* It was an unfamiliar room. Such noise could be quite common in here. Likely nothing more than the breeze through a crack in the wall. *Nothing to be jumpy over.*

The hairs on the back of her neck weren't so convinced.

She backed away from the bed, watching the curtains. Nothing emerged from beyond the black drapes. Clara cocked her head. When had the hissing subsided? She strained to find a sound in the silence. Nothing stronger than the sigh of the wind shut outside. *A breeze through the cracks.*

The hair clip returned to its brethren as she abandoned the mirror and any thoughts of tending to her hair. A bath would soon soothe her nerves.

Light and soapy warmth greeted her presence in the adjoining room. Here, as if shunning the dreariness of its sister chamber, everything was white and silver. From the tiles under her slippers and adorning the walls to the silvery clawed feet on the bath. As for the bath itself... Why, she'd never seen a tub of such size that wasn't used for laundry or tanning.

A few tugs on the laces and her gown came free, the shift following fast behind.

She slipped into the bath. Water lapped at her neck, the rest of her body was calmly cocooned in liquid warmth. Bubbles sloshed about on the surface, dozens of little iridescent orbs practically inviting her to burst them. Unable to resist the call, she slipped a nail into one of the bigger bubbles. It popped in a spray of tiny drops.

A tray lay across the foot of the bath, silvery and burdened with soaps and bottles of varying sizes. She tapped it with a toe. The bottles shifted, glass clinking against each other. A sweet aroma emanated from them, each fragrance battling for control over her nose. She hadn't seen such a collection in the smaller bath she'd last used. Was this how most noblewomen lived? *Perfumes and glitter.* Clara plucked a sponge from amongst the bottles. *They can keep it.* Tipping her head back, she idly began to scrub.

Her gaze wandered across the ceiling. At some point, someone had decided painting it would be a good idea. The light bluish-green tiles were speckled in bubbles and every other tile had been bedecked with either seashells or fish. Her head rolled to one side to eye were the wall met the ceiling. Here, they'd painted bright, rocky-looking branches. They rimmed the room, their knobbly fingers spilling down the walls.

Clean, she stood, tepid water slopping against the bath's white sides. The air had abandoned its muzzy warmth, turning instead to a chill that had her desiring to sink back into the bath.

She hurried to the stack of beige towels on the small table beside the door. They had to be the first commonly-coloured cloth she'd seen in weeks. Just like she was used to back home. Shivering, she picked one up and started rubbing at her chill skin. They even felt the same.

Beside the towels sat another pile of cloth, this in the black and red more prevalent around the rest of the Citadel. Clara took up the top bundle. As expected, it unravelled into a nightdress. No doubt the other item was to be her dressing gown.

Dressed and warm once more, she took up the candelabra and, after extinguishing the candles within the glowing bathroom, stepped into the black tomb of her bedchamber to snuff out the other candles.

Soon only the soft glow of the lit candles in her hand held back the darkness. Soft and hypnotic, the trio of flames swayed on their wicks. Yawning, Clara strolled over to the bed.

The hissing picked up again as she touched the curtain. She frowned at the blackness draped before her. It didn't sound much like wind through a crack anymore. In fact, it sounded angry.

Steeling herself, she jerked the curtain open a ways. Something rustled within the darkness. The candlelight barely disturbed the shadows beyond. She fancied seeing the same thing shifting about on the blankets. The light glinted on what she prayed, and feared, was an eye.

Clara stiffened as if she'd been doused with cold water.

She ran for the door to scrabble at the key. *Turn, come on, turn!*

The hissing had stopped. Clara didn't dare to look behind her and see why. She jiggled the key some more. The lock clicked open. The door hit the wall with a bang.

"Tommy!" Her scream echoed down the stairs. As it faded, she caught a sigh coming from whatever it was upon her bed. Should she go down to him?

The rapid tap of feet on stone answered her. Torchlight invaded the darkness of the stairwell, preceding Tommy as he burst through the doorway. "Clara!" He clasped her arm, the fingers stronger than she remembered. "What's wrong? Are you hurt?"

She pulled free of his grip. "No, I—" She tipped the candles towards the other side of the room. "My bed…" Clara met his dark eyes and bit her lip, suddenly unsure. *He's good with animals.* What if the beast was dangerous? Would he be able to cope?

He peered over her shoulder and frowned. Hooking the torch into the sconce outside her room, Tommy took the candelabra from her unresisting hands. He strode across the room, footsteps sure and his stance more like the man he was than the child he often seemed to appear.

Clara grasped the doorframe. She should've sent him off to look for someone else. Whichever person would've been more suited to dealing with this. *One of the guards.* Even the men down in the stables would've been a better choice.

Tommy jerked the curtains fully open.

A sleek, white form burst forth from the darkness. Hissing, it flapped and scrabbled its way around the room. The animal slammed against the curtained windows. Wings beating madly against the fabric, it kicked free of them with a honk.

Heading to the other side of the room, it barrelled into the screens. The crash as they fell set it off into a fresh bout of startled honks and shrieks. The bird then skittered along the ground, aiming for the open doorway at Clara's back.

She recoiled from the oncoming beak. Spinning to flee down the stairs, Clara bumped into someone standing just at the top of the steps. She clung to them, not daring to lift her head. Bare skin lay under her hands, hairy and warm.

Arms wrapped around her, the muscles tense. Behind her came the animal's frantic honking.

"Gotcha!" Tommy cried.

She dared a peek over her shoulder. With the creature still, she could see exactly what type of beast had invaded her new room. *A swan*? No mistaking the large white body or long neck. How had something so large found its way in here?

"Don't worry, Clara," Tommy said, gently stroking the animal's neck. The swan wriggled in his arms. Yet it didn't look to be as earnest in its escape as it had before. It could only be Tommy's influence on animals. "It's just a bird."

The sleek head swung about. One red-rimmed eye slowly measured her as it regally suffered Tommy's handling.

Clara shuddered, burying herself deeper into the strong arms holding her. The man mumbled soft words she couldn't quite make out. A hand, obviously unused to soothing anything more than a favoured pet, brushed her hair in short, jerking strokes.

"Shall I take her outside?" Tommy asked.

Movement came from the man's head, his chin brushing her shoulder. Tommy obeyed the order in the quiet, simple way she'd always seen him handle animals.

She watched him carry the swan off into the darkened garden, a fresh chill forming in her stomach. If Tommy stood over *there*, then who was holding her? *He wouldn't dare*. Clara pushed away from the bare chest, glaring up at Lucias. "What are you doing here?" She tugged at her dressing gown, drawing the front close. "You said I'd be free of your presence this evening."

Those dark eyes stared back, humour crackling in their depths. "I did not intend to intrude on your solitude, but I'd also instructed Tommy to have word sent to me if you were in need of assistance." One side of his mouth twitched upwards. "Granted I was expecting it to be something a little more sinister than a rogue swan." He chuckled, his gaze lifting from her to the night-darken windows. "She must've flown down from the rooftop garden."

There was another garden up there? Why didn't they ever tell her these things? "You've a swan living on the roof?"

Lucias lips parted to reveal a flash of teeth. "Actually, we've a mated pair living up there. They arrived some years ago from Port Dank as a gift to my father."

"Well it's gone now." Clara spun, deliberately turning her back to him. "Don't you think you should also be leaving?"

He sighed. "Look, you won't want to sleep in the same bed a swan has been using for a nest. Allow me to offer my own chambers for the night."

Clara glared at the dark hulk of her bed. She could've been asleep by now if it hadn't been for the accursed bird. Her skin crawled at the thought of what could be hiding in the blankets, of the tiny creatures that could be quietly infesting the dark sheets. She fought to suppress a shudder, her stomach quivering in retaliation. "It'll take more than a mere bird to get me to share your bed." She could find another spot. There were still chairs and, if it came to it, there was always the floor.

"I'm capable of sleeping elsewhere. My bed has already been warmed and I can guarantee you'll have nothing else in the sheets with you." A boot scuffed along the stone, loud in the stillness of the room. "Including me."

She peered at him over her shoulder. He'd moved closer, the torchlight throwing shadows over his face. There didn't appear to be anything other than sincerity in his voice. What if it was a ruse to get what he wanted from her? He could've easily had the swan put there whilst she was dining. Could she dare trust him? Should she?

Clara pulled her dressing gown tighter around her, the

neck of it biting into her skin. "Lead the way," she snapped, pushing past him to descend the stairs.

He'd caught up to her by the time she'd reached the bottom. Side by side, they walked through the halls in silence. Every so often, torchlight would glitter off his sword as he toyed with the hilt. She'd never seen him without the weapon, although he must remove it from his side for the belt sat askew on his hips as if hastily donned.

Had he been abed when she'd called for her page? Obviously the command had been made since Tommy's arrival. Or had it? He always seemed to know what went on between her and the guards. Had he just adapted the situation with her page to suit him? *All I need to do is cry out and he'll appear?*

Her stomach churned at the thought, bubbling in her indecision as she struggled with the idea. She knew few people who would drop everything to come to her aid. *Especially with a mere bird.*

"You seem more distant than usual," Lucias murmured. "Are you well?"

She jerked her gaze from the sword hilt, her cheeks burning. "I'm fine." Clara stared at the hallway stretching before them. This was not the passage she recalled from her first night here. The corridor seemed wider than most and the carpet under her feet felt thicker. They left this path for an even broader hallway. Here, tapestries and paintings adorned the walls.

Where was he taking her?

Candles lit the way to a large pair of doors. Black wood shone. Light reflected off the door handles that, despite the polish, had an eerie unused look about them. "My chambers." He shoved the doors wide open. The faintest of whines issued from above. More doors greeted them, equally as dark as the first set and just as large. "The bedroom is straight ahead." He bowed as she entered the room. "I will see to it you are never again disturbed by any animals in your room."

Clara bit her tongue, thankful he could not see her face. She'd rather *he* was the one not disturbing her. "Good." The dark shape of a third pair of doors lingered on the edge of her vision. She ignored them, swiftly crossing the tiny room towards the bedroom.

Her skin tingled in the unmistakable way that could only mean she was being watched. Clara spun, flattening herself against the door and no longer sure what to expect after finding a swan in her bed.

Lucias still stood in the entranceway, quietly staring at her. "You should wear your hair down more often." His lips curved into a minute smile. "It looks nice."

Clara frowned. Did he not think she was well aware of how her hair appeared to others? *Like a waterfall of blood streaming from my scalp.* Not exactly something she wanted to embellish. Perhaps Gettie was right. Maybe the Great Lords did have more than a drop of bloodthirstiness in them. "Goodnight, my lord." Opening the door, she slipped through the gap and firmly shut the heavy panel behind her.

The warmth of a blazing fire hit her, burrowing into flesh she had not realised had been so cold. Her gaze traversed the room, taking in the dark furniture of black and red. Naught seemed out of place. Compared to the room she'd been given, this chamber had a positively cheery air about it.

Yet the sensation something wasn't quite right pulled at her.

She hadn't expected to ever find herself in this room. Now here she stood. In the heart of the Citadel. The last place she wanted to be. *I should've asked for the key.* Would he have given it to her? She sighed. Even if he had, the servants surely possessed others. No one kept a single key to a simple bedchamber.

Tentatively relinquishing her hold on the door handle, Clara scurried towards the fireplace. A poker, thick and heavy-looking, leant against the hearth. She grasped it, the uneasiness in her gut dulling with the solid weight of iron in her hand.

An armchair sat by the fireplace, the dark shape of a book nestling in its old cushions. Beside it stood a table with a platter lying atop its dark surface. Clara stepped closer, peering at the silver tray in search of a less bulky weapon. It bore naught but a few crumbs and a half-full tankard of beer. He had eaten alone?

She searched the room again. The nagging feeling still lingered. If only she could put a finger on it. What was she missing? Her gaze slid across the walls. Something was wrong with them, she knew it.

Odd. Not much could be hidden. There weren't even any curtains for someone to hide behind. *No windows.* Clara spun, checking each of the bricked surfaces in turn. Nowhere could she see a single pane of glass.

She glanced at the doors, suddenly feeling cold despite the fire at her back. There was one way into this tomb-like place, no place to hide and the corridor beyond being her only means of escape. She was more trapped here than back in the chambers he'd gifted her.

Creeping up to the doors, she pressed an ear against the wood. Silence. Clara lifted the poker high and flung the door open. Darkness greeted her, relieved by the faint twinkle of polished handles from the opposite door.

Frowning, she shut the door again. Twice he had done as he'd said. Perhaps she could trust his word. To a point. Or was it just some ruse to get her into his bed? *Well, I am already in his chambers.* Granted, without him, but he must see this as a step forward.

She'd have to be extra careful with her words and actions over the next week. And search for a way to get both Tommy and her out, regardless of what vow she'd made. She hadn't asked to be kidnapped and dragged before him.

The bed lay at the far end of the room, its shadowy bulk rimmed in black and roofed in red drapes. Someone had already pulled aside the curtains facing the fireplace, exposing the dark bedding.

Clara prodded each lump in the covers. Nothing moved. Leaning the poker against the mattress, she clambered under the sheets.

Fluffy blankets readily embraced her, fast luring her into a half sleep. Stretching, she slipped her hand beneath the pillow. Something hard and cold greeted her fingertips. Wrapping her fingers around the handle, she withdrew the item from its cover.

The blade glinted softly in the dim glow of the fire. *He sleeps with a dagger in his bed*? The sword she could understand. Almost. But this? He actually expected to be attacked in his own bed. *By who*? *Me*?

Biting her lip, she returned the weapon to its resting place. Surely not. He'd lifted her off the ground without breaking a sweat. Had easily brushed off the best of her attacks. Lucias couldn't consider anything she did to be more than a mild annoyance.

Burrowing deeper into the blankets, Clara closed her eyes and let the soft crackle of the fire lull her to sleep.

Chapter Twelve

*T*he door gave a faint squeak that was nevertheless loud in the silence emanating from the room beyond. Clara halted in the doorway. Shelves of books clung to the walls, making a maze of the room and stretching high enough for the top rows to require ladders.

He's in here? Hard to imagine anyone would bother venturing into this place. The study had a look about it that spoke of many years of disuse. Tables and cabinets dotted the space between bookshelves, the glass doors of the latter dull in the morning light. Some things, like the top rows of books, had gone grey with the dust.

But Gettie was adamant he could be found here.

The ruddy glow of a fire peeked around the end of a cabinet, toying with the glass and dancing along the display of figurines cluttering the shelves within. The soft rustle of a turning page punctuated the crackle of burning wood.

Around the corner, a pair of chairs akin to the one in his chambers sat before the hearth. A figure, cloaked in flickering shadows, lounged in one of the seats.

Between the chairs stood a table and on it, lying innocently beside a tankard, was a dagger. Clara gasped. Although the firelight stained the metal, she was sure of it being the same weapon she'd seen last night. *He took it.* Stole it right out from under his pillow whilst she slept. And she hadn't even stirred.

Faint against her footsteps, she caught the scrape of a blade being drawn across the table's surface. His hand had fallen upon the hilt, his fingers slowly lifting it into his palm.

If Lucias had returned for the weapon, he would have stood right next to her. Perhaps even leant over her unconscious form. She shivered. He could've done any number of things to her before she'd been in a position to stop him.

Except he didn't. He'd all the power to make her obey his wishes and he didn't bother to use it. Was this some sort of game to him? "That dagger was taken from your room last night."

His fingers withdrew from the hilt. The dagger rocked on the table, glittering in the firelight. "Naturally." Another rustle of old paper filled the silence. "I'd no desire for you to accidently cut yourself."

She halted at his side, her hands planted firmly on her hips. "And the poker?" What would be his excuse for moving it?

Lucias glanced up. "The what?"

Clara frowned. She'd placed the poker near the head of the bed, practically level with the pillow. How could he have missed seeing the slim rod and not stumble over it? "You *did* go into the room after I was asleep, didn't you?"

He chuckled. "I assure you, I have not yet returned to my chambers. And I certainly did not attempt such a thing last night." The book snapped shut with a dry thump. "Believe me, I am well aware of how unwanted my presence is." Balancing the book on his knee, he reached for the tankard. "I sent Gettie."

"Like you did this morning?" She could well recall the ghastly image she'd woken to. Of the old woman looming over her, a mere shadow against the candlelight. A good thing Gettie had already taken the dagger away or the Citadel would've had one less servant. Clara still wasn't sure how to feel about the woman. She *had* admitted to being Gutting Gettie, the monster who'd terrorised the men of

Neardim. Except, the old woman just didn't fit into Clara's picture of a ruthless killer.

A brow twitched upwards. The tankard lowered from his lips, the bottom gently resting atop the book. "My apologies. I was unaware she'd woken you."

"You didn't send her in?" Had the woman then decided on her own when to wake Clara? But the servants were meant to be under Lucias' full control. *They get sent all over the kingdom.* There had to be certain decisions they could make on their own. *Orders that can be warped.* Had Sirius not twisted his lord's orders on how many women to bring before Lucias?

"I haven't been beyond these walls since last night."

She took in the rumpled twist to his clothes—a simple, linen shirt added to the pants and boots he'd worn last night—and the unkempt mass of his hair. "You spent the night here?" She recalled the lonely tray and its remains of the meal she'd found back in the room. *He must spend so much of his time...* "Alone?"

"Utterly, save for my books." He waved his hand about, indicating the room in a sweeping arc, and beamed. "I used to come here often as a child, seeking solace in the tomes and scrolls of old."

"I wouldn't pick you for the scholarly type." He certainly didn't fit with her vision of them, which had more in kin with robes and glasses than leather and swords. Nor did they have any right being quite as muscular as he.

"Oh?" His shoulders trembled in a silent laugh. "I more or less had to be. My father insisted on his heir having at least *some* knowledge of the kingdom he was to govern." He shook his head. "I grew so tired of the history he forced down my throat. The battles we've won over the centuries, the internal politics..." The words faded into a weary sigh. "To think I first came here of my own accord looking for answers. For truth."

She shuffled on the spot, cold despite the roar of the fire. "And did you find it?"

Lucias drank deeply from the tankard, those dark eyes unwavering as he stared at her over the rim. He sighed again, the sound amplified by the tankard before he lowered it. "If you mean I discovered my father hadn't lied to me, then yes."

"You suspected your father was lying?" Clara had thought—truly hoped—his paranoia was a current thing, but if he'd been in the habit of distrusting his father's words even as a child... then maybe the souls weren't what made the Great Lords insane.

"My father lied practically every time he opened his mouth. But it didn't matter by then. I'd fallen for the tales all these scholars and travellers told of other lands. Places *I* could never go." He laid a hand on the book still balanced between knee and chair arm. "*This* has always been a favourite of mine."

Clara peered at the title embossed on the front. "That book..." *The World Beyond*. She'd bought a tattier version on the morn of her kidnapping. Had he somehow known? It couldn't be possible. Only two people in the whole world would've known of her purchase. And she was one of them.

"Quite the humorous read." He patted the leather cover as if it were some old and faithful hound. "Although I must say the kingdoms wouldn't be quite as pleasant as they're depicted in these pages. They've many myths about us and we're often viewed as... unwelcomed visitors."

Hugging herself, she rubbed at an arm. "The kingdom or its lord?"

"Both." Lucias leant back in his seat and nodded at the curtained window. "Tell me, what do you see?"

Clara marched over to the thick drapes and jerked them aside. The room sat high enough to offer a beautiful view of the surrounding land. She leant against the glass. Below sat Everdark in shades of grey and beige.

Her chest constricted at the sight, even though Everdark was dull against the vivid green backdrop of the land. Near lifeless in appearance. All her life she'd only ever wanted to leave the place and now... "I see a home I can never return to."

"And beyond it?"

Her gaze lifted, following the winding path of the Murkwater. It meandered by fields and forests, past the faint suggestions of other villages dotting the green, and then finally vanished into the forests standing along the border. Beyond the trees sat the milky-blue haze of the steppes. "A land I'll never get to walk over."

"You could," he said, his breath warming her neck, "if that is what you wish."

Clara stiffened. *I didn't even hear him move*. And now he stood between her and the only way out. She should never have turned her back on him.

His hand brushed against her side and she shivered as it slid down to settle in the subtle curve in her waist created by her skirts. "You've certainly more chance of wandering this world than I."

"Because of your mother's desire to kill you?" She slunk along the window, keeping her movements small in the hope he wouldn't notice. "I don't understand why she desires your death so intently. Surely you cannot be blamed for your father's actions."

In the faint reflection on the glass, she saw him grimace. "She does it because of what her people believe. We've become their nightmares, the tales they tell to scare unruly children." His arm wrapped around her waist, gently drawing her back to him. "To those beyond the kingdom's borders, I'm just one in a long line of Dark Lords," he whispered. "A line that has gone on too long by their thinking." The bitterness in his voice hung in the air, lifting the hairs on the back of her neck just as much as his breath did. "People who have barely heard of my family will envision me as just another parasite who drains men of their souls."

Clara spun to face him, tearing free of his grasp. "But you do." *And kidnap young women*. Just as his father had done with his mother all those years ago.

"To the exact same men their laws would rather see hang. At least here they can be put to good use and serve the kingdom."

"Men like Tommy?" How many men, and women, had been accused of crimes they hadn't done and suffered having their souls wrenched from their bodies?

His gaze slid to the windowpane, although unfocused as if he stared at some unseen place. "It matters not what land you go to," he murmured, "sometimes innocent people get unjustly punished." He leant forward, his hands resting on the wall behind her. "And if I have not at least sired an heir before this accursed barbarian arrives to take my life, then the real wicked men will either die with me or be set free. Such a fate is far more unjust than anything I could do to the people."

She jerked back. The corner of the windowpane greeted her with a vicious dig between her shoulders. Her eyes watering, she struggled to think of anything beyond the paralysing burst of pain radiating down her spine. "Y-you mean you don't know either way?"

"The only way to be certain is for me to die. I'd rather the world didn't find out in such a way." To her right came the squeak of his hand on the window. "Just imagine... the village being set upon by the same murderers and thieves it sent me."

In the film of her tears, Clara could see it all so clearly. If they did not die with their master, the as-for-now-servants of the Citadel would pour down the mountain in a vengeful avalanche of death, taking what they could and destroying what they could not. "The watch will—"

"The watch?" His lips twisted into the ghost of a sneer. "They would not be enough to stop such men."

He was right. She hated to agree with him, but he *was* right. She'd heard the young men who'd joined the watch boasting on how they never had to do much. *Just watch.* The tasks of tracking and imprisoning criminals were ones best left for the lord's men.

"Such a scene would play out across the kingdom. Some of the more fortified towns along the border will withstand the initial assault, but between here and them?" His shoulders flexed, sending ripples down his sleeves. "If they don't fall beforehand, they will when we are invaded." He stepped closer, pressing her against the wall. The musk of linen and warm skin filled the air between them. "I must beget an heir to keep the kingdom safe, both from internal strife and invasion." His breath fell hotly upon her face. "And, of course, to beget an heir, I require a woman."

"Me?" she squeaked. Her cheeks burned. What a foolish thing to say. Of course he meant her.

His lips slowly curved into a soft smile. "You are my preference, yes." He leisurely curled a lock of her hair around his finger. "I know it is unlikely to mean much to you in light of the circumstances, but you possess many of the qualities I desire in the mother of my child."

"Like being a virgin of age?"

The soft puff of a laugh escaped through the gap between his lips. "Those points are important, in the beginning at least. But fleeting. I was referring to the lovely strong mind you're harbouring behind such a sweet face." Releasing her hair, he caressed her cheek. "I've no doubt there's a cunning lurking in the depths of those rich brown eyes, equal, perhaps, to your compassion. You'd have done well in the Ebony Court; those stuffy nobles at Ne'ermore wouldn't quite know what to make of a woman like you."

Clara jerked her head away, fighting to quash the scorching fire in her cheeks. "So my lack of willingness to be here, to be used as you wish, means nothing?" Her arms had become pinned at her side. A bit of wriggling gave her the room to slip them between their chests. Such a position wasn't much better.

"Nobles of all kingdoms arrange—"

"I'm not of noble blood!" With her back braced against the wall, she shoved. He didn't budge.

"Yet your marriage was still being taken care of for you.

I'd have thought you would've seen me as an improvement on the alternative."

"And now you know better," she snapped, attempting to push him away again. She'd no intention of allowing her mother to shuffle her off to be some man's wife, first or second. At least the cobbler she could've escaped. "And if you think it so beneficial to have it all *arranged*, then why has it not been done for you?"

"There hasn't been a marriage in the family since the fourth Great Lord." Frowning, he glanced down and seemed to notice the placement of her hands for the first time. "In any case, apart from there not being any ladies of age—none *I* know of at least—it's an old belief too much noble blood weakens the next generation's ability to handle the power."

Something had happened back then. She could see it in his eyes. Something horrible enough to have them forsake wives and legitimate heirs. *They go mad in the end.* Was the madness what had happened to the fourth Great Lord? Had the magic, the souls, warped his mind so much he'd attacked his wife? She couldn't bring herself to ask.

"But your parents... your mother." If Lenora truly was of the Raven Household, then she'd be no less noble than any other lady of the court. "She—"

"It's been a couple of successions since any noblewoman has shared a Great Lord's bed." Taking up her hands, he softy ran his thumbs over her fingers before releasing them to step back from her with a sigh. "Besides, the Raven line has its own small measure of power."

But not as dark as the Great Lords' magic. Nor could it be as strong, otherwise Lucias wouldn't have existed. Clara inched along the wall. What did it mean for him? Would it prove to give him the edge his predecessors simply hadn't had access to? Or was he doomed to grow insane quicker than his father? She shivered, the thought of *him* going mad chilled her insides. Whether he did or not, *she* didn't mean to be around to find out.

"My lord!"

Clara jumped at the voice. The answering hiss of Lucias' blade being half drawn had her flattened against the wall without a sound. Did he expect her stand idly by whilst he slaughtered someone?

He slammed the weapon back into its sheath as Tommy appeared around the cabinet, his brown eyes wide.

Puffing, the boy staggered forward a couple of feet before propping himself on a nearby bookcase. "There... there's..." he gasped, a shaking finger pointing behind him, "m-men... on the Road!"

She peered out the window. The Road's winding passage took the mountain in great swooping arcs, allowing the sole path towards the Citadel to be visible from many perspectives. Here, she could only see a couple of corners, but coming up the Road, flanked by men on horseback, trundled a carriage.

"Endlight colours," Lucias murmured over her shoulder, although Clara couldn't tell the precise shade of the dark lacquer. He grasped her hand, drawing her out into the main section of the study.

Clara stumbled, desperately trying to free herself from his grip before she became tangled in her skirts and fell. Who had come all the way from Endlight to this dismal place?

And could they take her with them?

CHAPTER THIRTEEN

*T*hrough the halls they went, him striding along the carpet and she skittering behind like a two-toned leaf. Lucias released her hand as they reached the steps leading out into the courtyard and the green-lacquered carriage that now dominated the area. The golden image of the setting sun had been embedded in the carriage doors, its metallic sheen glittering in the noon light. *Endlight*. The first defence of the western border.

At the far end of the courtyard, so close yet no more accessible to her than the freedom they boasted, the gates swung shut.

Guards and mounted soldiers bustled about the yard, making a mockery of the paltry show the lord's men had shown when she'd first arrived. Two men, one near bald and the other blond, stepped out of the carriage.

If she were to judge by their clothing—finely-made leather armour—and the way they stood in the centre of this apparent chaos, neither one was a mere commoner. Both held themselves with a sort of rigid grace that spoke of a great wariness honed by years of living on the border and the perpetual danger of invasion. Was Endlight where the kingdom's lords learnt their paranoia?

Lucias strode down the stairs and, as if they were of one mind, the two strangers faced the Citadel's maw of an entrance.

"Ah ha!" the older of the pair bellowed. "There he is! Come here, my boy." Extending an arm, he drew Lucias into a hearty embrace. The thump of the man's hand on Lucias' shirt bounced around the courtyard. "Couldn't be having with travelling this far inwards and not welcome our new Great Lord, now could we? Especially what with being in spitting distance of your doorstep." He swung to stand at his lord's side, keeping Lucias close with an arm draped over his shoulder. "Tell me, lad, how've you been faring since your father's unfortunate passing?"

"Well enough." Lucias' mouth curved into a simple smile. "I see rumour travels as it always has."

"Swifter than the crows fly, my boy," said the old man with the nod of his head. "Thought you'd be knee-deep in young women by now."

Lucias laughed. Clara had never heard such a sound from him before. He *had* laughed in her presence numerous times, but not like this. Never so open and at ease. "I assure you," he said. "One is quite enough."

"Bah! Take it from me, lad, they wear out far too soon."

Clara halted on the top step. The man had to be in his seventies—like Sirius—yet he held himself far straighter than the hunched figure who'd greeted her upon her arrival. *Stronger too.* His shoulders, like those of the younger man, were broad and appeared to be well-muscled despite his age.

Lucias glanced over his shoulder. Untangling himself from the old man's grasp, he beckoned her closer. "Gentlemen, may I introduce my dear mistress, Clara." Taking up her hand, he brought her before the two men, keeping her just out of arm's reach of either one.

The pair eyed her. She seethed under their gazes. The younger man's face was politely neutral. But the old man... She could all but feel his eyes undressing her. She didn't think she had ever been so glad for the high collar of a gown than she was right now.

"This," said Lucias, indicating the older of the pair, "is Farris—"

"The esteemed Count of Endlight and his son, no doubt." Clara curtseyed. "My lords," she murmured between clenched teeth. Lucias seemed awfully at ease with the pair. Was there any hope of convincing the two men to take her with them?

"Quite a fine maiden you've got there." Grinning, the count gave Lucias a nudge in the ribs with his elbow, the force of which had the young lord rocking to one side. "Would've thought you'd have cured her of the blushing by now, my boy."

"Father," the man's son said with a cough. "Don't go embarrassing the girl." He gave her a low bow. "I am Thad, dear lady, and it is my utmost pleasure to be meeting you."

With her heart racing terribly, she made no move to stop him from kissing the back of her hand. His eyes were so intense, more sure of themselves than Lucias'. *And so green.* Although no man had any business having lashes so light and fine. She curtseyed again, her face heating even further. "The pleasure is mine, my lord."

Hovering on the edge of her vision, she caught Lucias' frown. His hand squeezed hers, the pressure silently drawing her back to his side. Jealousy, raw and boyish, glimmered in the cracks of his usually calm facade. Could she use it in winning her freedom? Clara tucked the thought away.

Lucias' arm wrapped about her waist, pulling her closer still. "You seem to have brought quite a number of guards for a simple trip across peaceful land."

"*He* deemed it a necessity." Farris waved a hand at Thad as his son straightened. "Especially for the journey home." He shook his head, the wispy remains of his hair dancing in the breeze. "In all my years, we've never needed to bear arms near the heart of the kingdom."

Lucias released her as, with his boot heels grinding in the dirt, he twisted to face the fair-haired man. "What news could you have possibly heard that would move you to do such a thing?"

Thad's lips, generous in their width and thickness, twitched into a grim smile. "Your mother."

Lucias snorted. His arms folding, he drew himself up. He still couldn't attain the other man's height. "So, you let her pet break through then?"

"Break through? Our scouts report your parents never reached the border."

He jerked back as if the man had struck him. "She's *in* the kingdom? But my father... I could've sworn he died on the plains before Ne'ermore not—" He shook his head. "I thought, after so long, she would seek her home."

Clara smothered a gasp. Lenora was so close? No, she couldn't be. It had been a fortnight since Clara's kidnapping. There was still a few more weeks before the new moon.

No time. The woman would reach the Citadel well before Clara's time was up. What would it mean for her plans to escape? *He will insist on an answer.* And Lucias would no doubt inflict his own response on her when she refused.

Farris coughed. "What man could guess a woman's reasons?" The joviality fell from the old man's face. "I dare say returning to Ne'ermore now would leave the truth of your death shrouded in doubt for her, no matter what the barbarian swears. Clearly she seeks to ensure with her own eyes if not by her hand that the line ends with you." His gaze fell to Clara. "Is it wise to keep her here?"

Without turning, she could feel Lucias' eyes on her, considering his next move. She knew he wasn't going to sit back and wait for her to decide any longer. He would come to her bed and take what she didn't want to give.

Tears filled her eyes, dashing the world into shimmering blobs. She swallowed, sniffing back a sob. Ducking her head, she swiftly wiped her face dry. Whatever he decided, she would not make it easy for him.

"I think it would be difficult for her to serve her purpose elsewhere," Lucias said.

Farris eyed his lord before turning to stare at Clara. He rubbed his chin, those brown eyes seeming to delve deep and pluck free the answer he sought. "You harbour a wild flower within these walls and yet... You've not transplanted her into your own bed?"

Lucias chuckled and glanced over his shoulder at her. "There has been some resistance to that particular line of thought."

"Resistance? Bah!" He tossed aside his lord's excuse with a wave of the hand. "What sort of women are they raising in Everdark these days?"

She stared at the pair, unbelieving she'd heard them right. Lucias planned to rape her if she did not concede and here he was laughing about her attempts to be free of his attentions. *And Farris laughs along with him.* These were the people who ran the kingdom? An old lecher and a would-be rapist? She eyed Thad, half expecting him to change before her eyes. What sort of distasteful beast would he turn out to be?

"Come now, father," said Thad, a soft smile moulding his lips. "You're merely jealous you didn't hear about this, or her, earlier. If all Everdark women are so spirited, then perhaps Brenna will prove just as interesting for you."

Clara gritted her teeth, disappointed Thad had fallen in line behind the other two. But still, if the count wanted interesting, he should've tried courting Penny instead of the mayor's title-grubbing daughter. The short woman would've given him enough *excitement* to last the rest of his life. Although, Penny would also have shortened it considerably in the process.

The old man frowned at his son. "Brenna?"

"Your next wife-to-be, father. Her name is Brenna Goodheart."

"Of course. Of course. I remember now. Brenna." Farris' lips stretched into a smile. "Goddess willing, it shall prove to be an exciting marriage indeed. Brenna Goodheart." He clapped an arm around Lucias' shoulder and led the way up the stairs. "I do hope she's not *too* good, eh?"

Clara idly trailed behind them. Close enough to hear the

pair without being too obvious in listening. Perhaps they would divulge some small piece of information she could utilise in her escape. Give her the edge she so desperately needed.

"Brenna's got a good temper, I know that much." Lucias shook his head. "You'll have your hands full with that one."

Laughing, Farris slapped the young lord on the back. "You wouldn't want them any other way, lad. Not for long. Keeps the blood pumping." His free hand waved in the air. "Why my dear Jen and I would argue all the time."

Clara frowned. She'd never heard her parents speak a harsh word to each other, never mind arguing. Yes, they'd have mild disagreements on some things, usually about whatever she'd done wrong, but never about themselves.

"Ah, Jen." Farris gave a lusty sigh. "Now there was a woman who knew how to get what she wanted. No other girl carries such a fire as she did."

"How many women has it been now since Countess Jennah's passing?" Lucias asked. "Six?"

The old count chuckled, broad shoulders bouncing. "Hardly, my boy, hardly. Brenna shall be my *third* wife."

And they all die as this man's wife. Clara bit her lip, sudden pity welling in her chest for the dark-haired woman the count would be marrying. How did two women die whilst in the care of the same man?

"She's the eighth, if you include the mistresses and don't count the brief flings," Thad murmured from his place beside Clara. Glancing her way, he gave her a knee-wobbling smile. "It is perhaps not my place to ask such things, but... dear lady, you appear somewhat troubled. Are you well?"

She had not inspected herself in a mirror since yesterday morning and now had a sudden urge to do so. Any reflective surface would do. It was an odd feeling. Foreign, for her appearance was not something she dwelled on. At least, not when it came to enhancing. Much of her time before a mirror was methodical and tended to aim towards dulling the extravagance of her hair. How ill did she look for him to comment?

Clara drew herself up and mustered a smile she didn't feel like giving. "Of course. I was just thinking." The count had gone on ahead, dragging Lucias with him. She and Thad were as alone as they could be without arousing suspicion. If there was ever a time to enquire about Lucias' past and Thad's loyalties, now seemed promising. "Lucias said he used to spend much of his time away from here at Endlight. Were you and he close?"

They climbed the first flight of stairs in silence. Then she noticed his shoulders shaking and those wide lips of his pursed with self-contained laughter.

"Do you find humour in my question, my lord?"

"Not at all, dear lady." He flashed her another grin. "I was just expecting to have at least been given the time to settle in the guest rooms before you began your interrogation."

With her cheeks burning, she turned her face from him. The echo of the count's laughter rang out from somewhere on the floor above. What did they speak of for Farris to find it so amusing?

"My lady," Thad said once the noise had died. "Do you so utterly distrust the words from his mouth that you must seek out proof?"

Clara halted at the top of the stairs. She had not expected for him to glean the reason behind her questioning so quickly. "Will you answer me or not?" she asked, each word clipped.

"We are like brothers, my lady. Like brothers." Thad sauntered down the hall a few steps ahead of her, the tap of his boots the only sound to be heard. "It is my turn to seek out answers, yes?" His gaze swept over her slowly and caused her to blush anew. "I believe I am entitled. I'm certainly interested to hear the reasons behind why he would pick someone like you."

She bridled at the remark. "And just what is wrong with someone like me?" Had he expected to find his lord's mistress used to be one of those women who took a man's coin and let him use their bodies? Lucias had already given his opinions on choosing someone of *that* particular background. She sorely wished he'd reconsider.

Thad held up a hand. The candlelight glittered off several fat rings and the idle realisation that Lucias did not adorn himself in such a fashion crept through her thoughts. He was plainly clothed for a man who ruled a kingdom. More soldier than king. "I meant no disrespect to your personage," Thad said. "It's just I would've thought he'd choose someone more mature... Somewhat closer to his age."

His age? Clara stiffened. She had no idea how old Lucias was. She'd been assuming, utterly hoping and fearing, there weren't many years difference between him and her. "And what, precisely, is his age?"

Thad's fair brows shot up. "He's twenty-six come the spring. He hasn't told you this?"

She shook her head. *He tells me nothing*. Only what she needed to know to serve his wish and several truths she knew were most likely revealed only in the hope it would drive her faster towards compliance.

Twenty-six. Come the spring. Although, he wasn't expecting to see out the autumn months let alone the winter. It didn't seem right for Lucias to be so young when the lines on his face belonged on a far older man.

"Well, I suppose it'd be difficult to find a woman your age who's not already promised to another man." His gaze ran over her again, this time with a more clinical eye. "You're what, twenty?"

"I'm seventeen." Was it possible Lucias also thought her to be older than she truly was? Could her path to freedom be as simple as informing him of the error? *Doubtful*. She knew Penny to be a few months younger than herself, Brenna was of a similar age, eighteen she believed, and Clara would wager the other two young women also were.

She bit her lip. If Lucias hadn't known beforehand, he would by now. And, just as clearly, did not care about the nine years between them. Why should he when Brenna was happy to marry a man old enough to be her grandfather?

"I see," Thad murmured. "About the same age as him, then."

Blinking, and not entirely sure she'd heard right, she frowned. "But you just said he was twenty-six."

He nodded. "I was referring to his time at a certain house whilst posted at Port Dank. You're like him as he was then." He leant close, his eyes bright and piercing. "He at least told you this?"

She recalled Lucias making some mention of brothels and the women who worked within along the way. It hadn't been a topic she'd wanted to hear then and it certainly wasn't something she wanted to be reminded of now. "He told me of certain houses." Stepping back, Clara resolutely crossed her arms. "It was quite enough for me, thank you."

A soft, warming chuckle escaped the wry quirk in his smile. "And from the sound of your displeasure, he made it seem like he was through those doors on a regular basis." Thad shook his head, brushing aside his fair curls as they fell across his face. "I assure you, my lady, he did not frequent them as often as you've been led to believe."

Knowing Lucias had stepped foot into one of those houses at least once was more than enough for her liking. "I did not misinterpret him *then* anymore than I did his earlier threat."

"He *threatened* you? This is still Lucias we're talking about?" The fine curves of his brows pulled down when she gave a curt nod. "What did you do?"

Her hand flattened against her chest. "Me?" Amazing how smoothly he had jumped to such an accusation. "What did *I* do?" They were indeed much like brothers, sticking together in the face of a common enemy. "Oh yes, so quick to put the blame on me." She was not the felon in this. "I did *nothing*." Her teeth ground together in her efforts to keep a civil tongue. "Including not falling into his bed in a timely manner."

His eyes narrowed. "He would not seek to push you on it."

She jerked away from him, glaring over her shoulder. "Then it would appear you do not know him as well as you thought."

He stared at her, those green eyes digging, searching for a hint of a lie. His mouth opened, a question forming on his lips.

"There you two are!" Lucias said.

Clara stiffened. The slow, steady pounding of his boots rumbled down the hall between them. How much of their conversation had he heard? What would he do to Thad if he began to perceive the man as a threat?

"I thought the pair of you had gotten lost." His arm snaked around her waist, clasping her to his side. Before she could realise what he was doing, she'd been gently coaxed into facing him. "Trying to lure her away, are we?" he asked Thad over her shoulder. There was sweetness in his voice, a hint of boyish teasing. But the cold, guarded glint in his eyes spoke differently. Lucias fully believed his old friend would attempt such a thing.

Perhaps she could prove him right.

"I wouldn't dream of it," Thad replied, "but it seemed Father was intent on bending your ear some more. How could I resist getting to know your mistress a little better?"

There it was. A flicker of distrust brushed Lucias' face. So faint and swift she would've missed it had she not been expecting it. Jealousy glowed sharp and cold in the heat of his eyes. She found it strangely sweet.

Logically, she knew the reasons behind his suspicion were little more than scraps of old brother-like resentment. Thad, with those gorgeous eyes and stunning smile, must have drawn quite a lot of womanly attention. No doubt it was a sore spot in their friendship.

Even so, applying such reasoning did little towards shaking the fuzzy warmth glowing in her chest. Lucias, who had kidnapped her and threatened to force her into accepting the mantle of mistress, believed her to be precious enough to be stolen from him.

She smirked. *That* she could use.

Chapter Fourteen

*C*lara walked the hall leading to her chambers. She was alone since Lucias had procured Tommy's services for some errand that, as far as she could determine, was on behalf of the Count. Her stomach, previously content with the satisfying weight of the evening meal, now rolled a little in response to her unease.

Having been settled in rooms somewhere on the floor below, the two men had dined with her and Lucias. Farris had spent much of the night talking to the young lords, his warm laughter booming across the room.

It was a welcome change from the quiet dinners she usually shared with Lucias, although she could've done without the old count's attempts at speaking with her. Most of his innuendos were so crude and obvious that they made her face heat just recalling them. She'd been grateful for the way Lucias quickly put a stop to it.

After she'd agreed to not flee, Lucias had tried to get her to talk more about herself, his polite inquiries centring mainly on her family and life in Everdark. Clara had no desire to be reminded of what she would never see again and chose to be deliberately unresponsive to each question.

He would then move on to talk of the places he'd been. Not in the bragging manner she commonly heard from the worldlier folk on the streets, but in a soft and casual tone as if trying to pique her interest. Although a number of cities sounded intriguing—like the large merchant piers that made up Port Dank—she'd resisted the urge to ask questions.

He'd eventually stopped talking at all during their meals.

Now, remembering how animated his face had been as he conversed with the two men, she felt an odd pang of regret. Perhaps, if she'd allowed him into her life a little bit, she could've convinced him to let her go before these men, and their news, had arrived. Not much hope of it now. Not with Lenora practically at the gates.

The need to escape grew at the thought. But could she make it possible anymore? She'd been unable to find a way out in the last two weeks. How was she going to discover a means of escape now? Surely he'd have her brought to him soon.

Her foot touched the first step leading up to her chambers. Perhaps, now his time was shortened, he was already up there, waiting for her to innocently walk into the room. *And then...*

She shuddered, flinching from the mere thought of what he would soon do. Was she safe whilst the count and his son were here? Surely Lucias would not attempt to impose his desire on her with free men wandering his halls. *As if they would hear me scream.*

Even if they did, she doubted they'd come to her aid. Both men must be aware of what the Great Lord was capable of doing to them. Yet, there'd been no hint of fear in their greeting. Perhaps they'd forgotten Lucias was now the one capable of taking their souls.

Or did they have a countermeasure? Her history of the kingdom was not as advanced as it would've been had she a noblewoman's teachings, but she recalled not all the lords of old had gone against the first Great Lord. Perhaps there was some sort of ancient agreement with the nobles who now guarded the borders.

She frowned, recalling the tales Lucias had told of his

ancestors. Could the crazed rulers of old be trusted to abide by their own laws?

"My lady!"

Thad? She spun at the call to find him marching up the corridor towards her, his face set in a purposeful glower.

"A word, if I may?"

Clara nodded for him to continue. What matter was of such import it would have him seek her out?

He clasped her by the elbow and gently led her a few paces from the stairs before speaking. "I saw you flinch when he touched you earlier today. And you watch him as if you're expecting Lucias to change into some *beast* before your eyes." He bent his head close as they continued walking, his warm breath dancing against her ear. "This threat he has made to you. What is it?"

She glanced up and down the hall. There were no corridors branching off here, no rooms with doors for an eavesdropper to listen at. They couldn't be any more alone than if she'd taken him into her chambers. And she'd already had Lucias in there, although granted he'd left upon her dismissal.

Her cheeks warmed at the reminder of how she'd spoken to him. Her gaze swung back to Thad, the heat in her cheeks burning hotter with each passing moment. "If I tell you," she whispered, "will you take me with you when you leave?"

His lips flattened into a thin line as they continued to walk. The fair brows lowered further until the inner tips touched. "I don't think he would approve."

Of course Lucias wouldn't want her taken from here. That was the point. Allowed to be free of the Citadel, Clara would spend the rest of her life ensuring he could never find her again. The rest of *his* life, at least. "If you don't help me, he'll rape me."

Thad's steps faulted. He righted himself, walking on for some time in silence. "I highly doubt he'd force you. He loathes men who stoop to such actions."

Men like the old Great Lord. Clara frowned. Did it mean Lucias also despised his own father? She could see how people could believe it. Just as she could imagine how Lenora could grow to hate her son enough to want him dead.

"And what is Lucias' stance towards the men who'd steal a woman straight off the streets to be their mistress?" She trembled, hugging herself as she recalled the deadline he'd given her. "He has made it plain if I do not choose to go to him before the new moon, then he'll come after me. And now, it seems my time has run out."

"This is the threat he so willingly gave you?" Thad's jaw tightened as she nodded, his green eyes hardening. "Then I shall speak with him, get him to rescind his words."

"No!" She darted forward to block his path. "You'll only make it worse." Lucias may have already decided waiting was no longer a viable option, but he had not spoken a word to her about it. She didn't want to find out if he'd risk forcing her whilst these men were still here. "Please, just take me with you. It doesn't even have to be all the way."

He rubbed his jaw, his fingertips audibly scraping against his unshaven skin. "Say I did entertain this notion of taking you—"

"And Tommy," she blurted, her face ablaze. How could she have almost forgotten about taking the poor boy? She'd need to bring him with her if he was to keep his soul.

Thad frowned. "Who's Tommy?"

"He's my page," she said and, when his frown deepened, realised she'd have to explain further. "He's not under Lucias' control." No point telling him the reasons behind why or she'd never convince Thad to take either of them.

"You speak of the boy he sent to Everdark? How... interesting." He stared at her a little too long for her comfort. Did he suspect she hadn't revealed the whole truth? Or did his thoughts take him down some path she hadn't yet considered? "Very well. Say I took you, and Tommy, with us when we leave." He circled her in slow, measured strides. "Now then, supposing Lucias does not attempt to retrieve you, how do you intend to pay your way?"

Pay? She hadn't given much thought towards what she'd do after escaping the Citadel. She supposed Tommy would do fine working with the horses. He'd certainly cope well enough to cover his travelling expenses. But what service could she possibly provide? Her cooking and cleaning skills were barely passable, at least according to her mother. Perhaps they'd be enough for a trip across the land? There wasn't much else she could offer.

Clara lowered her head. "I will do whatever you ask," she murmured, her mind still elsewhere.

What would she do if Lucias *did* come after her? She didn't intend to linger anywhere close by to make it easy for him. Surely he'd seek to replace her rather than waste the precious time he had travelling the kingdom to track her down.

Thad crossed his arms. "Even if my price is no different than what you are running from?"

Her head snapped up and she took a frantic step backwards. He seemed to be far stronger than Lucias. Even without the aid of the Great Lord's sorcerous ways, if Thad decided to take her to his bed, she wouldn't have much of a say in it.

"Peace, dear lady, it was only a question. You need not tremble so." His strong, calloused fingers brushed her chin. He tipped her head up, holding her gaze. "I am a married man and I would not dream of betraying the woman who, at this moment, carries our third child."

He had a wife? *Of course he does.* A man like Thad would not reach his middle years without having been married at least once. The evening chatter had revealed he was the count's eldest child and, as such, he would've been in need of an heir himself. *And he has three of them.* No doubt with a lady who adored him.

Her skin prickled as she eyed his face. Endlight was on the border. Not just any border, but the first defence between the kingdom and whatever the court at Ne'ermore threw at them. How merciful would invaders be towards children?

Unable to look at him for long, Clara settled on a casual inspection of the hall. She didn't think she wanted to know the answer.

"Please," he sighed. "Do let me speak with him. The magic is reputed to do strange things to a man's mind, but I don't believe it has warped his ethics so much as to threaten rape."

"You think I'm lying." It would be a natural assumption. Believe the person you know rather than the one you didn't.

"Not at all, my lady. Seeing how you act when he is beside you, the silent dread radiating in your eyes..." He shook his head. "As much as I wish it were not true, I can fully believe you heard what you did. But I cannot accept he would knowingly threaten such a thing, especially unprovoked."

Shaking, her eyes stinging with influx of angry tears, Clara balled her hands.

He held up a hand before she could open her mouth. "I'm not saying you provoked him or you would deserve such a fate if you had. Merely that I believe he has misspoken, perhaps in anger, and is unaware of his words."

Looking into his eyes, seeing the soft unease lurking within, she knew Thad would not help her. For the sake of his own children's lives, he wanted his lord's heir to at least be in the making almost as much as Lucias desired it. Any woman would probably do in Thad's mind. She was just the most convenient.

"Do you think he also misspoke when he had me kidnapped?" Lucias may not have given the order to collect five prospective women, but he had told them to seek at out a mistress. Had chosen to keep her here. "I am a prisoner."

"A prisoner?" Thad paced before her; five steps one way, then turn and take another five steps. "Has he mistreated you since your arrival? Struck you, perhaps? No, he's never struck a woman in all the years I've known him. Starved you, then?" He halted before her, his eyes hooded. "You look well fed to me. He even allows you the freedom to walk these halls unescorted." One finger waggled at her as if she were some child. "If these are things you believe a prisoner is entitled to then, my lady, I think you have led quite the sheltered life."

She stared at him. "He allows it because he knows I'm trapped here." A prison was still a prison no matter its size. *I have no freedom.* No doubt Lucias would've become less lenient if she had continued with her escape attempts.

"As is he."

"He can leave whenever he so chooses."

"But has he?"

Clara lifted her chin, staring down her nose at him. If he wasn't going to help her, then she wasn't about to give him any more information.

Thad shook his head. The faint sneer tweaking his lips flattened out. "You needn't speak a word. Your silence is answer enough. There is nowhere else he could go which is as heavily defended as this *and* manned solely by the lord's men." He rubbed his forehead, brushing the hair aside. "Has he told you what will happen to the kingdom if he dies heirless?"

Her thoughts fell on Everdark and the hundreds of people claiming the village as home. All of them blissfully unaware of the danger in living so close to the Citadel. "Of the *risk*, you mean?" There was always a chance the soulless men would die with Lucias. She wished there was a way for him to evade the death he seemed so certain of. He'd undoubtedly be more amenable to her request of freedom without the threat of the executioner's sword hovering over his neck.

"Clearly he did not inform you of the near disaster brought upon by the third Great Lord's nearly heirless death."

The *third* Great Lord? "That was many successions ago." Did they honestly expect her to have memorised every detail of Lucias' ancestors? She could barely recall Lucias was the eleventh Great Lord, and only because she'd had the knowledge stamped into her as a child. "How would you know what had transpired back then?" How could a man be *nearly* heirless? Surely it was either one way or the other.

"Lucias spent much of his younger years at Endlight, training and fighting. Before then, when his father had considered him too young to travel, *my* father would have me spend my youth here. I learnt much about the Great Lords, perhaps more than any nobleman outside the bloodline ever has."

"Then *you* tell me what happened if you know it so well."

"Best if you asked him. It is not my place to speak of it." He peered at her. "Nor would it be a wise move for me to aid his mistress in fleeing. I can talk with him though. Perhaps it would be enough to have him revoke his decision. I cannot, however, force his hand. He *is* our Great Lord after all."

"Our *Dark* Lord," she muttered, sharply recalling what Lucias claimed to be the name used by the neighbouring kingdoms for his ancestors. *And now for him.*

"He told you of that, too." Thad clasped his hands behind him. "You must know it to be naught else but a name. Given first to the fifth Great Lord and handed down through the successions."

Judging by the bitterness she recalled in Lucias' voice, she would've expected Kerwin to have been considered the first Dark Lord. *Just another parasite who drains men of their souls.* The memory of his words, spoken just this morning, floated to the surface. She set her jaw, fighting down the unexplainable sadness welling in her chest. Even with everything she'd seen, all she had heard, Lucias didn't deserve to be lumped with his murderous ancestors.

"We've attacked most of the neighbouring lands in the past," Thad continued, "and they're rightly wary of us doing so in the future. Whether it'll happen in our time we've yet to see, but they have never fully understood why the kingdom allows her Great Lords do what they've always done.

What the foreign lands fear the most has always been their..." He frowned at her. "...their magic."

"Odd." She crossed her arms, holding them tight to her chest. "I would've thought they'd be more frightened of their ability to steal souls."

The fair brows twitched upwards. "Yes," he murmured, seemingly to himself, "he would've told you *that*."

"Actually, I stumbled upon his little secret." Would Lucias have revealed such a fact to her had she not discovered it? *He would've had to eventually*. But, by then, she'd have been too late to save Tommy.

"Then you must stumble into some strange places, my lady."

"I was following Tommy," she haughtily replied, her cheeks burning new.

"Your page?" He rubbed at his chin. The look in his eyes suddenly became a little too keen for her liking. "However did you manage to convince him not to take the lad's soul?"

Clara stiffened. "I promised to stay. *That* is the only reason I am allowed to wander these halls at all and why I must take Tommy with me when I leave." Sick guilt twisted her stomach. *If only he hadn't been caught*. She could've been far from here by now. *I could've left him to his fate*. It hadn't been an option then, she would not consider it as one now.

His lips pressed into a thin line. Thad stared at her for some time, before finally speaking. "I see." He gave a quick bow. "I must be off. There is much which needs discussing before the morn. I wish you a fair night's rest, my lady." He strode down the hall from whence he'd came, his determination pounding out in each footfall.

"Please," she called out. "Promise you will not speak with him on this."

Showing no sign of having heard her plea, Thad disappeared around the corner.

Dread crept up her spine as she listened to his fading footsteps. What would Lucias' reaction be once the pair spoke? She wasn't sure whether he'd dismiss her claim or, with his pretence at civility revealed for what it was, turn around and do the deed before the men left.

With the chill air pricking at her skin at every step, Clara hastened up the stairs to her chambers where she locked the frail wooden barrier of her gilded prison. There was one thing she could be truly certain of. No one was going to help her find a way out. She would need to do it on her own.

Chapter Fifteen

*T*he kitchen pulsed with a life of its own. Big, bubbling pots sat on the stoves and the delectable smells coming from within tweaked at her nose. People bustled about the room, working at various stations.

Tables dominated the centre of the room. It was here the vegetables and meat was diced or minced by quick, skilled workers. The prepared food was taken from these tables to be dumped into some of the pots where more people stood, occasionally dipping their spoons into the water to stir the contents.

Other people worked at lumps of dough, picking it off the floured boards only to throw the blobs back down with a sticky slap. At the far end of the room, where three oven doors took up much of the wall, a tray of uncooked loaves was being placed into the kiln. One of the men walked by with another batch and the hot aroma of freshly-baked bread drifted up to greet her.

Clara's stomach growled. No one had come to wake her. It wasn't as if they could've done more than knock if they wanted to keep their lord's illusion of her being in possession of the only key. She'd padded down through the Citadel's halls alone, eventually finding herself here.

She stood next to one of the heavy tables running down the centre of the room, basking in the warmth. It reminded her of home. Not of the pokey kitchen where her mother cooked, but of the Feast Day bustle when tables filled the streets and the air gained a spicy tinge.

The wet *chonk* of a blade hitting wood brought her back from the edge of reminiscing. The noise hadn't been loud, but some sounds, like steel slicing through flesh and bone, didn't need to be.

She spun to find Gettie watching her. Several plucked chickens lay before the woman, spread out in various stages of dismemberment. The bird on the thick cutting board directly in front of the woman already lacked a leg.

"You'll find them in the courtyard, mistress." The chicken's other leg was removed with a single swing. It seemed the Gutter of Neardim had found an excellent use for her blade-wielding skills.

Clara swallowed, her stomach fluttering. "Who says I'm looking for them?" She had idly wondered where the three lords had vanished, assuming they'd be in the study or the training grounds or some such place doing whatever noblemen did when they gathered.

One grey brow twitched upwards. Another chicken was lifted onto the block. The cleaver swung again and the frail ribcage didn't stand a chance. "No one, mistress. Nevertheless, they can be found there." The woman nodded towards a nearby table upon which sat a basket of apples. "Do be sure to eat a little something before you leave, mistress."

Clara paused in her hesitant shuffle towards the table, her hand already lifting to pluck a red and yellow apple from the basket. *Leave?* Did Gettie suspect she'd try to escape whilst the count and his son were still here? She peered at the woman, finding naught but sincerity in the old face. Gettie must be meaning the room itself.

Snatching an apple before another word could be said, Clara left the kitchen to resume her quiet wandering along corridors that stood bare, save for the occasional torch or candle.

She adored the servants' ways far more than the grandiose halls of above. Not as labyrinthine as the passages just below her feet, these lesser ways wove through the Citadel's underbelly and eventually became one with the larger halls. Munching on the crisp apple, Clara sauntered through the corridors she knew would lead to the entrance.

The courtyard was alive. Although, if the Citadel's kitchen could be compared to a carefully maintained beehive, the scene before her was a kicked anthill. Men scurried about the Endlight carriage. A team of horses were harnessed to the vehicle, others had been saddled and were now being led to riders, both of which she assumed came from the border city.

Thad, dressed in fancier attire than the serviceable leathers he'd arrived in, stood on the stairs leading into the chaos. A horse was brought before him and, adjusting his gloves, he trotted down the steps.

Clara trailed after him. "You're leaving so soon?" She'd hoped they'd be a few more days. Just long enough to think of a way to escape at the same time as them and leave Lucias thinking she was on her way to Endlight.

He halted in inspecting his mount's straps, turning to regard her. "Ah, dear lady, so nice of you to see us off." He inclined his head as the dark figure of Lucias strode across the courtyard towards them. "As I was explaining to Lucias, father wishes to collect his betrothed before sundown." He grinned at her and her cheeks warmed. "You're welcome to join us, my lady."

Lucias planted himself before the older man, his dark brows lowered. "She cannot le—"

"You know you are also more than welcome to come with us, Lucias. Bring her with you." He clapped an arm over Lucias' shoulder and Clara flinched, unsure if Thad had also marked his lord's sword hand twitch. "She's not a prisoner, now is she?" The man's voice suddenly gained a certain steely quality. Had he already spoken to Lucias? Her stomach knotted. What had been said between them?

Lucias' dark brows pulled down further. His handsome jaw twitched as his face took on a definite 'younger brother' scowl. "I suppose there's no harm in a brief excursion to the village." The words were stilted, his voice monotone. A child repeating something he'd been taught but did not believe.

The village. They were permitting her entry into Everdark? She could easily lose him on the streets. Clara took a deep breath, barely able to contain her glee. "I'm not going anywhere without Tommy." She flinched as Lucias' glare switched to her. She'd sounded far too eager and perhaps, given the barely agreeable mood he was in, asking for the boy to join them was a step too far. He had to know she wouldn't leave without Tommy. What better anchor was there for her than to keep the boy here instead?

"Sirius!" Lucias bellowed, his gaze not once wavering from Clara's face.

The head servant scurried seemingly out of nowhere to his lord's side, wringing his long-tortured hat every step of the way. "Master?"

"Have my horse saddled and whatever mount my mistress' page is using."

The man paused in his dash to obey. "And one for the mistress, master?"

"No." Lucias dismissed the idea with a wave of the hand. "She will ride with me."

The Endlight entourage, already prepared to head off, spent their time rechecking straps and adjusting clothes as they waited for the horses. Clara shuffled on the steps, watching as Thad mounted and trotted down the line of men. There didn't appear to be much room for another person atop the horse's back. Yet she was to somehow share Lucias' black brute of a horse. *He knows.* Lucias had to suspect she'd attempt to flee once outside these walls. What better way to ensure she hadn't much chance of succeeding than to enforce their closeness?

Tommy emerged from the stables, leading two horses. He handed the reins of Lucias' steed to the beast's owner, then clambered into the saddle of the smaller brown creature and joined the waiting group.

Lucias swung into the saddle in one leap and, after nudging the destrier to stand parallel to the stairs, offered her his hand.

She gripped it andhe air around her waist hardened. A strangled gasp caught in her throat as she was lifted into the air and onto the beast. The horse snorted, wriggling underneath her in a most disturbing fashion.

Clara shuffled in her position behind the saddle. At least this particular creature had enough of a rump to carry her. Her skirts slithered against the glossy coat, giving her the most uneasy feeling of sliding to the ground without actually falling. The horse took a lurching step forward. Unsteady and fearful she would indeed slip free after all, Clara wrapped her arms around Lucias' waist. Her wrist dug into the cold steel of his belt buckle. How was she going to stay aboard whilst they travelled down to Everdark?

"Your mistress looks rather uncomfortable," Thad said, giving a nod in her direction. "You should let her ride one of the palfreys."

Clara stared blankly over the man's broad shoulder. Was she hearing right? He wanted her to ride a horse on her own. Her gaze flicked to his face, her cheeks warming. Surely he had *not* just winked at her.

Through her chest, pressed hard against Lucias' back as it was, she felt him grunt. "She cannot ride and I do not wish to risk her neck."

"The carriage then? Be more comfortable than the bony behind of your old nag."

"I mean your father no disrespect," Lucias said, his voice dropping until it was quiet enough to not carry across the courtyard. "But I wouldn't leave any young woman alone in his presence."

Thad chuckled. "One day we'll look back and wish we'd the same fervour at his age as he does." With a few clicks of the tongue, he urged his shaggy horse to the forefront of their little parade.

"I'd settle for just living to his age," Lucias whispered

once the man had gone.

Clara clung tighter to Lucias, partly because they'd begun to move out, but also because of the welling urge to comfort him. He believed he was going to die. Sooner than he had originally thought, too.

And yet, although she'd angered him, seemingly frustrated him to the edge of his patience at times, he had not attempted to get much more than his first try at a kiss from her. Of course, if she allowed kissing, even once, he may insist on a lot more than she was willing to give.

Would he have been this persistent if his mother wasn't set on murdering him? She hoped the answer was no. It was almost enough to make her sorry she would betray his trust in her word, but not enough to want to stay. She would escape before this day came to an end. Clara may not have a horse or the ability to ride it, but Tommy had both. Together, they would be free.

A hand closed over hers. She twitched, jerking back and nearly pulling free before recalling she was perched rather precariously aboard a moving animal.

"You are awfully silent." His fingers gently stroked over the back of her hand and across her wrist, setting both to tingling in a pleasant and disturbing fashion. "I'd have thought you would've tried to talk me into letting you go by now."

"If I left, you would take Tommy's soul." Did it not bother him that her compliance was based on protecting another man? *Why would he care?* As long as she stayed and eventually gave him the chance he wanted, then undoubtedly the reasons behind it didn't matter to him.

"And why would I?"

"That was the deal." Had he somehow forgotten the arrangement? "He's meant to be a criminal after all." More like accused of a crime he did not do. What use would he have for the jewels the merchant swore he'd taken? Even if it were true, the watch should've found them on him. Yes, he stole from the stalls, but no one ever objected to him taking a handful of food now and then. It'd been that way for so long he was practically part of the streets.

Lucias sighed. "You saw the two men he arrived with. Whatever the lad did, he does not deserve their fate."

"You're letting him go then?" she asked, unable to believe what she was hearing. The boy had arrived at the Citadel as a criminal and he was to be given more freedom than her?

"I didn't say that. He has settled well within the ranks." He shifted in the saddle. "And he seems content enough with his duties."

Tommy? He would have her believe the carefree child she'd known for years was content with being someone's errand boy? She couldn't accept it for truth. "If you're trying to convince me to stay here willingly, it won't work."

Lucias stiffened, jolting her backwards. "Of course," he grated, "I would not wish for you to feel *imprisoned*."

She groaned inwardly. Thad *had* spoken to him. How much had the man told his lord? "But it doesn't stop you from neatly shutting me away from everyone, does it?" Trapped. Unable to find any means of aid. Lucias must revel in watching her escape attempts, she was sure of it.

His shoulders bounced as he chuckled. "Thad's right, I should've given you your own horse. If only so I could see your face now. You are most enchanting when you're angry, although you hide it well. There's considerable spirit flashing behind those dark eyes."

She glared at the back of his head. If he wanted to see flashing, she was more than welcome to grant him all the twinkling stars he desired.

"And I bet you're now pouting those gorgeous lips you so rudely deny me a taste of."

Clara bit her bottom lip. She *had* been doing exactly as he said. How had he been aware of her pulling such an expression without being able to see her face? She wouldn't have noticed if he hadn't pointed it out.

"Now you fall silent. I thought you would be overjoyed to

be in Everdark again. Is it not what you wanted?"

"Not quite," she mumbled. Yes, she wanted to walk the streets once again, but under the mantle of freedom, not bound in these silken shackles.

She risked a look at the Road lying beneath them. They had reached the lower section now. The cobbles here were worn smooth from the carts and horses of those coming and going from Everdark. Little to trip her up and leave her at his mercy. She could easily jump to the ground and run.

To where? Her gaze lifted to the nearby woods. Distance made it naught but a dark green lump hunkering on the edge of the wide, unbroken grassland. She'd be out of breath by the time she touched a single tree. And, even without his ability to halt her from afar, Lucias would've caught up with her long before she reached such dubious safety.

No, she needed a more immediate hiding spot. She needed the rabbit warren of the village.

Clara watched as the green-lacquered carriage, flanked by its mounted escort, pulled ahead and through the city gates. Lucias' halted his destrier in the middle of the road. Her heart jumped as the beast edged sideways and pawed at the ground. The powerful muscles of the animal's hindquarters rolled beneath her.

She fought to keep her balance whilst her thoughts raced. Why were they stopping? Had Lucias changed his mind and intended to return to the Citadel? She licked her wind-dried lips. Did he guess her intentions once within Everdark's walls? She'd given her word, yet she had always planned to break it. *Like he did.*

For him to have broken the deal first by declaring he would not take Tommy's soul stung a little. Of course, she was glad the boy would be safe, but she hadn't expected to find her careful planning would be all for naught. Or knowing she'd given up her freedom for even less.

"It always grows in my mind when I'm away," he murmured. "Yet, every time I return, I'm struck by how small it seems close up."

Everdark was big for a village and owed its size to the converging trade routes. But, from what she'd heard from Lucias, her home was no Port Dank, full of trade from beyond the sea. Most of the merchants who came through Everdark were of the common kind, bearing mundane wares from nearby farms. The buildings stood in neat lines, pressed together as one long house and stretching off into the haze of smoke, which even the noonday sun could not disperse. People and carts filled the pockmarked streets, their bright clothes breaking up the dull greyness.

She tightened her grip on Lucias' waist as he kneed their mount into a lazy trot and caught up with the carriage. They made their way through the crowds swirling around them. People stopped to stare at the passing group and Clara frowned at the awed faces fixated on the carriage. Lesser nobles came to Everdark, but it was clear this was a special delegation.

Did they know their Great Lord rode amongst them? Such knowledge could prove to be a problem. It hadn't occurred to her before now that the crowd might attempt to stop her from fleeing.

The shaggy rump of another horse suddenly blocked her view. Clara jerked upright, finding Thad had joined them at the rear of their small parade.

He urged his mount closer, leaning towards Lucias. "Thought you'd gone and lost your nerve for a moment or two there." Thad's green eyes glittered sharply as he surveyed the crowd. "You know your mother would have a good deal of trouble blending in here."

Lucias sat straighter in the saddle. An arm slid along hers as he grasped his sword hilt. "She is capable of blending in anywhere. It is part of her power."

"It's not absolute and the giant she travels with surely couldn't escape notice." A grimace formed on the man's lips. "In any case, seeing the people would not be able to reveal to her where you are, she would attempt the Citadel first, would she not?" Thad scrubbed at his chin as Lucias made no indication he'd heard. "Why haven't you chosen to hide yourself in the village anyway?"

Clara was pretty sure she knew precisely why Lucias chose to stay within the thick walls of the Citadel. Although hiding in the village might keep other people safe for a time, their safety was not the sole reason he didn't choose that path. Where else but the Citadel could he lock her away and be certain she would break?

She stared at Lucias' back and then the crowd. *He carts me about like some simpering damsel.* Worst of all, a small part of her liked it. Just as she adored the silk and the room he'd gifted her. Was this how people broke? Not all at once, but bit by bit. She couldn't break now. Her home was too close to give in.

"It wouldn't matter if I were to stay here or elsewhere," Lucias said. "My mother would find me. If I stay in the Citadel then there's no chance of innocent people dying."

Until she kills you. Clara swallowed in an effort to relieve the tightness in her throat. Then the soulless men would be free and everyone would suffer. First the criminals would come, then the armies sent by Ne'ermore and the other neighbouring kingdoms.

Her gaze returned to the crowd. All those faces. She could picture them frozen in horror as their way of life crumbled beneath the feet of death.

Laughter drifted up to scatter her thoughts as they rode past a less crowded street. Here, the children had not halted their play. They seemed altogether heedless of the carriage rumbling by, their little forms darting amongst the adults with uncaring glee. She wished she was still young enough to join them in their bliss.

"Ben!" a woman shrieked as she pushed through the crowd, her arm outstretched towards a small boy. "Come back here!"

The lad, no more than five years of age, ignored his mother to run towards the front of the carriage.

One of the horses reared, the driver issuing a stream of

abuse. A similar flow of words came from Lucias' mouth. His mount launched forward just as she caught sight of the boy tripping and falling before the wheel.

Despite the driver's efforts to halt the harnessed team, the carriage creaked onwards. Time seemed to slow. Clara shut her eyes, her heart pounding hard enough to leap out of her chest. Any moment now and the boy would be crushed beneath the iron-bound wheel.

The collective gasp of the crowd hit her ears. She opened her eyes a fraction, feeling bolder when no pained cry of a wounded child followed.

The carriage wobbled in the air, just high enough to miss the boy. With her chin pressed against Lucias' shoulder, she could feel him shaking. How much effort did it take to lift a carriage?

The destrier swung around, destroying her precarious seating. Clara slipped to one side, her descent halted by her hold on Lucias' waist. The muscles under her fingers tightened. Any moment now and he'd gain control of the situation, then draw her back onto the horse.

She released him, letting herself fall. Her feet tapped the cobbles.

Clara dashed into the crowd, shoving aside those who barred her way. No one called for her to stop. No magic snaked out to snatch her into the air. She dared to glance over her shoulder.

Lucias was nowhere to be seen.

Hitching up her skirts, she raced through the streets, rounding one corner after another. The familiar maw of an alley neared. She nipped down it. A wooden fence, covered in faded posters, barred the far end. Kicking the boxes aside, she tugged at the boards. One gave and she slipped through to the other side.

Flattening herself against the brickwork, she listened for some sign of pursuit.

The clop of a hoof greeted her ears, but the sound fast became the steady plod of a carthorse. There were no shouts over the general clamour. Had she lost him then? She didn't think it'd be so easy.

Clara peered out into the street. Few people walked here. The lone cart rounded a corner and vanished from sight. She hurried across to another alley, turning off to follow a narrower path between the buildings. Cold and slimy things squelched underfoot. Other things, things she wanted to think of even less, gave with a crunch.

With much relief, she left the alley, and her slippers, behind. Having been sheltered by the sun, the cobbles were gently cool against her skin as she scampered across the street to squeeze down the last alley. Here, sheltered by an L-shaped wall, stood the back way into their home. Clara prised a wobbling brick from under the door, sliding the key out of its hollow bed.

The lock clicked. She froze, her hand flattened against the wood. Flakes of paint drifted to the ground. Fourteen days had passed since she'd been taken. The last words from her mother had not been kind. But they never were.

Clara pushed the door open. It didn't matter. She'd done it. She had finally returned home where she was safe at last. Better to be here, where freedom meant stepping outside, than shut away in some fortress.

Chapter Sixteen

Warmth greeted her, followed fast by the musty smell of wood and cloth. Although her mother had tried several times over the years, nothing could banish what Clara had always considered as the storage room's oddly comforting aroma. She strode past the shelves lining the walls with their bolts of wool and linen, halting as she stood in the doorway.

A curtain partitioned this area from the main shop. Pushing the old sacking aside illuminated the battered doorframe. She ran a hand up the age-polished wood, her finger instinctively settling into the old grooves where her father had carefully noted her ever-changing height.

She twisted to take in the storage room. Her gaze swept over the shelves and drawers. Here sat the chair, banished to the dark corner because of the wobbly leg, where she would practise her sewing as child. Her father had always meant to get it fixed. She peered at into the gloom. There, tucked away behind crates and cases, stood the old seamstress' dummy her mother never quite managed to be rid of.

Little seemed to change within this room. The years came and went. The bolts of cloth may arrive in whatever colour the seasons and the fashions dictated, but there would always be cloth. Just as there would always be the dummy, the chair and the notched doorframe.

Taking a deep breath, she left behind the storage room

and its memories to enter the main room beyond. "Mum?" she gently called into the silence. Listening brought only the haphazard snapping of the fireplace. Clara crossed the room to part the doorway curtain and peer out into the shop front.

No sign anyone had recently been here. By the silence in the kitchen, she could also rule out there. Upstairs? No, ever since her father had passed away, her mother rarely ventured into the upper rooms during the day. *The workshop.*

She padded down the hall, a rhythmic ticking starting up and growing louder as she neared the closed door at the far end. The sound stopped as she twisted the doorknob. She opened the door to find her mother turning in her seat to face the intruder.

Clara smirked at her mother's shocked face. She'd never been able to surprise her mother before now. To suddenly appear, barefooted and silken skirts ruined, she must be a dreadful sight. "I escaped him, Mother. I've come back home."

Her mother stood, her hands flying up to plant themselves on her hips. "Well I never," Marian breathed. Her auburn brows, generous in their sprinkling of grey, pulled down and increased the wrinkles. Those eyes, a lighter brown than Clara's, glared at her as if she were some ancient enemy. "Not only do you have the hide to show your face, you have the audacity to march in as if you belong!"

Clara flinched as if she'd been slapped. She had been, in a way. Something deep within her breast certainly stung. "But... but I came back..."

"To burden me!" Marian threw her arms up. "I struggle to keep the home my husband died in and you seek only to give me another mouth to feed."

"I can work." She waved a hand at the sewing machine. It'd been a wedding gift from someone on her father's side. Not exactly new back then, it was now a clunky thing.

The machine itself had been bolted to a table that bore hints of once having a painted edge. Bits of thread and material lay scattered about the wrought iron feet, the pile at its thickest just around the enormous pedal that drove the stitching beast.

"I can clean, fetch materials, take orders." Just like she used to in the days before her kidnapping. Only this time, she would never complain again.

Those hard, cold eyes bored into her. Clara squirmed. What else could she offer? *There is nothing.* All Clara possessed of worth was herself.

Finally, after what seemed like forever, her mother harrumphed. "You can't do a thing in that gown. Just look at it! Anyone would think you'd crawled your way home through a midden after a romp in the cattle yards." Her mother rummaged through a pile of suspiciously familiar clothes sitting beside the old, padded chair produced a simple smock. "Here." Her mother threw the item at Clara. "Put this on."

She did as her mother ordered, both eager and reluctant to be rid of the gown. Layers of black and red pooled at her feet. She hesitated at relinquishing the chemise, which hadn't suffered the same abuse as the outer layers, only removing the soft undergarment at her mother's sharp nod.

Clara stepped away from the clothes to dress, the smock's rough weave scraping against her skin as she pulled it over her head. Next to the silk she'd worn, she might as well have draped herself in sacking. After several years of use, the smock had even taken on the off-white colour of canvas.

Her mother picked up one of the many layers that made up the gown's skirts and vigorously brushed at the fabric. Dust curled about the silk, settling back onto the folds. "What have you been doing in this?" She held up her hand before Clara could think to speak, heedless to the dark horsehair clinging to her palm. "No. I do not wish to hear. It is painful enough to know you will not go before the altar untouched. I couldn't bear to hear any more."

Clara swallowed. *She thinks I'm no longer a virgin.* Could such a reason be why her mother was less than keen at seeing her again? She recalled the response given upon informing her mother of her imprisonment. Mentions of compensation, of *money*, dominated the page. *It was all she wanted*. Clara could suffer such knowledge.

"I thank the Goddess your father is not alive to witness this."

"Did you not fully read the letter I sent? I was *kidnapped!*" Did her mother believe she'd been a willing participant in their lord's search for a mistress? "I haven't been outside the Citadel for two weeks."

"My dear girl, you protest prettily enough, but *this—*" Her mother brandished the handful of silk as if it were some mighty sword. "—this is not a gown one gets without offering up something in return." A brow twitched upwards. "And you have little to give a man of his breeding." She shook her head, the thick braids of her hair gently swaying. "What sort of man will take you now?"

"Does it matter?" What did she care if a man wouldn't have her because of rumour? If he would believe idle hearsay before her then she'd be better off without him.

"Do you plan to be a spinster for the rest of your life, my girl? Working yourself death just to survive, burdening your poor mother more than you seek to do now?" Marian clutched the lace at her throat. "My only hope was Terence would take you, even if you are tainted, but—"

"I'm not marrying him!" Clara had barely escaped one man she wanted nothing of. How could her mother be thinking of marrying her off to someone else? *And to Terence.* The cobbler from down in Main Street. She shuddered at the thought.

"He is a good man, Clarabelle. No reason to think anything else of him. He treated his first wife well, even got her the best doctors he could afford when she became ill."

Yet his wife still died. It wasn't Terence's fault. Sometimes an illness grabbed hold and refused to let go no matter how much money you threw at the doctors. And Terence Cobbler was a man with a fair bit of money to get things done. "The man has *children* my age!"

Her mother nodded. "Children who'll be moving away to follow in other trades no doubt, leaving their poor father all alone. He'll need help." She bent to gather up the rest of the discarded clothing. "Assistance only a young woman could give."

Clara clamped her teeth together. If Brenna ever had a daughter, and she prayed the Goddess would see fit to grant the woman sons instead, this was exactly how she would be with a little girl. "What is it you're trying to have me do, Mother?"

"I'm attempting to do what your father should've had arranged years ago!" Black and red silk shimmered in the lantern light as her mother threw up a hand and waved it about. "Ensuring you had a life which wouldn't demand you to prostitute yourself in order to eat has been our goal since your birth." The dress, dangling half-folded in her arms, hit Marian's skirts with a hollow *whump*. "You don't make it easy for me."

Easy? Because she wouldn't roll over and allow her mother to dictate how her life went? The idea her father had also been behind this plan was absurd. "I am not marrying Terence, Mother." Her father would never have agreed to such a thing. He wouldn't seek to force a man older than himself upon her.

"You will." The words snapped the air; sharp and precise, bearing the edge of heat encased in an unruffled facade. "It had all been arranged before your... unfortunate incident with the new Great Lord."

"But I—"

Those brown eyes snapped out a warning. Marian Weaver had not finished speaking. "He should be willing to marry you despite your lack of—"

"Stop!" she shrieked in an effort to be heard through her mother's calm, and equally relentless, prattle. "I'm not marrying—"

The clothes slammed to the floor, landing in a rumpled

heap. "You will do as you are told." Marian strode towards her, kicking aside the gown she'd so carefully folded. "Are you not *my* daughter? Is this not *my* house?" She jabbed at Clara's unprotected shoulder. "Whilst you are under this roof, you will do as *I* say!"

Clara stepped back out into the hall. "I'm not a child anymore." She was seventeen, not seven. If her mother considered her old enough to marry, then she was certainly old enough to decide who it should be to. She would not be bullied into a marriage to some man who had children older than she was. If she had to live under another roof to get the chance to choose, then so be it. "You can't make me do a damn thing!"

Her mother's hand lashed across her face, snapping Clara's head around. "You will not speak to me like that."

Clara glared at Marian. "I assure you, I won't. I'll never speak to you again." With her cheek stinging from the blow and hot tears blurring her sight, she ran back towards the storage room. The curtain tore as she hit it.

She stumbled across the room. Her shoulder smacked into the door. Abandoning the battle in wiping the tears from her eyes, she blindly scrabbled at the handle.

Daylight flooded the room, turning the world beyond into a shimmering pool of white and grey. She entered the glittering realm, slamming the door shut on the remnants of the home she hadn't before realised was lost to her.

Sheltered by the L-shaped wall, her back pressed against the wood, she scrubbed a sleeve across her face. "I wish Dad was here," she mumbled. Her father would've made everything seem right again.

"How strange. I've been thinking the same thing over the last three and a half weeks."

Clara jumped at the sound of Lucias' voice. Her hand grasped the door handle before she could think. But there was no freedom to be had in the rooms beyond. *I can't go back.* Going back would mean submitting to the fate her mother offered.

Steeling herself, she peered around the end of the wall.

Lucias leant on the other side, his back pressed against the brickwork. His destrier stood in the alley entrance, blocking her only way out. "Was home not the bright and cheery welcome you thought it would be?" He offered a small, sympathetic smile. "It never is, you know."

She stared at him through the last of her tears, marking the weary lines on his face. He'd returned to the Citadel because of his father's death. She forgot how short a time it'd been since the old Great Lord had died. *Barely a month now*. Perhaps because Lucias didn't seem at all bothered, showing no outward sign of his grief. Her father had died two years ago and she still missed him.

On the other hand, did Lucias actually have the time to waste in grieving for the loss when his mother was coming to kill him? "How did you find me?" How long had he been standing here?

He shook his head, a low chuckle escaping his lips. "I trained with the scouts on the southern border, spent many summers hunting across the Endlight moors with the nomads and you ask me how I found you?"

Clara sidled along the wall, inching further from his side. "You tracked me through the city?" A horse would not have navigated the path she took. She peered at his boots. They were dirty, in a lived-in sort of fashion, but far cleaner than they should've been if he'd trod the same alleys as she.

"I'd no need." Lucias' smile carried a grim edge. "A woman dressed in black and red stands out in a crowd rather well. More so when she decides to nip through the alleyways. All I had to do was ask." His gaze ran over her, those dark eyes narrowing and undoubtedly marking the lack of the gown she'd fled here in. "Why are you dressed in naught but a shift?"

She flattened herself against the wall, suddenly aware of the little she did wear. "These are my normal clothes, my lord." The smock was baggy, serviceable and came to her knees. The perfect attire for busying herself about the house, but not exactly something she'd choose to wear on the streets. "I am a commoner, after all." He must be aware.

And he doesn't care. Certainly not if much of his lineage had originated from common stock. *To help keep the madness at bay.* What, in the name of that goal, had his ancestors stooped to in order to ensure their reign continued?

"Where are the clothes I gave you?"

"My mother has them." Clara caught his brows twitch, puzzlement flitting across his face. "She no doubt plans to sell the fabric, my *lord*," she muttered. "As compensation."

"For the loss of your unpaid services or the inability to marry you off now you are apparently no longer a virgin and possibly carrying my child?"

Heat flooded her cheeks, blazing its way across her face. Marian was right. Someone of her low breeding didn't get fancy dresses without reason. Lucias may have gifted the gown to her, but he would also be expecting remuneration. He truly believed she would yield and give him an heir. Compared to a child, a gown or two was pittance. "You heard?"

One corner of his mouth lifted. "Your mother has a good set of lungs."

She thought back to the day of kidnapping, of the cry that had scattered pigeons. Her mother belonged at the forefront of an army, bellowing orders as she slew her enemies. "Runs in the family." Clara could've sworn neither of them had been loud enough to hear from the street. Had Lucias found her faster than she'd thought and used the time to eavesdrop?

"And undoubtedly the temper does as well." He strode deeper into the alley, his face set into a determined scowl. "Come. We must return to the Citadel."

Clara backed up until she hit the far wall. "Don't you dare touch me!" She had not gained her freedom only to be recaptured.

"Again, there is fear in your eyes," he snarled. "What is it you expect me to do to you?" He waved a hand at the walls. "Pin you against the brickwork and have my way?" His lip quivered in a sneer. "*Force* myself on you in an *alley*?" His brows drew together. "Do you believe I would stoop to such wickedness?"

If it got the deed done, then why not take her here and now? She glanced at the crates around them, searching for a weapon. Her hand fell upon the nearest board. It felt loose enough to come free at a tug. "You lay one finger on me and I'll scream."

Lucias gave a cold smile. "No, you won't because then I'll be forced to do something you do *not* want me to do." Closing in, he grabbed her outstretched arm before she could move or utter a single world. "Don't scream." He pulled her close as she tried to wriggle free. "Don't struggle. Just listen. Please."

She obeyed, held by curiosity. *Please.* He'd never spoken the word to her before.

"There is to be a banquet held at the Citadel tonight in celebration of the impending wedding. I'd like you to be there."

Clara glared at him, her hands balling. "I don't have a choice, do I?" She could not allow herself to be placidly returned to the Citadel like some stray cow. If she did, she would become his prisoner again, and for good as he'd hardly give her another opportunity to escape.

"You have no home here."

"I'll find another." She'd enough skill to become an apprentice. Someone in the village would be willing to take her on. And if not here, then there were other villages. "I'll live on the streets until then if I have to. It's safe enough." How hard could it be if Tommy had survived all these years?

"Nowhere is so safe for a young woman, especially one who cannot defend herself." He tilted her face to one side. His thumb, cool against her skin, hesitantly brushed her cheek and she flinched as it stung anew. "Did she hit you?"

Clara blinked, finally lifting her gaze to look at him. Lucias glared straight ahead, although not at her, for the focus seemed elsewhere. His black brows knitted together, shielding eyes that had hardened. The firm line of his lips compressed with visible distaste. Was it concern? For *her*?

"I'm fine," she blurted.

"Fine?" His eyes took on a feral edge. "No one has the right to touch you in such a manner." He released her, marching towards the door. The weathered wood rattled. Hinges groaned under the unseen force.

"Wait." She grabbed his arm, desperate to halt him. Her fingers dug into the hard muscles, but she could not turn him away. "Stop it!"

"She struck you." His lips shuddered into a sneer. "Her own daughter. Is this common behaviour for your family?" He faced her, a faint shimmer of light dancing in his eyes. "Do you not wish to seek retribution for this act?"

"Whatever for?" Her mother had always been physical when it came to dealing out Clara's punishments. Even her father had resorted to the belt in her youth. But she'd seen the result of worse handling. Her parents weren't harsh, never cruel and, although she never believed it at the time, all the reprimands she'd endured over the years were not uncalled for. "What would you do to her if I said yes?"

"Anything you desire."

Anything. All the power he had under his command, waiting to be wrought at her word. She could do whatever she wished. All she needed to do was give her consent. *And be in his debt all the more.* Letting him deal with her mother would just be another little hook to ensnare her. "N-no." She shook her head in case he hadn't heard. "I just want to leave." Her cheek was not so bad and the mark would be gone in the morning.

With his hand firmly grasping his sword hilt, Lucias silently inspected her.

Her untouched cheek joined the other in its burning. She planted herself before him, her arms folded tightly across her breasts. "If you plan on taking me back to the Citadel, then let's be off." Her gaze flicked to the alley's entrance and the destrier still standing there. "Otherwise, move your flamin' horse."

His forehead creased. One brow rose as he eyed first her, then the door. His mouth took on a sour twist. "Tell me, Clara, do you enjoy being a martyr?"

She jerked back. "What are you talking about?"

"First you give up your freedom for the street urchin." Lucias marched over to his mount's side. "Now you attempt to sway me from seeking out your mother by promising to return to the Citadel." Grasping the black leather saddle, he leapt aboard his mount. The horse, seeming larger now it bore a rider, swung to face her. "You clutch your grievances to you like a child's blanket, forgetting you are not entirely blameless for your current situation."

"So I deserve everything I get?"

The horse snorted as he kneed it into the alley's tight quarters. "I could give you a great deal, Clara. Whatever you wished."

"As long as I give you a child."

He gave a sad smile. The horse shifted and threw his face into deeper shadows. "That choice has always been yours," he whispered.

She shook her head. What choice did a prisoner have? "You took away my right to choose."

"Oh?" Leaning over the horses' neck, Lucias thrust his hand towards her. "Then what is it to be this time, Miss Weaver? Do you seek to suffer even further by enduring hunger on the streets, or will you swallow your fierce pride to join me in the feasting and the comforts of a warm bed?"

She clasped his arm. "As long as that bed does not include you."

He grinned back at her with a mischievous twinkle in his eyes. Something both firm and yielding wrapped around her waist. Her feet left the ground. Clara stiffened as his magic coiled down her legs, writhing against her thighs and gently encouraging her knees to bend. Lucias lifted her over the horse to sit her, sideways, before the saddle. The unseen hold on her shrank into a thick sash-like harness, clasping her tight.

Her stomach flopped. Why had he not tried to stop her from fleeing earlier? Had he suspected she would not find this a suitable haven?

Clara wriggled on the spot, trying to find a comfortable position on the animal's withers. The horse's body rolled beneath her, coarse hair tickling her unprotected legs, as the horse backed out of the alley and onto the street. Her smock slipped down one shoulder. She struggled to cover her bare skin, her face growing uncomfortably warm.

The destrier, at his rider's sudden and sharp command, leapt into a gallop, jolting a scream from her throat. Keeping her eyes squeezed shut, she clung to Lucias. Flattened against his chest, the harsh leather of his jerkin rubbed at her exposed shoulder.

She peeked through her lashes, jerking upright when she saw the buildings were no richer than those of her home street. This wasn't the way to the village square. This was the way to the western gate. "Aren't we going to the village hall?"

Lucias shook his head. "You've already led me in quite the merry ride through the village and, although I won't deny tracking you was thrilling, we've wasted much time. Farris has no doubt acquired his bride and is making his way back to the Citadel." The streets before them filled with people and he pulled the horse into a lazy trot. "We must be there when they arrive."

Peering over her shoulder, she caught the plain, boxy form of a carriage disappearing around a distant corner. Lucias aimed them down a side street where the crowd was thinner and urged the horse into a canter.

They caught up with a line of carriages, escorted by the Endlight guards, just as the last one trundled through the gates.

Lucias pulled the destrier alongside Thad's less impressive-looking mount. "You were faster than I anticipated," he said.

The older man offered a grunt, one brow twitching upwards as he faced them. Clara shrank against Lucias' bulk
as her presence was noted. He had to have seen her fleeing.
What did he think now to see her back in their company and
wearing far less than she had earlier?

"Are we done here?" Lucias asked.

Thad's gaze flicked from his lord's face to hers, those
green eyes heavy as the fine brows drew together. "That we
are, my lord. That we are."

Chapter Seventeen

*C*lara stared blankly at the remains piled upon the dishes along the dining table. Bits of what had once been slabs of lamb and beef were dotted down its length, interspersed with the picked carcasses of whole chickens and a few bigger birds that might've been geese. Of the bread she'd smelt during her morning foray into the kitchen, only crumbs were left. A few platters still bore whole vegetables, fruits and pastries; the last survivors of the feast.

There were mostly desserts left but, with her belly having already reached a comfortably full state, she could barely stand to glance at the delights the servants had presented the room. Not even when the pungent scent of warm cinnamon tickled her nose and set her mouth to watering.

Her gaze lifted from the near-empty platters, once again straying to where Lucias sat at the head of the table several chairs up from her. How alive he seemed, laughing along with Thad and Farris. Courteous in his discussions with the village council as well as the handful of nobles and wealthier merchants who'd happened to be passing through Everdark at the time.

Almost a different person.

There was movement to her left, slow and bordering on imperceptible. Someone halted just on the edge of her vision. Something gold glittered in the candlelight.

"Wine, my lady?" The figure dipped forward. A heavy,

golden jug slipped into view.

She nodded, unable to stop staring at Lucias. He'd forsaken his normal leather attire for once, opting to clothe himself in a red and black embroided vest and shirt with equally dark trousers, their style service-worthy much like the clothing the count and his son wore. The black hair, which he so often let hang freely, had been tied back, allowing the candlelight to soften his features.

Having given up the more modest of the two gowns she possessed, Clara wore the low-cut dress the women had first made for her. Yet, even with her shoulders and good deal of her chest bare, she could still be considered overdressed when compared to Brenna.

The woman who would be the next Countess of Endlight all but hung her breasts on display to everyone within the room. And as for her skirts, why Clara would never have dared to wear something that showed so much leg in public.

She wasn't quite certain why the count had bothered with the trip down to the village to collect the woman only to then have the council follow them up to the Citadel for a feast. Enquiring had led to a simple answer: tradition. It had puzzled her no end until posing the same question to Thad led to the foreign lord expanding on Lucias' abrupt reply. Any man born in Endlight, especially if they originated from the moors just west the city, was expected to claim his bride the night before the wedding if not earlier.

Clara poked at what was left of the jellified substance in her bowl. She'd known the original inhabitants of Endlight had once been part of a smaller kingdom, absorbed centuries ago during the border disputes of old, but it hadn't occurred to her they would keep their ancient traditions. How wildly marriage customs swung from one side of the kingdom to the other.

And such a barbaric custom. Such a scandalous thing would never be allowed in Everdark. Her whole life, Clara had been bludgeoned with the litany of what was expected from good girls. Sticking to it meant she wasn't even allowed live with her intended husband before their wedding, let alone partake of intimate acts.

What did the Goddess think of Endlight's women coming before the altar in such a state? Or did the nomads, along with those living within the nearby city walls, still worship another deity? One who was obviously lenient when it came to a person's morals.

Her spoon slipped and clanged against the bowl. Such a divinity seemed the perfect being for men like the Great Lords to worship. What better excuse could they have than custom?

A sharp bang on the table brought her back to the nobles clustering around Farris. The old count was laughing, again, and attempting to speak through the dreadful wheezing. "You should've... seen the look... on his face!" He slapped the table once more and clutched at Brenna. The woman had perched herself upon her future husband's lap like a child, her nearly fully-exposed bosom bouncing distastefully close to his face.

Clara's gaze swung back to Lucias. He was listening to the count's story with the expression of one who had heard it many times before but was still a little embarrassed to hear it again in such company. Seeing such a reaction, Clara was almost sorry she'd positioned herself just beyond normal hearing.

Another outburst of laughter from the old man had Lucias grimacing and shaking his head. He glanced her way, his lips softening into a smile that had her cheeks ablaze in seconds.

Gripping the delicate stem of her goblet, Clara held the cool, crystalline bowl to her chest. She sipped the pinkish liquid within, wrinkling her nose at the bittersweet aftertaste. How could anyone drink this stuff?

Her gaze travelled down the table to the men and women draining glass after glass of wine. No one seemed at all bothered by the flavour. She took another hesitant sip. Less tart than the last and a touch fruity, almost reminiscent of the plums her father used to buy every year.

"You look bored."

Clara jumped at the voice, almost spilling the half glass of wine. Her gaze darted to where Lucias sat, or at least had been sitting. The men and women around the empty chair still laughed and chattered amongst themselves. How hadn't she noticed his disappearance?

"I admit, I am not entirely fond of these gatherings myself." Lucias collapsed into the chair beside her, the heels of his booted feet resting upon the edge of the table. His arm draped over the chair back, an empty goblet dangling from his fingers. He gestured with it to a passing servant and the glass was filled with a deep red wine. "I wouldn't recommend drinking too much." He nodded towards her goblet. "It can go straight to the head of the inexperienced."

She rolled her eyes. Brenna had drunk two glasses during the meal and was now working her way through a third. Surely if the woman could consume so much without any ill effects, then so could Clara. "I'd have thought you would prefer me in an inebriated state."

Twisting in his seat, Lucias shot her a dark look before sipping quietly at the deep red wine. He stared at her over the crystalline rim for some time before finally lowering his glass with a sigh. "It's about what you expect of me, isn't it?" He gave a small smile, his eyes glittering with a deep sadness. "So I don't suppose you'll believe me if I swore it would be the last thing on my mind, would you?"

Jerking her shoulders back, Clara looked away under the pretence of taking another sip. Bitter wine brushed her lips. He sounded genuine, but she couldn't bring herself to believe his words. What better way to have her comply with his wishes than to get her drunk?

The music, which had been softly playing as they ate, grew louder. Gentle notes flowed from wood and string, soft and with a hint of a spring to encourage movement. Clara fast found her foot swinging from side-to-side to the alluring beat.

All around her, people left the table and the group clustering about the fireplace. She tracked the migration, both the stately and the more spirited, to the once vacant floor at her back. There, the people began to dance.

Clara's gaze proceeded to follow the pattern of feet and skirts as they twirled about with the music picking up speed and volume. A part of her longed to join in the dancing, although she couldn't bear to do so alone like she often did at the fairs in Everdark. No, she'd need someone to join her who wouldn't be expecting anything further. *Someone like Thad.*

She glanced at Lucias. His attention had swung to the dancing couples, the tapping of his boot heel on the table joining in with the rhythm. The memory of his face, the jealousy that had flared in his eyes when she and Thad first met drifted to the forefront of her thoughts. He seemed somewhat at ease right now. Certainly more relaxed than before the Endlight lords had arrived. Perhaps it would be best to not aggravate him.

But who else would dare to ask her other than Thad?

Lucias drained the last of his wine and, with the chair legs skidding along the stone, sprang to his feet. "Would you care to join me in dance, Miss Weaver?"

Of course, he *would dare.* Clara stared at his outstretched hand as if it held a dagger, frantically thinking of an excuse he would believe. "I—"

He took the half-full goblet from her unresisting fingers. "Come now. If I am to restrain myself from the thought of ravishing you in my bed, then at least let me have this one dance."

She glared up at him, content to leave him standing there. Restraining himself from her, was he? He spoke as if he was doing her some great and trying favour. Clara raised her hand, itching to slap him.

Movement, or rather the cessation of it, on the edge of her vision caught her attention. She suddenly became aware of the room's stillness. The chatter she'd been ignoring earlier had died to whispers, leaving only the hushed notes of the musicians' fading melody. People were watching them, watching *her*. Waiting to see what she would do.

Blushing at the scrutiny, her fingers alighted on his forearm. She silently allowed herself to be drawn to her feet and escorted to the dance floor where he gently swung her around to stand before him.

He took a step backwards and bowed. Her face burned hotter and, aware they were still being watched, she curtsied. Lucias held out his hand for her. She clapped her palm against his, biting her lip in instant regret as her fingers, not protected like the rest of her gloved hand, throbbed. Taking a deep breath she drew herself upright with some manner of grace.

Lucias pulled her close, his other hand falling to her waist. His chest pressed heavily against the stiff-panelled corset she was suddenly thankful to be wearing. "How good a dancer are you?" he whispered, softly twirling them to the music's beat.

"Adequate," she admitted, raising her voice as she spun out to arm's length. "Enough to know this is a courtship dance." She bobbed again, him with mimicking the genuflection.

His shoulders shook with a minute, cheerless laughter. "I thought you might prefer the *Display of the Peacock* over others." The smile he gave matched his laugh. "Although, I'm afraid my plumage is a touch too dark to attract a mate with. Even then, I'd have little time to make a woman my wife before she became a widow."

Clasping one hand and facing his back, she followed him as they trotted in a circle. "So you'd rather waste your time on a woman who denies you everything?" Clara gave him yet another bow. They changed hands and circled in the other direction before ending up back in his arms.

"Ah, but I am apparently set on raping you come the new moon." His voice was small and carried with it the hint of a question.

Clara stiffened.

Lucias guided them across the floor, not seeming to notice her sudden lack of response. "Is it not what you told Thad?"

So Thad has *spoken with him.* Despite her plea to not get involved. Her stomach clenched, bile sliding up her throat. She swallowed, desperately trying not to let her thoughts show. "I spoke only of the deadline you imposed upon me. Of how you said I could either come to you or be raped."

"That's not what I said!" he hissed, tipping her backwards and forcing her to cling to him.

"But is it not what you meant?" She gasped as he hauled her upright, bouncing back onto her feet with a jarring hop.

Step for step, they followed the music's soft notes in silence, his dark eyes glittering with the candlelight. At least, she hoped the flickers of light came from the candles. "No."

No? Clara tripped, barely feeling the tendril of his magic right her. *Choose how I will come to him or he decides for me.* Obviously she had no intention of going to him. So what else would he mean if not force?

She spun away, then back into his grasp. "Your mother will be here soon." To kill him. And her, if she couldn't convince him to let her leave before then. Perhaps Thad would have more luck. Although, now she'd seen how the soon-to-be-wed couple were in public, she was hesitant to share a carriage with them.

His eyes hardened, the faintest spark of blue danced in their depths. "She will."

"You've little time left." Then he would die. *Because he is his father's son.* It didn't seem fair Lucias was to bear the brunt of his mother's vendetta again the man who'd kidnapped her several decades ago. Yes, Lucias had been the outcome, but he could hardly be the one to blame for his father's actions.

He sighed. "I know."

"What will you do?" He had to have some plan to survive

the barbarian's assault.

"I…" His steps became wooden, his face even less expressive. "I will wait and accept the fate our Goddess has given me."

Death. And the land would be destroyed. Its people butchered or worse. Could the Goddess truly be so cruel to her people and allow such a thing? "And what of our deal? If I leave, what will you do with Tommy?"

"Take him with you if you think you need to. Had my death not been so certain, I would've liked him to stay and be fully absorbed into the ranks."

She pulled back to glare at him. "You know I won't let you take his soul."

He shook his head. "Poor choice of words, I see. No wonder you think the worst of me." His mouth curved into something too small and sad to be considered a smile. "I swear, Clara, I do not intend to take the lad's soul. The boy is harmless and works in the stables well enough. Given time, and training, he could've been an excellent stable master. Guess there's not much chance now."

"*Tommy?*" Surely they not speak of the same man. Yes, he was excellent with animals but, as far as she knew, he'd never given orders to anyone.

"You'd be surprised what he takes in and what he can do when you stop treating him like a child and more like the young man he is." He chuckled, his gaze drawn to something over her shoulder. "I see it didn't take her long."

She twisted her head, straining to see what had caught his eye. With a flick of his hand, he twirled her around. Clara gasped as her back struck his chest. The doublet didn't offer much padding and the muscles beneath were firm.

He wrapped his arms about her waist. "Farris has finally drunk himself to sleep." Resting his chin on her shoulder, he gently swayed them from side to side. "I've a feeling I know what she'll do now."

Brenna had abandoned her husband-to-be's side to drag

Thad out onto the floor. The way she twirled and gyrated against the older man set Clara's face aflame. Did Brenna have no morals? Upon her arrival at Endlight, and her subsequent marriage to the count, Thad was to become her step-son. Yet she chose to dance in such a way as to suggest she was betrothed to the younger foreign lord instead of the count.

And in front of her parents. Clara glanced at the crowd. No one seemed at all bothered by the pair. She couldn't even find the woman's parents. Why, if Clara had attempted such an act before her mother... Well, her mother probably wouldn't have cared so long as a wedding was involved.

Brenna had to be aware of being just another in a line of young women. Clara suspected the woman would be looking to ensure she was not brushed aside when the current count died. What better way to do so than seduce the next in line? *Even so...* She sighed. It just seemed wrong.

"If he's still the same Thad I remember, she's wasting her time." Lucias' quiet laughter shook her whole body. "He's not going to be interested. She'd have been better off trying her luck on his eldest."

"Not interested?" Clara mumbled. "He is a man, she has a pulse." Was it not the only requirement of all men? *Especially those of Endlight.* And Thad had probably taken his own romp through the city's brothels.

Lucias' snort of amusement blew past her ear. "You think this is the first time a woman has tried to lure him into their bed? Thad is no fool. He takes steps to ensure he's not the least bit tempted whilst away from his wife."

She eyed the dancing couple. Brenna wasn't holding much back. A man would have to be dead to not react in *some* fashion. Clara was certain if the countess-to-be were to take it any further, it would require an extreme decline in the woman's decency. "Steps?"

"I believe it's some sort of herbal remedy they use on the men posted in Endlight's border towers. To keep them focused on the task at hand and not on the nomadic women of the nearby moors."

"I see." Was this why Lucias had seemed content to allow Thad to be alone with Clara? But it did not stop the jealousy. *Sibling rivalry.* Was Thad's presence responsible for the more amenable Lucias? She couldn't see why he'd bother when Thad was married and uninterested. Or had the foreign lord's arrival merely shown the true Lucias? "You and he, you were close once. Like brothers."

"Once."

The music had taken on a dreamy note. Clara leant back against his chest, letting her mind wander along with the music. So Thad had not lied about his closeness to his lord. Did it mean he'd spoken truthfully about everything else? What about Lucias' treatment of women? Seeing this more open man, she could well believe Thad had known a different young lord.

The magic twists their minds. And people suffered because of the apparent destruction letting go would cause. But what had Thad said? Something about a Great Lord dying. "How are you here if one of the Great Lords died without an heir?"

"Hmm?"

Clara spun to face him, the memory returning in full. "The third Great Lord," she pressed, "Thad said he died nearly heirless. How is it possible?" The more she thought on it, the less sane it sounded. There had to be a living lord for there to be an heir.

"Oh, *that.*" He grimaced and shrugged. "He suffered a heart attack, nothing unusual about it."

"And the nearly heirless part?" A man died with or without an heir. There could be no *nearly.*

Lucias gave her a wolfish grin. "He was in his marriage bed at the time." The smile faded into a frown. "I'm surprised the story hasn't lasted. It had to be one of the kingdom's worst days. The soulless portion of the army went crazy. I know for a fact they destroyed half of Everdark before stopping."

She could recall old tales of some dark day in the village's long history. When Everdark had been subjected to what the storytellers grimly referred to as the three r's: raid, ravish and ruin. The village would've been smaller back then and yet, for them to decimate half of it in a day... She'd thought such destruction had come *before* the first Great Lord took command, not after. "So why *did* they stop?"

His frown deepened, his lips twisting sourly. Clearly this was not a topic he wished to talk about. "His wife had conceived."

"And it was all back to normal? Just like that?" Hundreds of lives tipped upside-down and the army, like some parasite bent on destroying its host from the inside, just... stopped.

"Of course. There was, technically, a Great Lord again."

A mere spark of life, still vulnerable and easily destroyed, yet it had enough power to halt hundreds of murderers. Small wonder Lucias, even with his time shortened considerably, still persisted in convincing her to bear his child.

If she had but known the certainty. Could she have let him? "You told me the servants breaking free after your death was only a possibility." She'd been demanding her freedom when the whole kingdom was destined to drown in its own blood.

Giving a weary sigh, Lucias brushed a tendril of her hair to one side. The back of his finger slid across her cheek, leaving a warm, tingling trail. "I didn't want your decision to be swayed by past events."

He'd lied, knowing the risk, knowing she was more likely to refuse than comply, just so he could give her a choice? "But they *will* break loose."

"Yes, and the kingdom will fall with me."

Clara stared at him as if they'd never met, looking into his eyes in search of the truth. Lurking in their depths, peeking out from behind the mask of false gaiety, sat the cold certainty of approaching death. Of there being naught else left to do but wait until it came. This feast was more than a celebration of the impending wedding, this was also his wake.

And, in some small way, Lucias was already dead.

Chapter Eighteen

*C*lara danced across the floor. The music and her partner had changed several times over the hours. She
currently followed Thad in the slow steps, her neck craned
to watch as Lucias danced with Brenna.

The woman's methods of dancing had not altered with
the men and he appeared to be enjoying her attentions far
too much. "He should not lead her on so." Did Brenna not
think of how she dishonoured herself with this display of
wantonness?

Over her shoulder, she caught Thad's whispered chuckle.
"What is so amusing?"

"You." He gave a smug grin as she glared at him. "Anyone would think you're jealous. Small wonder he continues
to pursue you."

She gave a derisive snort. Her? Jealous of what Brenna
did with Lucias? "I've never heard of anything more absurd." If he was willing to let the woman debase herself in
such a fashion, then Brenna was welcome to him. "I'm surprised you let her get away dancing as she did." She eyed
him, thinking back to Lucias' mention of the foreign lord's
use of herbs. "Or is it because your darling wife isn't here to
monitor you?"

Thad smirked and her cheeks warm ever so slightly. "Do
you think Brenna is the first young woman to try seducing
me?"

Clara shook her head. She couldn't believe a man like him had gone through life and only caught the eye of one woman.

"My dear Thalia, like most of those not born under Endlight's jurisdiction, has adapted well to our city's less conventional ways." His full lips twisted wryly. "Although it took her many years to accept that a man can admire a woman without further interest."

She glanced over her shoulder at the dancers. Brenna had moved on to another nobleman, pressing herself tightly against the unknown lord as they swayed to the movement. All around them, it seemed men and women were doing more of the things that were best done in private.

Truly, only a handful danced as sedately as she did with Thad. *No interest*? And what of when the woman was being persistent?

The gruff rasp of someone clearing their throat brought her back to the more immediate people around them and Clara belatedly realised they had drifted towards the long dining table. Lucias stood nearby, polite enquiry plastered upon his face.

Thad relinquished his hold of her hand and waist. "If you will be so kind as to excuse me." Bowing to the both of them, he returned to the far end of the table and his sleeping father's side.

Lucias collapsed into a chair, pulling her onto his lap.

She wriggled, struggling to get free of his arms. "You apparently enjoyed your little frolic with the bride-to-be." If she could just get him to loosen his grip for a moment, then she stood a chance of... well, standing.

"It was refreshing at first," he admitted, giving her an excessively toothy grin. "But it begins to bore after a time." His arms tightened around her. One corner of his mouth twitched upwards as she fidgeted on his lap. "I wouldn't persist if I were you."

Clara frowned down at him. She shouldn't keep trying to win free, should she? Certainly not from his point of view.

She squirmed a little more, noting how Lucias' breath hitched at each movement. He leant back a ways, tipping his hips slightly upwards.

She went rigid. Realisation put a soft warmth in her cheeks, which was steadily stoked into an inferno by his throaty laughter.

"I *did* suggest you should stop." He lifted a leg, tipping her against his chest. His breath, lightly touched with the smell of fermented fruit, brushed her lips. "Why *do* you fight me so much?"

Why? Why wouldn't she? He'd kept her prisoner. Was it not reason enough?

Ignoring Lucias and his question as best as she could, Clara tracked the path of a servant bearing a tray of glasses. The man walked by the chair. She snatched a full glass and drank deeply of the dark liquid within.

Lucias watched her, his dark brows lowered in a heavy frown. "How many of those have you had?"

She shrugged. This had to be her third, or possibly fourth, glass. Surely not enough to affect her mind. Why her thoughts had never been clearer than they were now.

Lucias prised the empty glass from her fingers. "I think you shouldn't have any more."

"*You* are not my keeper." This close, he was quite handsome. A little rough around the edges from a lesser courtly life than the refined Thad, but she could soon fix that. Leaning forward, Clara closed her eyes and puckered her lips.

His fingertips brushed the base of her neck. The hand slid up and into her hair. Then, much to her surprise, he gently coaxed her backwards. "Go to bed." Unseen bonds wrapped about her waist, hauling her to her feet. "Sleep and sober up."

Suddenly released from the magical grip, she staggered backwards, her passage halted by the table. She hadn't noticed it whilst dancing, but the room seemed to spin. *Sober up?* She wasn't drunk. *I tried to kiss him.* Groaning, she cradled her head. What was wrong with her? Perhaps seeking her bed would be a good idea.

Sticking to weaving along the tableside and groping across the walls, Clara made her way towards the heavy doors. Her stomach didn't feel right. A touch on the leaden side and a whole lot on the bubbly. She clutched the door handle with one hand, the other firmly hugging her middle. *Blasted wine.* No one told her it had this sort of effect. Was she going to be sick? *Please, not here.*

"My lady," a deep, unfamiliar voice spoke, "do you require assistance?" The man's hand clamped onto her shoulder.

She flinched under the man's touch, more forceful than she expected. Letting the unknown hand steady her, she tipped her head up to stare blankly at his face. Her gaze dropped to take in his clothes. Simple servant garb in dark greens and golds. *Endlight colours.* One of the guards who'd come with the carriage.

The man opened the door, letting her stumble through the gap. "Come, my lady." The guard took her by the elbow and began to lead the way down the hall. "I'll escort you to my—" He gave her a glassy smile. "—I mean, *your* quarters."

Clara paused, for a second, since the guard was still moving and took her with him. Something about the man felt off. Even the hall didn't look right. If only she could focus long enough to figure out what was wrong.

His arm wrapped around her shoulders. A finger slipped under the edge of her gown, casually tugging at the low neck line of her gown over her shoulder. "Not far now, my lady." He steered her towards a door, opened it and urged her through with a soft push.

Clara took a few numb steps into the room beyond. Shouldn't there have been stairs? She halted to blurrily stare at the red curtains framing the far window. This wasn't her room. She spun to make her way back out the door and walked straight into the guard. Flattening her hands against his chest, she pushed back and attempted to skirt around him.

"Now, now, love." The man threaded his fingers through the corset laces, trapping her. "Don't be shy." He grabbed hold of her chin and tilted her head up. "How 'bout you give us a taste, eh?" He licked his lips with a long, shudder-inducing suck.

Clara struck out, her hand connecting with his cheek. His fingers slipped from her face and she jerked back, held by his grip on her clothes. An inept kick of her leg in the direction of his groin had him releasing her before she could connect.

Free, she staggered across the room, frantically searching for a means of escape.

A half-burnt candlestick sat on the table. She dove for it, sliding across the tabletop. Her fingers curled around the candlestick's heavy base just as he made a grab for her. Rolling onto her back, she jabbed the makeshift weapon in the man's direction. The candle smacked into his chest, cracking near the base to dangle on the wick.

The man lunged, and his fingers encircled her arm. He squeezed, his thumb pressing into the soft underside of her wrist. Her hand went numb and the candlestick fell from her limp grasp.

Thumping her back against the table, he dragged the skirt up her legs, grumbling as his hands fell upon the bloomers she wore underneath. Each side of the cloth grew tight then loosened with an almighty rip. The cool air brushed her most intimate of places.

His tongue snaked into her ear. She tossed her head, attempting to hit him. He leant more of his weight on her and sucked at her neck. When she fell still in a moment of shock, he buried his face into her cleavage.

Lifting his head, he moved again, the brush of his chest on hers revealing he was creeping upwards. His breath, rank with smoke, huffed against her lips.

She clawed wildly at a face she could no longer properly see through the tears. Her fingers scraped along flesh, her nails dug into every ridge they found.

The man jerked back with a yell, clutching at his eye. Snarling, he swung. The back of his hand lashed her cheek.

Clara fell to the floor with a yelp. The acidic mix of blood and bile filled her mouth. Blinded by her tears, she groped across the plush rugs. Searching for the way out. To open the door and call out. Someone was bound to hear her.

"Where do you think you're going?" he growled.

She screamed as he grabbed her hair. He threw her onto her back. His hands pawed at her, clawing frantically at the corset laces. Trapped under him, Clara fought back with everything she had left. She squirmed and writhed backwards along the floor, seeking for a way to slip free. Her fists thumped hard against his shoulders until her hands were sore. The man hunched over to worry at her clothes. Her teeth sank into his shoulder at the sound of shredding fabric.

He slapped her again. "Be still!" The hem of her gown lifted, once again sliding up her legs. "You give it up for him, whore." A leg that wasn't hers brushed against her inner thigh. "You can give it up to me." Another leg followed the first, spreading her legs wide. "I said be still!" The hand came once more, leaving its stinging mark across her face.

Whimpering, her tears rolling down her face in unstoppable waves, she turned her face from him and closed her eyes. Why had she come back here? *Lucias*. He'd said she would be safe. Had brought her here to *keep* her from harm.

The man grunted. His weight shifted, his belly pushing against hers. Somewhere beyond the ringing in her ears, a faint click brought her eyes open a fraction. Light glistened through her lashes.

Tilting her head to one side, she could just make out the door, its outline broken by what seemed to be the nearing form of another man. *Two* of them? *Sweet Goddess, no.* She wanted nothing to do with this one. *Someone, please, help me!*

The shadowy form bore down on them, revealing itself to

be Lucias, his face warped in rage. He grabbed the man, dragging him off her.

Swearing at the interruption, the guard swung at the intruder.

Lucias ducked. His fist slammed into the other man's stomach as the Endlight guard lurched forward.

The man spun about, his arm raised for another blow. He froze, hanging in the air as if coming up against a clear pane of glass. Clara watched as, his grey eyes widening, the struggling man's head drew level with his lord's.

Lucias' eyes glowed with the same silver-blue sheen it had in the dungeon. "How dare you," he snarled. He pulled the man closer and spoke further. The words drifted lazily into her ears, not quite loud enough to make out, yet they pulled at something deep within her.

The man ceased his thrashing. Now it was *his* eyes that took on the unearthly hue.

Lucias set the man back on the floor. "You will go to the highest window you can find." Ice ruled his voice. "There, you shall throw yourself from it."

"As you command, my lord." The man marched out the room, his movements akin to that of a wooden clockwork soldier. The door slammed shut behind him, rattling a nearby vase.

Shivering, Clara hugged her knees to her chest. She huddled where the guard had left her on the floor and watched the vase rock back and forth. Fresh tears welled. She joined in its tiny motion. Back and forth. He'd been so close. She could still feel his breath on her neck. The heat of his thighs on her now cold legs.

What if he'd succeeded? Would Lucias have let her go, tossing her aside like some soiled rag? Or would he have seen it as an opportunity to storm through gates that had already fallen? Clara hugged her legs a little tighter. She'd been beginning to think she had been wrong about him, but now, anything seemed possible.

Movement to her right. Quick and shadowlike. Something behind her ripped, then something else, heavy and metallic, hit the ground with a dreadful clang. She dashed the tears from her eyes and uncurled from the ball she'd scrunched into. What new horror awaited her?

A hand brushed her shoulder. Clara screamed and shrank from the touch. She lashed out, the heel of her hand meeting the other's chin before she realised who she'd struck.

Lucias groaned and rubbed at his jaw. Those dark eyes glittered with repressed anger, silvery-blue specks dancing in their depths. "Easy, Clara," he breathed. The dark red cloth of a curtain lay at his feet. "He can't hurt you now." He threw the curtain over her shoulders and she realised her corset lay open, the shift beneath torn, leaving her breasts bare for all to see.

Clara trembled beneath the coarse fabric. Her stomach clenched. She swallowed. The bitter tang of bile coated her tongue. A horrid rasp filled her throat, sharp fire following quick on its heels.

Unable to stop, she bent over and emptied her body of the night's feasting. The rug she'd almost been raped on fast became stained with the contents of her stomach.

It was when she was breathless, retching with only saliva dribbling out at each heave, her throat hot and raw, that she was capable of sitting up. "Sorry," she rasped, wiping her mouth on the curtain's edge. She sniffed and spat out the last wayward chunks.

Lucias stared at her, his lips compressed into a thin line and brows merged in concern. "Feel better?"

Talking hurt and swallowing felt like she'd a thistle wedged in her neck. But the gentle nod she gave him wasn't much better. Clara shrank deeper into the curtain as he left her side. She couldn't stop shaking.

A fire flared to life within the cold hearth, eliciting a harsh squeak from her tortured throat. The firm clasp of magic embraced her, lifting her off the floor. Unresisting, she floated towards where Lucias stood next to the fireplace.

Settling her on a nearby stool, he strode over to the bedside table laden with another candlestick and water pitcher. He picked up the pitcher and poured its crystal clear liquid into the cup. "Drink this. It should help."

Clara gulped down the chill water. She felt it slide into her stomach, its passage soothing her burning throat. She hunched over the cup, softly rocking.

Lucias crouched before the stool, mutely watching her. He raised a hand to her cheek, his fingertips cool against her skin. She flinched and he drew his hand back.

A new fire burned in his eyes. This one of slow, murderous hatred, of witnessing the exact thing he despised above all else. Was Thad right? Perhaps Lucias had never had any intention of raping her. What, then, would the alternative be if she did not come to him?

"Do you think you can walk?" he asked.

She nodded.

"Let's get you to your room, then." Straightening, he gently aided her to her feet. "You'll be safer there."

Safe. She wouldn't be safe until the men were gone. Clutching the curtain to her chest, Clara leant against him, finding some small comfort in his arms as he escorted her out of the room and down the hall. There was no one else around. Not even a hint of a passing servant. Lucias must have followed her as they left the dining hall. Had the guard seemed so suspicious to him?

Her legs wobbled as they climbed the coiling stairway to her chambers. Lucias' grip across her shoulders remained firm but distant, his magic doing much of the work in holding her up. The door swung inwards at flick of his hand. Holding the candelabra aloft, he led her across the dark room and to her bedside where he gently had her sit.

The candlelight danced in the wind as he set the metal base on the table. He crouched at her feet, taking up one of her hands. "Do you require me to remain nearby whilst you change?" His brows lowered and his mouth bore an uncertain tilt. "I could have a few of the servant women stay the night if you'd feel better with some feminine company."

She bowed her head and drew the curtain tighter around her neck. "No."

He nodded slowly. "I guess I'll leave you be."

Clara squeezed his hand as he stood, refusing to let it slip free. "Don't go," she whispered. Glancing up, she saw him hesitate.

Lucias stared at her for what seemed like hours then finally sighed. "I—I'm not certain it would be appropriate given the circumstances. I should be getting back to the main hall before my absence is noted."

"Please? Just until I fall asleep." In reality, she did not want him to leave at all. No one else was better suited to keep her safe; he'd already proven it to her.

His eyes narrowed. "Very well." He pulled free of her fingers as a chair squeaked along the floor. Lucias collapsed into the seat. "Until then."

She used the bathroom to change into her nightgown whilst Lucias, under strict instruction to stay out, no matter what he heard, waited on the other side of the door. She could hear the leisurely tramp of his boot heels as he strolled alongside the connecting wall.

Clothed in an outfit that was at least whole, she snuggled under the sheets, grasping his hand when he bent to pull the blankets higher. Her fingers entwined with his, she closed her eyes.

It was some time later when Clara felt his hand slip free. She rolled her head to one side, her mind slowly rising out of the fogginess of light sleep. Candlelight glistened through the cracks between her lids.

"Hush." The word was barely a whisper, the breath of it hot against her skin. The blanket lifted over her shoulder, engulfing her in sweet warmth. There was the hesitant touch of a finger brushing her cheek, then the light faded away and all she could hear was the soft tread of retreating footsteps.

CHAPTER NINETEEN

*T*he pale light of dawn had well and truly left by the time Clara joined the waking world. Now noon was in danger of passing and her head still felt as if someone in heavy boots danced upon her skull. To have been woken by the cheerful figure of Gettie also hadn't helped.

Like many of the party-goers, Clara sat in the gloomy dining hall and stirred her soup, endeavouring not to let the spoon hit the bowl as she drew lazy circles. She'd drunk half of the brownish liquid and her tongue still had a decidedly papery feel to it.

Someone at the far end allowed metal to clank with porcelain. A few people closer to the sound groaned. Clara winced as a fresh pang stabbed through her brain. Upon awakening, Gettie had given her some sort of vile-tasting tonic that was meant to help. Clara fervently prayed it would start working soon.

The chair beside her screeched backwards, the sharpness prickling its way up her spine and into her brain. A pair of black leather boots hit the table with a heavy thump. "And how do we fare on this glorious day?" Lucias enquired in what, had her skull not been threatening to split in two, would've been a wonderful sing-song tone.

"Sod off," she mumbled.

He chuckled, the sound hammering inside her head. "That bad, huh?"

She peered at him, twisting her head and squinting to keep out the flare from the torches behind him. "Why are you so flaming cheerful?" she asked through gritted teeth. He would've easily drunk twice as much as her, and no less than the others who now nurtured their aching heads, yet he seemed completely unaffected by the previous night's indulgence.

Lucias' grin gleamed brighter than the sun. "Still feeling a little under the weather, are we? I can fix it."

"Gettie's already given me something for it."

His grin widened. "Ah, but my way works." He sprang to his feet, the chair rocking on its legs as it squeaked backwards, and offered her his hand. "Would you like to know the secret to it?"

Was that a trick question? Of course she wanted to know how he didn't suffer the same ill effects as everyone else. She grabbed his hand, instantly regretting it as he pulled her to her feet and all but dragged her out of the hall.

They made their way through the familiar corridors leading to the main stairway. A handful of servants passed by on their way out of the Citadel, each man carrying a number of chests bearing the setting sun emblem. *Endlight's men.*

Clara watched the men moved on, solemn in their task. Not a one of them as much as glanced her way. Had they heard about their comrade and the punishment Lucias exacted on him?

"Do keep moving, my dear," Lucias said as he disappeared down another corridor. "You'll never get there if you stop to ogle every servant on the way."

Dear? He'd never called her dear before. Clara lifted her skirts to keep up with his brisk pace. The women had made two dresses upon her arrival and Lucias' subsequent choosing. With one of them given up to her mother and the other ruined, she'd been delighted to find they'd kept the serviceable attire she'd worn upon her first arrival. A pity her boots, with their soles in heavy need of repair, had not sur-

vived, for her dark red slippers didn't exactly match the outfit.

Her head swam as she trotted after him. Around her, the
walls became less and less opulent. Paintings in their or-
nate, if not gilt, frames gave way to tapestries, which in
turn dwindled to bare stone. Underfoot, the long stretches of
carpet had finished with the last of the landscape paintings.

She'd been this way before. It'd been the first time he
had seen her in the gown the Endlight guard had destroyed.
Where was he taking her?

Just when she thought she could go no further without
being sick, Lucias stopped.

Clara halted beside him. Her brain felt as if would pound
its way out of her forehead. She leant on the pillar, pressing
her cheek to the stone's cool surface until she was certain
she wouldn't vomit.

Instead, she sought the strength to face whatever cure
Lucias proposed. Peeking through one eye, she peered
around the smooth curve to discover nothing more than the
unoccupied, dusty stretch of the Citadel's training grounds
waited beyond. "*This* is your big secret?"

"One of the best," he said, laughing as she stared at him.
"Go on, try it."

Did he expect her to believe this would work? *Well, it
does heal the injured.* What did she have to lose?

She stepped out onto the compacted dirt to stand just on
the edge, bathed in the noon sun. There was no need to
move further. An odd pinching tingle bore its way into her
skull, then gradually faded. Her cheeks warmed as if sun-
burnt. She groaned as the aches melted away.

"Feel better?"

Clara nodded. She'd never felt so well. The pain in her
head was gone and her face... She hadn't realised her
cheeks still stung until they no longer did. She gently prodded her skin and massaged her jaw. No one had mentioned
either way and she hadn't dared to even glance in the mirror this morning to see the truth, but the man's blows

hadn't been light and must have left some decent bruises.

"Wonderful!" Lucias clapped his hands together, untainted delight creasing his face. "Would you care to join me for a heartier meal than the swill the kitchen dares to call soup?"

Her hands flopped to her sides, slapping against her skirts. He'd murdered a man just last night. Clara could still picture the stiff, doll-like look on the guard's face as Lucias commanded him to die. Yet he acted as if it had never happened.

She grabbed Lucias' bare arm. "What did you do to the guard last night?" It'd been something far stronger, and nastier, than the magic she'd seen him use in the dungeon. "You killed him," she whispered. Lucias had somehow ordered the guard to jump to his death and the man had obeyed as if he couldn't stop himself.

Lucias shrugged her off, the rage of last night twisting his lips into a sneer. "It was no less than what he deserved."

She shrank from the fury in his eyes. They flickered from his normal dark brown to silvery-blue, seething with the memory. He could've imprisoned the guard. But no, he chose death over all, disobeying the law of his ancestors. "I thought all criminals had their souls taken, not their lives."

Lucias sighed. "Usually, yes. But you were in trouble. It was late." He ran his fingers through his hair, pulling the wayward strands from his face. "I-I wasn't thinking straight and... It's a reflex. I didn't intend to do it, but once I had him—" He shrugged again. "What else would you have had me do?"

"What *did* you do to him?" She hadn't wanted to ask then. Now, with the nearing prospect of once more being alone with him and the dozens of men who obeyed his command, the need to know overwhelmed her.

He pressed his lips together, the skin fast grew white and thin. "You won't like the answer."

"I'll decide what I like. *Tell* me."

Those dark eyes stared at her for what felt like eternity

before he finally spoke. "It was a simple spell of compelling, akin to the soul-taking ritual." He waved his hand in the air, his mouth opening and closing as he obviously struggled to find the words he needed to explain. "It... overpowers the will. Allows me to... control a person, whether partially or completely, for... whatever means. At least, for a short time."

"Long enough to climb a tower?" Obviously it had taken the guard beyond the window ledge. Had the man been aware of what he was doing as he made his way to his death? Did the magic wear off before he hit the ground?

"Yes." Lucias' lips twisted with bitter wryness. "Or have a woman accept a man's seed."

Clara stared unblinkingly at him, her thoughts mostly still back with the guard's horrid fate. This power belonged to all the Great Lords? "Your father used this spell on your mother?"

"A great many times and, I believe, a few after I was born."

Since hearing his mother had been an unwilling participant in his creation, she hadn't given much thought to how his father had gone about getting her pregnant. Surely, with the magic they had at hand, the power to lift a body off the ground, it would be easy to pin a woman and have their way.

"You could do the same thing to me, couldn't you?" Compelling a person seemed such an obvious choice. There'd be no struggling, no screams. She wouldn't be able to resist. No more so than the guard. Or Lenora. *Sweet Goddess*. No wonder Lucias' mother hated both father and son so much. His father had done worse than rape.

Lucias shook his head, his face tightening in disgust. "No, I couldn't. There is no difference in whether I compelled you or took you kicking and screaming into my bed. Rape is rape."

"But you *could* compel me." Had he done so already? *Like in the alleyway*? Did he use this dark magic to convince her to come back? Surely it wouldn't have taken much. A small tweak to change her mind and keep her here. Would she have been aware of the intrusion?

"I could do many things, I just choose not to. Sure, I could take the easy route and rely on my magic for everything." Lucias shook his head again, his smile bitter. "I'd become no better than the so-called *Great* Lords of old and *exactly* what my mother believes me to be." He clasped Clara's hands with shaking fingers. "And the choice of lying with me has always been yours, although I'd hoped we would have the time I promised you, so—"

"So I would want to stay?" she finished for him. "Have you forgotten your men kidnapped me? Why would I ever choose to stay?" She thought her constant attempts to escape had proven she wouldn't stay if given the choice. *Then why did I come back*? She should've walked away and left him standing in the alley.

But no, she'd been once again locked in his prison and she had allowed it to happen. *Because he wanted me to be safe*. And he'd almost failed. Some half-drunk guard had nearly gotten what Lucias could not. The thought, and seeing how easy it had been for the man, must chafe at his pride.

Lucias frowned. "Clara, you have my word I did not order my men to take women off the streets, especially unwilling. They were meant to bring me no one else but Katharina."

She sharply recalled his surprise the first night they'd met. Her cheeks warmed anew as the memory returned in full force. Him standing there, wet and wearing naught but a towel, eyeing her whilst Sirius informed his master of the situation. "But it didn't stop you once we were here, did it?"

"Once *you* were here." He barked a gasping laugh, nervous, almost to the point of embarrassed. "I admit it was a poor execution on my part, but I couldn't risk having you slip through my fingers." He cupped her chin, his chill thumb brushing along her cheek. "Had I known Everdark held such a treasure, I'd have sought you out myself months ago. I would've wooed you in such a fashion that, when the time came, you would've eagerly chosen to be with me."

She pulled away from him. "Why would I choose to be with a dead man?" Shaking her head, Clara raced back down the hallway.

On the way back to the Citadel, he had promised to let her go as soon as she could decide on how she would make a living and where. Why was he doing this now? Did he think expressing such feelings would get her to change her mind? *I never should've come back.*

Lucias caught up to her as she reached the main stairs. "Clara, please. Let me explain."

She spun on her heel to face him. "Explain *what*?" she shrieked, the words echoing around them. "That in *any* scenario you can think of bar this one, I end up giving you an heir? Is *that* what you want to explain to me?"

"I didn't intend for you—"

"*Intend!*" She threw up her arms. "You haven't *meant* to do a single thing since I got here." His previous words came back to her. *Only Katharina.* Clara hadn't ever been his intended mistress. "Before, even!" She paced the width of the stairway, silently ticking off each thing he hadn't *intended*. Her kidnapping, her learning the full extent of his magic, letting her escape and, of course, there was the guard's compelled death. "You unintentionally ruined my life."

What horrors he could unleash on the world if he ever did something on purpose?

"By taking you from a home where your mother hit you if disobeyed? Or do you refer to the marriage you did not want? I have already agreed to let you go once you've decided what you wish to do with your life and where you plan to go from here. What else are you expecting me to do?"

She stepped close enough for their noses to touch. "If you're so ready to let me go, then why do you continue to speak of having me stay?"

One side of his mouth tweaked upwards. "Wishful thinking? I'm going to die soon and I... I just wanted a chance."

Clara stared into those dark eyes and found herself getting lost not into the cold, devious gaze of her lord as she once would've assumed, but the lonely, pleading eyes of a boy. *A chance.* She shook her head. "To do what? Have sex one last time?" He could easily pay for such a thing, even if the woman had to come here.

His lips made a vain attempt at smile, although it was small and watery. "To show you I could've made you happy."

Her? Happy with *him*? "You honestly believe you could?"

Lucias gave a short, self-mocking laugh. "I do have the power to give you all you desire, but since you claim the only thing you want is your freedom." He shrugged. "All you need give me is a how and a where, then you can take Tommy and go whenever you please."

"So say I wanted to go out through the gates right now." She strode out the front entrance and into the sunlight. "You would not stop me?"

She'd trotted halfway down the steps before registering the green-lacquered carriage sitting in the middle of the courtyard. Of the other carriages that had been here last night, there was no sign.

The guards twisted in their saddles as she came to the foot of the stairs where the count and his future wife stood waiting. There seemed to be a lot more armour on the men than when they'd first arrived. *They're expecting to fight their way home.*

No one said a word towards what they thought would be found on the roads to Endlight, but it was there in the way the guards moved. The subtle adjustments of steel and straps. The checking and rechecking that their weapons were close at hand. Even the wary manner in which they glanced at the gates.

Thad, also bedecked in armour and already astride his shaggy mount, halted before his father to give the count a nod. "They are ready to depart when you are," he said.

"What's this?" Lucias asked as he descended the stairs to join them. "Leaving without even a goodbye?"

"Not at all, my lad." Farris' eyes sparkled with a sort of secret amusement. He hugged his lord, almost lifting Lucias off the ground. "We didn't want to tear you from your lady's lecture." The count faced her, his arms wide open, and embraced her before she could refuse.

Clara stiffened, expecting him to do something highly inappropriate and was surprised when he tenderly patted her back.

"You be gentle with him," he whispered in her ear. "The lad hasn't been shown much compassion."

Her cheeks burned as if freshly slapped. How much had they heard?

Giving her another pat, Farris stepped back to waggle a bony finger under her nose. "Don't you go hurting your pretty voice with all your yelling." Winking, the count escorted Brenna to the carriage. He inspected the courtyard as his wife-to-be stepped inside. "We appear to be man a short."

Thad glanced up from the gauntlets he was adjusting. "Yes, Sean is no longer with us."

Clara swallowed, her heart suddenly racing as memory dredged up the guard's attack. *Sean*? Hard to think the man who'd tried to rape her had a name. She didn't even want to believe he'd been human.

"Oh?" Farris' bony hand fell to his sword hilt and toyed with the tassel. "Defected, has he?"

She caught the flicker of the mounted lord's green eyes glancing her way. "Actually, Lucias had him defenestrated."

The count's grey brows nearly reached the top of his head. "*Truly*?" He swung to face Lucias and, at first, Clara thought Farris would demand an explanation. "I do hope he wasn't too much trouble for my lord to clean up."

Lucias bowed his head. "Nothing my servants couldn't handle."

Farris peered at him, seemingly considering enquiring

further then deciding against it as he also lowered his head. "Well, we best be off. Long road to travel and all." The count rested a foot on the carriage step. "And you'd be best to bear in mind what I said, my lady," he called before disappearing into the gloom, the door closing behind him.

Clara watched the carriage and its armed escort trundle out onto the Road. The massive gates swung shut as they slipped from view. *This is it.* She was right back where she started. Alone with Lucias and his men.

Why did the thought no longer seem quite so bad? The world certainly held worse fates, which the Goddess could bestow upon her if she so wished. But this?

Clara glanced over her shoulder to find Lucias ascending the stairs, his hands clasped behind his back. *A chance.* It was all he claimed to want. A single chance to prove he could make her happy. *My lord, you are a fool.* He was to die soon, he should've been breeding like crazy. Had he not confessed to having no time for courtship? *He would've wooed me.* Was it not what he'd professed? Only the Goddess knew what he thought he was doing to her now. *If he'd the months to spare.* How many more days were left to him?

"Clara?"

She blinked, torn from her musing by his gentle voice.

Lucias had halted at the top of the stairs and was staring down at her, his brow furrowed.

Straightening her back and holding skirts high, she trotted up the steps. "You mentioned lunch?"

One corner of his mouth curved upwards. "I did, didn't I?" He took up her hand, tenderly pressing it to the crook of his elbow. "Let's see what the kitchen has to offer."

CHAPTER TWENTY

The massive door swung open at a gentle push. Clara halted, mindful the next move she took could easily become her last.

Lucias *had* left her side upon reaching the kitchen to spend the rest of the day in the training grounds. She hadn't bothered him then and she felt embarrassed to be doing so now. Especially dressed in the little she wore.

No sword lashed out to greet her. She took it as a sign to be wary. Was Lucias expecting her? Had someone else besides Tommy seen her heading towards his chambers? She peered into the room.

Lucias stood by the fireplace, half-dressed and with his back to the door, leaning a hand on the mantle.

The twitch of his upraised arm was all he gave as she walked into to room. "What is it?" He tipped his head back to drink. Firelight glinted off the glass in his hand.

Trembling, she swallowed the sudden unease clogging her throat. She'd come this far. Now to take the final step. "I've made my decision."

He straightened as she spoke, finally turning to face her. His mouth dropped open, a question touching his lips. Nothing came out.

She could almost feel his gaze raking her body, taking in the dressing gown and nightdress she wore under it. The answer to his unasked question, and her intentions, could've been no more obvious than if she had come to him naked. She already felt as if she bared far too much.

Lucias set down his glass and strode to her side. "Are you certain of this?"

Her stomach quivered at the words. No, she wasn't certain. She could never be *certain*. What choice did she have? *I could say no.* However, if she told him the truth, then the kingdom would most definitely fall. Death. Chaos. Her once beloved home in ruins. All because of her pride. "I am." At least this way, she could give the kingdom a chance.

His hands ran over her shoulders, his fingers sliding beneath her dressing gown. His touch warm against skin that had chilled during the trek from her chambers. "You know you can't go back once we have done this." The first layer between him and her slipped off to pool at their feet. The subtle chill of the room pricked at her bare arms. "She will hunt you forever if she gets wind."

Clara nodded, puzzled. She came to him, nearly naked, and he tried to dissuade her? Was this not what he'd wanted from the beginning?

She searched his face for something that would help her understand, at last catching the suspicious doubt lurking within his deep brown eyes. "Anyone would think you had changed your mind." Her gaze dropped to the sword still belted around his waist. Should she dare try to remove it? Her fingers twitched then stilled. "Do you not tire of always needing a weapon at your side?" she asked, hoping to divert him from any more questions.

"Hmm?" Lucias followed her downward gaze and touched the heavy brass buckle. "To be honest, half the time I forget it's still on." His eyes lifted, narrowing at her as he sucked on his bottom lip. "If you are certain..." he whispered, his breath a shuddering rasp. "Come." Taking up her hands, he led her to the bed, where he seated them both on the edge. "Clara, I..." His fingers slid under her chin, softly coaxing her head upwards.

Her lips parting ever so slightly, she waited for what

would come next. She'd never been kissed before. Kissing led to other things and her father had been far too protective of her to allow either to happen to his unwed daughter.

Sighing, Lucias pushed her back. "You're not ready for this. I can see it on your face."

She glanced away from his piercing gaze. Neither of them was wholly undressed and already her cheeks felt afire. "You've not the luxury of waiting until I am," she mumbled.

"Wh—"

Clara pressed a finger to his lips, stilling whatever words he wished to say. If she let him speak another word, then her resolve would waver. "You need to sire an heir." She leant against him, the bare skin under her touch warm. "The kingdom needs your child."

By the light of the fire, she saw his jaw tighten. "The kingdom."

"I can give you that babe."

His face darkened further. "So that's all this is about then?" He lunged forward with frightening speed, flattening her onto the bedcovers. A single hand wrapped about her wrists and pinned her arms above her head. "Yes, the *kingdom* needs my heir," he snarled. "Do you think it wouldn't be easy enough to get one? I could have forced the task upon you." Her nightgown slid up her legs, stopping as the hem reached her thighs. "I could've done the deed the first day you were here."

He jerked upright a little ways. The jingle of metal spoke of his belt unbuckling. A leg slipped between her knees, parting them with a gentle nudge.

The pounding of her heart filled her ears. She was well aware he could force her, whether through magic, as his father had done with Lenora, or through more mundane means. *Like right now*. He had settled firmly between her legs, his bare waist sitting just above her knees. It wouldn't take much for him to complete the deed. Rumour told her of how it was done. A few deep thrusts and... *Rape is rape*. His own words. She prayed he remembered them.

Lucias leant over her, a monstrous shadow framed by the firelight. "I don't think you quite understand how badly I've yearned for this, Clara, for *you*." Heat rolled off his bare skin. It burned through the thin cloth of her nightgown. "But is this what *you* want?" he breathed. "Do you truly want me to take you here and now? To fill you with my child?" His free hand caressed her cheek, sending a chill jolt through her gut. It pooled there, slowly growing warmer. "Do you *want* this?" He inched forward, pushing her legs further apart.

She shuddered, the sudden ache in her chest clashing with her fear. *I don't know.* A part of her screamed to say yes. Another part, spearheaded by the piece of her that still recalled the chill avoidance of her would-be rapist, just screamed. "I—" She tried to close her legs, a whimper escaping her lips as her knees met resistance in his strong, warm flesh.

Clara squirmed, trying to find purchase on the bed to haul herself free. Her shins scraped against the supple leather still encasing the thighs of another. Had he not... But she'd heard a buckle and yet... He was still clothed!

"Shall I tell you what I *don't* want?" he muttered, the breath of his words hot in her ear. "Let's start with your pity. Do you think *I* want to be remembered like *this*?" He thrust his hips forward. Leather rubbed against her thighs and drew a trembling gasp from her lips. Shaking his head, he released her arms and stood back. "No," he murmured. "You will *not* offer yourself to me because you *pity* me."

Clara sat up, hastily brushing her nightgown back down. Clutching her knees to her chest, she watched as, his back to her, Lucias retrieved his sword and the belt it hung from. The only item he had removed. "Then what do you want?"

He straightened in silence. "What I can't have," he whispered, the words all but lost to the jingle of metal and the faint crackling of the fire. The glitter of an eye was all she saw as he glanced over his shoulder. "For you to come to me."

"But I did."

"Because you wanted to?" He swung to face her, stilling the lie forming on her tongue. "Or was this for the *kingdom*?" A sneer twisted his lips. "Do you think me a fool? That I wouldn't question this sudden change of heart?" Anguish warped his face. "The last thing I wanted was for you to wake in the morning and regret this action or—and may the Goddess flay me to death if I even considered it—think I took advantage of you." His fingers raked through his hair. "What difference did you think this night would've made with what is to happen anyway?"

"It might have saved the kingdom," she mumbled.

"It would've cost you your life." He leant over her, his hands resting on the mattress either side of her legs. "If she finds you without your virginity intact, it would mean your death even if you hadn't conceived. I'm out of time, Clara. It seems I was when they brought you here and there's little point in you dying alongside me."

He sighed, the heat of his breath dancing down her exposed cleavage. "I was going to tell you this in the morning, but you might as well hear it now. A plain carriage has been procured for your passage to Endlight. It should arrive in the next few hours and be prepared to leave at dawn. Who knows, maybe you'll catch up with the count's entourage. If you do see them on the way, give my apologies to Farris and Thad, although I'm sure the former won't understand."

"A carriage?" she parroted, barely able to grasp the one fact. Her vision blurred as she tried to focus on his shadowy figure. "Y-you're letting me go?" Not once had she believed he spoke the truth of letting her seek out her own path in the world. To Endlight? Any closer to the border's edge and she might as well be in another kingdom. "You're exiling me." Of course he would. Nowhere *within* this realm would be safe after his death.

"Not at all, although do I strongly advise you seek to leave the kingdom entirely." He stood up, his shoulders stiff and square. "Several kingdoms away would be more prudent. The area around Endlight is usually guarded by nomads, so the path through there should be the safest. If you take the western roads after crossing the border, you'll stand a better chance of evading the advancing troops. They *should* stick to the caravan trails, although I cannot guarantee it."

West? "But—" Where could she go after leaving the border city? *In a plain carriage.* Like those from the village? Riding in one of them, she could be mistaken as the daughter of some well-to-do merchant. Except... "Travelling beyond Endlight will put me under the eye of Ne'ermore."

Lucias sat beside her, slowly nodding. "The safest city in the world."

Her brow lifted. "Safe?" But, of course, the city had never been breached. In an unmarked carriage, bearing naught but herself as cargo, she could slip straight through the gates. "For anyone?"

"Everyone but me." His smile was small, almost apologetic. "You won't be taking the journey alone. Tommy and Gettie will be travelling with you and I've made sure you'll have enough money to settle wherever you wish."

"Gettie?" she echoed numbly. "Why would you send the Gutter of Neardim with us?" Would the woman not go mad like the others once released?

He shook his head and chuckled. "Did you never wonder about the men she'd earned her title on? About what they'd done to deserve it?"

"Not exactly." The old stories certainly didn't touch on the nature of the slain men beyond their gruesome deaths. Often, they were explained as hapless victims whose only crime was being in Gettie's path. "Weren't they merchants?"

"You could say they were." Lucias scrubbed at his chin, the dull scrape of fingers over unshaven skin loud in the chamber's tomb-like silence. "Although you could also say they ran a rather exclusive trade."

Clara frowned. Neardim was on the western border.

There would've been a large number of skirmishes back when Gettie was young. Not like the wary peace they had now with the southern and western realms. However, such battles became an open market for slave traders. Their men would slay the kingdom's men and, in retaliation, the kingdom chose to imprison theirs. "They traded in prisoners? Wasn't it common along the borders?"

"Not prisoners. At least, not one's I'm aware of. They were a little more select."

"Women?" Such atrocities also weren't unheard of. Although reports of such happenings generally came from the east or the ports where women fought alongside their men.

"Closer." Silvery-blue light flashed in his eyes for a heartbeat. "They took children. More specifically, *girls*." His refined, and oddly handsome, jaw twitched. "From what I was told by my father, the men took Gettie's baby sister. I cannot say what exactly happened to the girl, but she..." He frowned and shook his head with a blustery sigh. "She died and, in seeking her vengeance, Gettie earned her unfortunate moniker. By the time the truth was discovered, my grandfather had already taken her soul and, once taken, it cannot be returned. I should know; I tried."

Sometimes innocent people get unjustly punished. Those were the words he'd spoken upon her asking about his soul-stealing power. He'd tried to right it and could not.

Clara thought back to the conversations the lord and servant had, to the way he treated the woman compared to the others. It'd been softer. Heavy with the knowledge she didn't belong here. *Just like Tommy.*

She could even see the reasoning in letting the old women travel with them. If he couldn't free her whilst he still lived, he would do so in death. And, should they happen across any sort of trouble on the way, Gettie could protect them.

Clara was no longer certain she wanted to leave. The last few days had shown her a side of Lucias she hadn't expected to find. Where she thought he threatened rape, he'd meant freedom. Come to him in her own time or leave with the new moon. Those had been her choices. There had never been any others. And when she'd found herself defenceless, in need of rescuing, he'd been there to save her. Little of her original assumptions of him were true.

"You should go." The doors parted without a sound as he stood. Her dressing gown rose from where it lay in a crumpled heap on the floor, drifting across the room to lay beside her.

Clara gathered it up and slowly wrapped the thin fabric around her shoulders. Even without looking up, she could feel him watching her dress. It was strangely exciting to know she was the sole focus of his attention. "So this is it, then?"

Lucias gave a stiff nod.

This is how he says goodbye? She finished tying the front of the dressing gown shut and drew herself up. "Will I see you in the morning before I depart?" Regardless of how he felt on the matter, she didn't want them to part this way.

He pulled away from her, his shoulders hunched. "It is probably best if we do not," he replied, his voice hoarse. "I may end up changing my mind." His laughter, cold and mirthless, echoed into the dark corners. "In fact, I think if you do not leave now, I will end up making you mine."

Was it not why she'd come here to begin with? Blushing at her forwardness, she sidled closer to him. "If I am to leave before your mother arrives, would it not be better if I did so with there being a chance of an heir?"

"No." He advanced on her, his eyes glittering with flecks of silvery-blue light. "She would hunt you forever." The words came rushing out in coarse whisper. "I could not let you go knowing that to be your fate. It is the only thing stopping me from taking you now, whether you be fully inclined or not." Standing in the full light of the fire, his bare chest heaving with each breath, he resembled some hungry beast straight from a fairytale.

Clara shook at the sight, uncertain whether or not fear

drove such tremors. She stepped back, trying to think beyond the glowing creature before her, and found herself pressed against the leather chair.

Lucias jerked her closer, a gasp exploding from her lips as he crushed her to him. She pushed against the firm bulk of his chest to steady herself. His fingers wove their way through her hair.

Unbidden, her head tipped back. The quick rasp of his breath bathed her lips in its heat. Closing her eyes, she clung to him. Willing. Waiting for him to claim even this small part of her.

"Just leave," he breathed. His hands left her head, sliding down her neck and off her shoulders. "Please, before I wind up doing something we'll both regret." The silvery-blue light had left his eyes, but the stark hunger remained. It burned through her mind, crying out to be sated in her flesh. To know her as only a lover could, to bask in the paradise of such discovery. And to fill her with him.

Clara shivered, suddenly cold and empty. Hugging herself, she stumbled across the room. Behind her came the dull thump of a body. She paused in the doorway. Looking back, she saw him hunched in the chair, his fingers digging into the fallen mass of his hair. "Lucias, I—"

His head snapped up, the face it bore was one of disfigured agony. "Get out!" The words echoed through the room, blasting into her ears over and over.

Clara flinched, jumping back as the doors shook, then slammed shut. She blindly stared at the dark wood. What had she been thinking? *I thought it was the right thing.* Let him have her for one night and give the kingdom a chance. She hadn't counted on him refusing her. *And he's sending me away.* There was still a little time left to him and he was giving it up. *To give me a chance.* It was exactly what she'd been trying to do with him.

Only she was too late to change his mind this time.

CHAPTER TWENTY-ONE

*S*omething poked her in the ribs, its full strength muffled by the thick blankets. *Just a little longer.* The prodding moved to a shake of her shoulder. Groaning, Clara rolled onto her back. Through the crack between her lids, she caught the dark shape of a person leaning over her.

Lying completely still, she carefully inched her hand under the pillow. Her fingers wriggled beneath her head in search for the carving knife she'd hidden there before going to sleep. Nothing? It couldn't be gone. She stretched a little further, worked her fingertips along the handle until she could close her hand on it.

She lunged for the figure, the knife blade extended before her.

The knife was wrenched from her hand. It hit the floor with a tinny clang. The man pushed her back onto the mattress. His hand clamped over her mouth, muffling her cries.

Clara fought the surprisingly strong grip. The man had a leg on either side of her, pinning her beneath him with the blankets. Out the corner of her eye, she caught the glint of candlelight running down the sharp edge of a sword, held at the ready in his other hand.

"Hush," Lucias breathed into her ear. "It's just me."

She stilled her thrashing, although her heart continued to pound wildly. As her vision adjusted, she made out more of his face. What was he doing sneaking into her chambers?

But I locked the door. How had he gotten in?

She rolled her eyes to peer at the dark curtains still ringing much of the bed. How long had she been asleep?

Lucias released her and stepped off the mattress. "Get up." The blankets flew off to one side at a flick of his hand, letting the cool air dig into her skin. "You have to leave."

Rubbing at her arms, she inched her way to the side of the bed. From where she sat, the dressing table's mirror showed the black expanse of curtain shielding the windows on other side of the room. Dawn would be some time in coming. "Now?"

"Yes." Lucias strode to the open door. Pressing his back to the wall beside the doorway, he stared into the darkness beyond as if expecting to be struck down where he stood. "Get dressed and make for the stables." He glanced over his shoulder, his lips twisting with impatience. "*Now!*"

Clambering out bed, she gathered her clothes. Forsaking the heavy gown, she pulled the thick shift over her nightdress. "What's happening?" Clara asked as she tugged her dressing gown over the bulk and crossed to the door. Her heart near stopped as he faced her.

She could see the answer in his eyes. The haunting fear.

They're here. His mother and the barbarian who was meant to slay Lucias. If the pair where not yet at the gates, then they were awfully close. "But we're safe, aren't we?" The Citadel had never fallen since its creation. In all the centuries of fighting, the kingdom had never been conquered. But this... this was striking at the heart, where no army had ever reached.

"For now." Lucias grabbed her wrist. He dragged her down the stairs, the patter of her bare feet on the stone echoing above the tap of his boots. "They haven't yet gotten in, but it can't be much longer." They entered the hallway. It stood empty. "I've sent Tommy ahead to the stables. Gettie should meet up with you there. Come." Gesturing with his sword, he set off down the hall.

Clara jogged beside him. Tommy and Gettie were accounted for. No doubt the rest of the Citadel's inhabitants would be left to their own devices, guarding for now and... Whatever they wished afterwards. *When Lucias is dead.*

What if he wasn't here when they arrived? No one said the Great Lord had to reside in one place. He could flee the Citadel and live another day. "What will you do?"

He slowed. "Me?" The lump in his neck bobbed as he swallowed. "I plan to use myself as a distraction. Lead them away from the gate and..." He gave the walls the best inspection they'd had in years. "...live long enough."

She grabbed his arm, halting them. "You don't have to die here."

Those dark eyes, heavy with grief, stared at the hand upon his upper arm, then at her. He smiled. "It's better this way. The kingdom will recover, eventually. Although her people will be under Ne'ermore rule by then. They'll adapt. Common people are surprisingly good at it."

Clara shook her head. By the time peace reigned again, much of the kingdom and her people would have suffered. *Anything* would be better than letting him die. Why had she not seen it sooner? Perhaps... "I could help." The barbarian was only a man. Men died every day. A well-placed crossbow bolt and so would he.

A boom ran through the floor. Lucias stared at her, his eyes widening. He'd heard it too. *Time's up.* They were at the gates. Nothing left now but to flee or die.

Lucias ran down the hall. She raced after him with her skirts held high. He suddenly veered off through a door. She followed him beyond the wooden panel and found herself standing at the top of a narrow stairway she never would've guessed had been there. *Secret ways.* Clara knew there would be. Was there a hidden way out after all?

She trotted down the steps, staggering and halting just shy of bumping into Lucias in the dark. He grasped her hand, leading her ever downwards and out into the hallway beyond.

Keeping his sword raised before them, Lucias led the

way along the corridor, their creeping footsteps muffled by the carpet.

He stopped at another door. Like the first unexpected stairway, this door appeared to be no different to the countless others pock-marking the walls. She thought if secret passages were anywhere, then they ought to be accessed by pressing a loose brick or some other canny mechanism, not via a simple door. How many secret ways through this fortress had she walked by without even suspecting they were there?

A mournful, groaning rumble echoed through the halls.

Clara froze. It had to be to be the gate falling. The shell had been breached, leaving the heart bare for the final blow. What sort of man could bring down the front gates of a fortress?

She glanced down at the hand still holding hers. It trembled. She squeezed his fingers. Rough, strong and terribly afraid.

"This way leads to the main stairway." Lucias took a deep, shuddering breath and, with the sharp tug of her hand, spun her before him. "But first..."

The sword clanged onto the ground. He grasped her head, his fingers sinking into her hair, forcing her to look up at his face. A dot of silvery-blue light began to glow in his pupil, spreading outwards until it encompassed even the whites of his eyes.

Clara jerked back, struggling to free herself from his hold. His fingers dug into her scalp.

Words spilled from his mouth, harsh and alien. They poured into her ears, their exotic lilt neatly ensnaring her. Although she couldn't understand a word of it, an unbidden thought surfaced in her mind. *You shall not be bound by your fear.*

She blinked as the words settled back into the depths. What had she to fear? If his plan worked, she'd be on her way to Endlight and his mother would never know Clara existed.

His hands slid down to cup her jaw. Lucias stared at her, those dark eyes rich with regret. Then he sighed and released her to pick up his fallen sword. "They'll most likely begin looking in the courtyard." Taking a candle from the nearby sconce, he shoved the door open with his shoulder. Lucias trotted down the stairs, Clara following close behind. "When we get to the main stairs, I want you to hide at the top and wait until I've drawn them out of your path."

She misjudged a step and stumbled down the next few. "I could help you," she said, picking up where she'd stopped and he...

He'd done something to her. *He compelled me.* Just like the guard. But to do what? Fight for him? She was already willing to do anything to keep him alive. "Give me a crossbow and I—"

"And you could do what?" Lucias growled. "Think! The walls were covered in guards, all skilled in archery, yet he made it through the gates. He's *in* the Citadel! Do you think one little girl is going to stop him now? You probably couldn't even fire straight." They reached the bottom. Firmly grasping the door handle, he stopped to glare at her over his shoulder. "I will *not* have you risk your life in such a foolhardy attempt."

Screams came from the other side of the door. The sound of death. Clara felt her skin prickling with fear and the shudder-inducing tingle running along her spine, yet it seemed to have no effect when it came to her thoughts.

She glared at the back of Lucias' head as he glanced down the corridor. Was this his doing? Had he wiped her mind of emotion? No, it was still there. But whilst her body tried to freeze her where she stood, her mind was having none of it.

"It sounds like they're almost across the courtyard." Lucias stepped into hall, motioning her to follow. "Hurry! We must reach the main stairs before they enter, or they may end up trapping both of us."

Carrying the bulk of her skirts in one arm, she trotted

alongside him as they ran through the hallways. The clang of metal and the screams of dying men grew louder. She stumbled, despite the flogging from her mind, her legs still fought to obey the terror she could not feel.

Beside her came the swift, sawing gasps of Lucias' heavy breath. How she wished she could take the fear from him as easily as he'd done for her.

They reached the last platform of the stairway as the doors below opened. They swung gracefully on their hinges, hitting the walls with a booming shudder.

Planted firmly in the middle of the doorway was a man.

Clara sank to her knees and peered through the railing. She'd never seen a barbarian. There were plenty of tales, but she never believed them or the blatant exaggerations about these people from a distant land. Watching the man as he strode through the Citadel's main entrance, she wondered if the storytellers had not done enough embellishing.

He was massive, easily nine feet tall if not more. His upper body was bare, leaving to all the view of his war-hardened form. Muscles bugled from places she wasn't even aware muscles could bulge. In one hand, he bore a sword not unlike the one Lucias wielded. In the other hand, sat an immense battleaxe. Both dripped blood.

Movement on the edge of her vision pulled her attention from the hulk of a man. Lucias was already halfway down the stairs, his sword dangling in his hand. She expected him to speak, or at least shout. The sight of him silently marching towards what he believed to be his death churned her stomach.

The barbarian watched his descent. "You face your death with honour, Dark One," he said, his accent thick and rolling. "Not snivelling like your father." He flexed his shoulders and hefted each weapon in turn. "May your gods look upon this favourably." Hoisting his axe aloft, he rushed at the lord.

The metal haft hit Lucias' blade with a dreadful clang. Lucias staggered backwards, and then, as the barbarian's sword came up, leapt to one side. The axe fell again, and for a second time Lucias blocked it, although how Clara couldn't quite grasp. His sword should not be holding up to such blows.

Apart from the grunts issued upon each strike, they moved in silence with Lucias slowly giving ground to the barbarian. She'd watched Lucias sparring in the training grounds a number of times, more than she would want to admit to anyone, and he always attacked the guards first. But here, although neither sword nor axe appeared to be clashing heavily with his blade, Lucias flinched at each blow. He didn't try to engage the man, even when she thought he'd the chance. All he did was evade and defend.

Clara frowned as the axe struck his sword, the half-moon blade grinding along the sword's length. Lucias winced as he had at every blow. It almost seemed as if his head was hurting the most.

His magic. Did he use it to hold the barbarian back? All that power. Enough to lift a carriage, to close and open the Citadel's massive doors with a mere thought, and he still lost ground to the barbarian. *I have to help him.* Lucias had no hope of defeating the man alone.

Their fighting drew them away from the entrance. The path down the stairs stood clear.

Keeping a wary eye on the duelling pair, Clara crept down the steps. Beyond the doors lay the bodies of several men. She halted in the doorway and fought to swallow the acidic fluid rising in her throat. Not a one of the men were whole.

Stepping around the blood splashed on the stone, Clara steeled herself and bent over the bodies. There was bound to be a weapon amongst them. She searched through the remains, trying not to focus on what she was seeing whilst hunting for a blade or bow. Something she could use. Any weapon would suffice.

A shadow, wavering in the torchlight, fell over the bodies. "Just where do you think you're going?" A woman stood in the doorway. The wind behind her toyed with the dark fabric of the once fine travelling gown, separating the torn sections of her skirts. "You don't think I wouldn't be prepared for when his little mistress tries to escape?"

Clara had seen Lenora's face before in the paintings the upper halls, although the real thing was a decade or so older than the image; grey peppered the hair that once shared the same colour as the bird her ancestors named themselves after. Yet the elegance Lenora of the Raven Household carried had only matured with the years. "I cannot allow you to leave." Lenora raised the curved dagger she clutched in her hand and lunged.

Clara leapt towards the woman. She grabbed Lenora's wrist, pulling them back into the Citadel. Lenora staggered forward, tripped and fell onto the carpet. Clara spun, aiming for the exit. A warhorse stood in the middle of the courtyard. Such a massive beast had to belong to the barbarian. She'd flee on foot first before attempting to mount the creature.

She pitched forward, dropping to her knees with Lenora's arms wrapped firmly about one of Clara's legs.

Clara lashed out with her free leg, kicking blindly in the hopes of regaining her freedom. Her bare foot landed on flesh, her toes curling around what had to be a face. Something metallic clattered off to her left. *The dagger.*

Scrabbling across the carpet on her hands and knees, Clara dove for the weapon. Her hand landed on the hilt at the same time as Lenora's. She tugged the dagger towards her and the woman yanked it back with a might Clara hadn't expected.

Clawing and shoving, they hauled the weapon back and forth. Lenora, for all her years, was too much of a match to defeat this way. Where could the woman possibly be drawing such strength from?

Clara kicked out, struggling to find an edge. She yelped as her bare toes slammed against an armoured shin. There had to be a way to take the woman down. Clara had to get the dagger off Lenora if she'd any hope of freedom.

Balling her hand the way Lucias had taught her, she aimed for the woman's face and swung.

Lenora jerked back, releasing the dagger, and Clara's fist connected with the stone floor. Sharp, crackling pain lanced through her fingers. She screamed, cradling her bleeding hand to her chest.

The dagger skittered across the stone. She lunged for it, pawing weakly with her free hand. Her fingers touched the hilt, a little more effort had them curling about the leather. She dragged the dagger towards her, the blade scraping along the stone.

The toe of Lenora's boot planted itself squarely in her gut. The air whooshed out of her lungs. Clara rolled onto her back. Tears streamed down her face as she frantically fought to regain her breath.

Lenora stood over her, those sharp blue eyes surveying her handiwork. "Why, you're just some chit of a girl. How typical." The woman wrested the weapon from Clara's unresponsive fingers. "Forgive me, child." She lifted the dagger high.

Clara stared up at the blade. The dagger shook, metal glinting in the torchlight.

"No!" Lucias roared.

Lenora's eyes widened. Clara could make out the wave of magic distorting the air as it wrapped around the woman and flung her across the room. She hit the far wall and crumpled to the floor.

Lucias cried out.

Clara rolled over, her stomach clenching with the terrible suspicion she knew exactly what she'd find.

A foot of steel poked out Lucias' back, glistening with his blood. He swayed, held upright by the blade. Lucias grasped the sword hilt. His head lifted, his gaze locking with hers. His mouth moved silently, his lips forming what she could've sworn was an order. One word.

Run.

The barbarian pulled the sword free with no apparent effort. Lucias screamed anew and, clutching at his stomach, fell to the floor.

Clara rose to her feet, cradling her broken hand against her aching stomach. *Run.* Any moment now, the once amiable servants would regain their souls. *Run.* They'd begin taking their revenge on the land that had sent them to this living nightmare. *Run.*

Hunched, she hobbled towards the door. *The carriage.* It could take her far from here. If she could but reach it. *And Tommy.* Where was he? Had he fled or fallen?

A hand, thick and strong, clapped onto her shoulder. Then a voice, harsh and heavy, demanded, "What do you want me to do with the girl?"

Chapter Twenty-Two

Groaning, Lenora clambered to her feet. Clara shrank back against the muscled bulk behind her as the woman leant on the wall and glared first at Clara, then at Lucias.

Pushing off the brickwork with a grunt, Lenora staggered across the room to her son's inert form. She bent over him as if to check whether or not he still lived. Giving a most unladylike snort, she kicked him with such force it snapped back his head. "You filthy little worm." Lenora dealt him another blow, putting her boot into his gut.

Crying out, Lucias curled into a ball.

Clara lurched forward, held back by the barbarian's grip. She couldn't believe he still lived. *For now*. Not for much longer, surely.

Tears streamed down his face in an endless torrent. He raised a bloody hand in supplication towards his mother, only to have her kick it aside. "Please," he whispered.

"What's this? Does the mighty and *great* lord beg?" Once again, Lenora slammed her foot into his stomach. Blood coated her boot. "Speak, you wretched cur. Speak your last words!"

"Don't hurt her." He stared at Clara, his blood-stained teeth gritted and his face a mask of agony. "*Please*. Take her with you."

"Her?" The woman swung around to eye Clara. Her lips

curved beneath the wicked hook of a nose, she looked for all the world like a nasty little falcon searching for an excuse to bite her handler. "Of course, your sweet heir. Protect the girl, protect the child." She bent low over her son. "You think I'm going to let another *you* walk this earth?"

"I—" Lucias gave a breathless cough. Blood tinged his lips. "She's not preg—" The words were lost as he coughed again, then fell silent.

"Do you think me a fool, boy? You cannot lie to me." She lunged at Clara, her hands clawed like powerful talons. Strong fingers grabbed her shoulders, hauling her free of the barbarian's grip. "Why else would he keep you here, hmm?" Lenora shook her and Clara found herself clinging to the woman with her uninjured hand to stay upright. "How can you be here and not carry his child?" With a sudden, hissing gasp, Lenora stilled. "How..." Her sharp blue eyes narrowed, emphasizing her beak-like nose. "He speaks the truth?" she breathed.

"He does," Clara spat, jerking herself free of the woman's grasp. Her left arm stung. Had she cut it? "My lord has not touched me." But he'd been so close. Had he guessed this would happen? Surely, he couldn't have known she would need to speak of her purity without falsehood. Wouldn't be able to guess the woman may take his words for truth. Then why did Lenora no longer seem quite so adamant?

They've their own magic. It wouldn't be something capable of facing the Great Lords head-on. Could the woman tell when someone lied?

Lenora glanced down at her son. "But—" Doubt flickered across her face for an instant and was gone.

"What's the matter, my lady?" Clara said through gritted teeth. "Does it bother you to know you *didn't* give birth to a monster?"

The woman gave her a flash of teeth Clara assumed was meant to be a grin. "They're all monsters, girl." Lenora nodded towards the barbarian. "Even *him*."

Seemingly not hearing the lady's words, the giant of a

man lifted his axe and tested the weapon's blade with his thumb. "Do you want me to kill 'im now, my lady?" He jerked the same thumb at Lucias' inert form. His head cocked to one side as he waited for an answer and the bound tail of his ashen hair tumbled across his shoulder.

The fine arches of the woman's brows drew together. "No. I wish to be as far from here as possible before he dies." She motioned the barbarian back with a wave of her hand. "And he will be gone before this day is out. Nothing can stop it now."

Clara flinched as Lenora's gaze swung back to her.

"Bring her along."

The barbarian advanced, his dark blue eyes hard. He towered over Clara by a good three or four feet. Although his chest was bare and his armoured legs spoke of enduring many battles, he bore little in the way of scars. His thick, calloused hands closed upon her shoulders. His arms, each one thicker than her thigh, barely flexed as he hoisted her off the ground.

Her knee jerked as he lifted her higher. She whimpered as the joint struck something cold and malleable, but also as hard as metal.

A strangled grunt passed the barbarian's lips and she slid out of his hands as, clutching himself, the barbarian sank to the floor.

Clara hobbled back a few steps from the hulk of man, her right knee throbbing. Had she heard Lenora's orders right? First the woman wished to kill her, then they planned on taking her with them. What were they up to? "If you think I am leaving with you..."

Those eyes, burning with a cold fire, snapped open to glare at her. The words growled through his throat with such ire, even though she couldn't understand them, he could nevertheless only be cursing. He knelt, a hand creeping towards his belt and the heavy knife sheathed there.

Lenora stilled him with the faint touch of her fingers on his shoulder. She eyed Clara; the falcon had found something interesting in her prey. "Do you know what will happen upon his death?"

"I do," she snapped. "And once he takes his final breath, you'll have sent *hundreds* of innocent people to their deaths." And here she was, lingering in what would become the heart of the maelstrom. *I need to get out.* She needed to find somewhere safe before it was too late.

"And you still wish to stay?"

"I never said I'm staying." Truly, she'd no desire to wait for when the madness struck and the land succumbed to those it had punished. "I'm just not leaving with you."

The barbarian had gotten to his feet. He sheathed his weapons, although he surveyed the room as if expecting an attack. Clara didn't want to think on why the Citadel had suddenly become so silent. Were the servants waiting for the man to depart? Had she been in their place, she would have. "Are we taking the girl or not?" he asked.

Lenora tipped her head back and glared at Clara down her nose, making the hooked feature take on an even bigger resemblance to a beak. "No," she finally announced in a clipped and precise fashion. "If she'd rather die here, then so be it."

Clara folded her arms, biting her lip as her hand sharply reminded her it was still broken. She'd no intention of staying. Leaving with them would've ensured her safety from the suddenly free men, but she'd no idea how far she could trust either person. What if the woman decided it would be better to kill her anyway?

The barbarian grunted and, with Lenora close behind, marched out the door.

She quietly trailed after the pair, clinging to the doorframe of the main entrance with its shattered doors. The remains of the men who'd given their lives to guard the Citadel lay at its feet.

Clara watched the pair mount the heavy warhorse. No one appeared to stop them. Not even as much as a single arrow dared to sing out in defiance. The murderer had walked in and now he left without a single care as to what havoc he had wreaked.

The horse thundered across the compacted earth and through the broken maw of the Citadel's entrance. Beyond lay the sun-bleached road leading down Mount Winding. She could leave. Nothing would move to bar her way now. The carriage would be waiting in the stable yard. It would be easy to take Tommy and depart. *Forever*. She took a step towards the lure of freedom.

Her foot landed in something damp and sticky.

Clara glanced down to find she'd marched to the edge of the carnage littering the steps. Now the area had her full attention, she could see more bodies amidst the courtyard's gloom. Bile rose in her throat as her eyes adjusted and she identified halves and bits amongst the corpses.

She couldn't leave. To do so now would be to let the kingdom fall, to have this carnage spread across the land like a plague. She glanced over her shoulder at Lucias. He should have been dead. Would've been if his mother hadn't decided to stay the barbarian's hand. He'd still die if someone didn't help him. *Like me*. Who else would dare?

Turning her back on the open gate, Clara knelt at his side.

For a second, she could've sworn Lucias had already left the living world. Blood oozed onto the floor, soaking into the black and red threads to blend well with the rug. Then, as she rolled him onto his back, his breath, near non-existent, gurgled out of his throat. The sword had pierced his abdomen. A thin cut, but straight through.

Tearing her dressing gown from her shoulders, she pressed her hand to the wound. Warmth quickly soaked through the thin fabric. The flesh underneath her fingers bulged in an unsettling fashion. Clara wasn't entirely certain when it came to the nature of a man's body, but she knew it wasn't meant to feel like this. Had the cut been the other way, she was sure Lucias would bear more resemblance to the men out in the courtyard.

As it was, he'd die, but the death promised to be slow and, should he regain consciousness, painful. *The training grounds*. If it could heal a man's arm when cut to the bone, then surely it could mend this.

Hooking her arms into the hollow area under his arms, she struggled to move him. His weight dragged at her arms, growing heavier with each footfall. The carpet snagged on his belt and pulled at his boots. Her broken hand screamed at the strain, her other arm, dull compared to the fire in her fingers, grumbled its own opinion on the matter. Sweat ran down her back despite the cool air.

Her foot slipped and she fell backwards with a yelp, losing her hold on Lucias' limp form. He collapsed onto her legs, a groan issuing from his lips.

Hot tears filled her vision. She slapped the floor, wincing as the movement jarred her aching arm. *I won't make it.* He was going to die before they reached the training grounds.

Panting, Clara brushed the hair from her face. Her body ached with a deep weariness. She wanted nothing more than to obey its call and sleep. *I can do this.* They couldn't be far now.

She pulled her legs free of Lucias' bulk. Her ankle throbbed as she clambered back to her feet. *I can do this.* He'd die if she didn't.

Her heel tapped the edge of a step and, muttering between her teeth as she hobbled upwards, she hauled him over. The chill stone underfoot fast numbed her soles, but now there was no longer any carpet, his body didn't drag quite as much.

Yet each lurching, backwards step took more effort than the last to make.

Clara stumbled, catching herself before she could fall. Lucias slipped from her arms and onto the floor. In the silence, broken only by her panting, came the rapid thud of footsteps.

Holding her breath, she listened. The sound was getting nearer. Who was coming down the corridor at such speed?

Did they search for her? For their lord? Who amongst the criminals sent here wouldn't wish to see him gone?

She hobbled to the nearest door. It was unlocked, the room beyond devoid of life. They could hide and wait for the person to pass. Her heart hammering, she tried to lift Lucias again. Her arms refused to bear his weight any longer. Grabbing the collar of his jerkin, she hauled. Lucias didn't budge.

A shadow, tall and wavering in the light, appeared on the wall. Clara tugged harder. Her aching shoulders protested. What she wouldn't give to feel a dose of fear right now, then she might actually have the strength to move him, even if only for a moment.

The shadow merged into a figure. A small, lean man. He paused before resuming his advance at a slower pace. Torchlight picked up the edge of a sword. She planted herself firmly between the person and Lucias. If she was to die here, then she wasn't doing so peacefully.

"Clara?" The torches illuminated a face she hadn't expected to see. Although, in the flickering light, the sweet, simple boy she'd known for years had vanished.

Relief washed over her, near stealing her ability to stand. Tommy was alive.

He stepped closer. "They told me to wait so I did. Then the man came and the others died. I waited until he was gone, but you didn't come." A worried frown creased his gentle brow. "We need to go."

"No." They couldn't leave. Not yet. "You have to help me." She crouched by Lucias. His breathing seemed shallower than before. They were running out of time. "We need to reach the training grounds. Do you think you can get him there?"

Those soft brown eyes lowered to examine Lucias. He brushed a finger across the dark stain marring the jerkin. His gaze flicked to her and his lips pressed together. Sighing, Tommy handed her the sword.

The hilt tilted in her hand, the sharp tip glancing off the

floor with a jarring clank. Her hold on the worn leather slipped and the sword hit the stone. The clatter of its passage rang out along the corridor.

Tommy grabbed the older man around the chest and, grunting, started the task of dragging him down the corridor. Clara hastened to maintain control of the sword before the noise drew less trustworthy men. She followed close behind the pair, absorbed in keeping the sword free of the floor.

They were further from the training grounds than she'd hoped. Too far for her to have made it before Lucias succumbed to his injuries. Tommy set a good pace, faster than she could've done uninjured. How much time did they have left? *It'll be close.* Hopefully the magic would work. *It has to.* She couldn't bear to think on Lucias actually dying.

Clara glanced up as she walked by a pillar. Another sat a few feet away, followed by the dark expanse of the training grounds. *Not far now.* Torches burned on each pillar, lending the area an air of undisturbed solemnity.

Beside her, Tommy lowered Lucias to the ground.

Her body tingled as she padded onto the dirt. The aching in her shoulders diminished then vanished altogether. Her ankle and knee, having puffed up in the walk here, shrank back to their original sizes. And her hand...

She dropped the sword to examine the swollen, purple fingers. It still hurt, but maybe mending bones took longer than knitting flesh back together. Hopefully the magic was working faster on the stab wound.

Clara knelt by Lucias' head. His breathing no longer seemed quite as shallow or laboured. She plucked at the jerkin, lifting the congealed mass around the cut to see if anything was happening. The wound still lay open, but his blood no longer ran as freely. That wasn't necessarily the magic's work.

Tommy suddenly dove for the sword, bringing the tip around as he stood and faced the dark corridor. "Someone's coming."

Now she was listening for it, the faint tread of feet reached her ears. She twisted around, eyeing the weapon racks on the other side of the grounds. No use trying to make a run for them. She'd never reach the racks before the person got here and, even if by some miracle she did, there were few weapons she could lift let alone wield.

"May the Goddess forgive me," Gettie said, "I thought he'd be dead by now. Just what do you think you are doing, girl?"

Clara swung to face the old woman. Gettie stood in the corridor, a large meat cleaver in her hand. Her gaze bore into Lucias. He didn't seem any better. Were they too late? Had the Great Lord's old magic finally released its prisoners?

"The training ground heals people," Clara said by way of an explanation. She smoothed back Lucias' hair, damp with sweat. His body trembled under her fingers. "It *will* heal him, won't it?"

Gettie threw up her hand. "Pah! Doesn't the lad tell you anything? The magic feeds off the Great Lord's strength. Look around you, girl!" She flapped her hand at the walls.

Without the stark daylight, Clara easily spied a chain of glyphs encircling the grounds. They seethed with pale blue light.

"It's struggling to mend him. If he hasn't got enough left in him to aid it, *nothing* will stop him from dying." The woman waggled a finger at her as if Clara were an unruly child. "You better pray there's enough magic left to make him stronger or we're all going to be in trouble."

"The magic still works." Her hand continued to tingle. Upon examination, it didn't look quite as purple as before. "I can feel it."

Gettie's eyes narrowed. "If you're hurt, girl, then you'd best stay out of there and let the magic work on him alone until he's stronger."

Lucias' brow moved, pushing against her fingertips. A soft puff of breath left his lips. She could've sworn it was her name.

Clara lifted his head and pillowed it on her lap. "It'll work." She bent over his body, lifted the jerkin and checked the wound. It'd grown smaller, the flesh within no longer quite so angry-looking. "He's healing." She gently wrapped her arms about his shoulders, briefly squeezing. *He's going to live.*

"Yes," Gettie mumbled, marching along the line of pillars with her cleaver at the ready. "I can feel it."

Clara stared at the old woman, her face burning with embarrassment. How could she have forgotten that Gettie, although kind and as protective as any grandmother, was soulless like all the other criminals? "I'm sorry." With Lucias alive, the old woman's chance at being truly free died.

Gettie paused. "It is not your fault, child, anymore than it is his." She nodded towards Lucias. "Things happen the way do and not all mistakes can be undone. It is the way of the world and there's little we can do about it."

"But you never should've been punished." The woman had only been protecting the innocence of young girls after all.

Gettie stared at her with a vapid smile. "But I *did* kill them. Didn't have to. Could've gone to the authorities." She shook her grey-haired head. "Chose the other path. You may not think I deserved this life, and it may be true, but it's the only life I've had. No point in regretting it at my age."

Lucias bucked beneath Clara's hands, starling her. His head thrashed, rocking between her knees, then stilled. A groan rumbled through his throat. His eyelids flickered open, slid shut, then widened. "W-what... how?" He blinked up at her, frowning. "Clara?" he croaked. "No, you can't... You ca—" He gasped for another breath. "You must go."

Her stomach fluttered. He'd almost died and his first conscious thought was towards her safety. "Don't be daft." She calmly brushed the hair from his eyes, holding his head still when he tried to object. "I'm not going to go gallivanting down the mountain with the one-man siege machine out there." The barbarian could still return. Lenora must be searching for signs of an uprising. Would the woman dare another attempt on her son's life so soon after the first had failed?

"You can't stay—"

Clara laid a hand over his mouth. The lips beneath her palm were soft and warm. "Hush now," she whispered. "Close your eyes. Rest."

"I'm sorry," he mumbled against her fingers.

"Don't think on it. You can apologise to me later." There would *be* a later. She was certain of it. "Right now, you need to rest."

His eyelids slid half closed. "Don't leave me."

She took up his hand and squeezed the fingers tight. "I'm still here."

Lucias rolled his head to one side, his cheek resting against her thigh. "I love you," he whispered.

"Hush now." Clara smoothed the hair back from his face. He loved her? She couldn't have heard him right. He had to be delirious with the blood loss. Healing such a wound, even with the aid of magic, must take its toll on the body. And he was so pale. How much blood could a body lose before it was too much? *But still...*

She bent and kissed his forehead. *He loves me.*

Chapter Twenty-three

*C*lara stood in the main entrance, clean and freshly clothed. The sun had risen whilst she'd washed away all traces of blood from her skin. In the dawn light there wasn't much left of the aftermath, just a few pools of red staining the earth and a thin column of smoke rising above the Citadel's outer walls from a funeral pyre.

With the barbarian gone and Lucias' life no longer in danger, the servants had appeared in force. She watched them mill about the courtyard. Some were beginning to repair the damage the giant of a man had done. Most of the men were engaged in the grisly task of removing what was left of those who'd fallen in the initial attack. The rest scoured the mountainside for any sign of Lenora and the barbarian.

"Mistress?"

Her gaze swung to the scrawny form of Sirius cowering at her side. He glared up at her, the stone-flat eyes carrying the last, fading trace of anger. What had he originally done to warrant this punishment? *Something to do with young women.* Was it rape? Murder? Both? Although he once again sat under his lord's thrall, she was too afraid to ask him.

"The damage report?" He clutched his sad, little velvet hat, wringing it tighter when she didn't respond. "You asked for it to be brought to you?"

"Yes." Lucias now rested in the hands of those more capable than she. It had taken a little more persuasion in getting the servants to listen to her. Was she not the Great Lord's mistress? The servants had all agreed this was true. So, should they not heed her when their lord was incapable of issuing orders?

The general consensus there had been surprisingly negative, at least until Gettie had voiced her opinion. They were hers to command so long as whatever Clara asked for did not endanger the lord. And so the larger portion of the men had gone to carry out her orders.

Movement flickered on the edge of her sight. She whirled about, ready to deal with the threat.

As if the mere thought of the old woman had summoned her, Gettie trotted up the stairs.

Clara waited until the old woman had reached the top step and regained her breath. "Have the fires been put out?" Hearing the far end of the stables had been set alight during the fighting wasn't the worst shock she'd suffered this morning. *I never even noticed the smoke.* She should've at least been able to smell it.

Even Tommy, who'd been hiding in one of the stalls, hadn't known about it until much later. Now the boy was busy fussing over the animals residing within even though no living thing had been close enough to be in any danger. Dead things was another story. At least those the barbarian had cut down would've died long before the flames could touch them.

"Yes, miss," Gettie said with a jerky bob. Despite the lack of any obvious threat, Gettie still clutched the heavy cleaver and there seemed to be a crackle in the old woman's eyes Clara could not recall being there earlier. "They finished putting out the last one as I came up here."

Clara nodded as she descended the steps, the two older servants trailing close behind. The stones at her feet were still wet where water and soap had washed away the blood. Her mind shied from the recollection of the remains she'd seen earlier. Apart from Lucias, the barbarian had left no survivors amongst those he'd faced. *They died guarding us.* Pressed into this life against their will and dying with their souls bound to a man they must have believed would also never see another dawn. "How many men were lost?"

"About four dozen, mistress," came Sirius' snivelling reply.

They crossed the courtyard in silence. Her gaze fell on the gaping hole the barbarian had made in the Citadel's defences. "And the gates?" she asked of the pair. "Are they salvageable?" One of the massive iron-bound panels lay in the middle of the courtyard, its thick planks possibly concealing more bodies. The other half of the gate hung from a single hinge and groaned in the wind, threatening to fall at any moment. She'd warned against anyone lingering near it unnecessarily. They'd already lost far too many lives. *And all to one man.* No wonder Lucias had feared the barbarian's arrival.

"I'm afraid only the lord will be able to safely remove the gate, miss," Gettie answered. "And then we will require extra blacksmiths to fix them."

Clara halted at the base of the stairway climbing up the wall. "Hire as many as you think we'll need." The sooner they had a gate, the better she'd feel. *It hadn't stopped him.* How had one man managed to do so much damage? "But we may have to move the gate without Lucias' help." She wasn't sure how much it would take out of him to lift the gate free, but she did know he'd be too weak to attempt it for some time.

Giving her a bow, the pair scurried off.

Clara ascended to the top of the wall, her skirts held high. This section above the ruined gates gave the best view of the terrain. Alone on the wall, she leant against the parapet and stared out at the land stretching before her in a carpet of greens and browns. If she squinted, she could make out distant villages along the roads.

Men dotted the mountainside, a handful on horseback and the rest on foot. She didn't have much hope of them finding Lenora and her pet barbarian, but they searched for the pair anyway. If anything, she prayed their aimless wandering would be mistaken for something more sinister.

And there are the pigeons. Her gaze swung to where the Pillars of Endlight sat on the horizon. Two of the messenger birds had been sent there at first light. The border guards would be ready to greet the pair. She prayed they would at least succeed in bringing down the barbarian.

Clara stiffened. Someone stood behind her. No one else was supposed to be up here, which meant whoever stood behind her must have come with the intention of seeking her out. Was there any chance of one soulless man regaining his soul with their lord hovering in the edge of death?

Her hand slid towards the dagger wedged under her belt. The past few hours had given her a new appreciation for why Lucias always wore a sword, even in the heart of the kingdom. She'd come to a decision whilst she was bathing. Never again would she find herself without a weapon.

"You know," Lucias said, "I was under the impression they were to obey only *my* command."

She twisted to face him. His skin had not yet forsaken its pallid colouring, blood and sweat still caked his hair even though his face had been wiped clean. "You're meant to be resting." Who knew how much blood he'd lost before they'd reached the training grounds? *Too much.* She'd almost fainted upon seeing the trail his dragging body had left.

"How could I think of sleep when I know they're so close?" He stared out at the land. Yet a blind man could tell he did not see the mountainside laid out before them. "They could return at any moment. I must be ready."

Clara sighed. She'd hoped such thoughts wouldn't reach him until much later when she could be certain there was no threat. "Why did you compel me?" How many times had he done so without her knowledge? The fearless sensation had been quite chilling, but she wasn't entirely sure she could've done what she did without his intervention.

Lucias' attention snapped back to her. "I sought to ensure you wouldn't freeze in a moment of panic." His cheeks darkened and those dark eyes, which had once looked upon her with such unashamed fervour, suddenly would not meet hers. "The side effect was... unexpected."

Side effect. He saw his life being saved as some happy by-product? "How do you feel?"

His eyes became unfocused. Haunted. What had he seen whilst standing on the edge of death? His hand, still stained in his own blood, rose to his abdomen, the fingers caressing the pink scar. "Whole." His head tilted like some bewildered dog. "Why are you still here? You're free to leave whenever you so choose."

Yet here I am. Commanding his men as if they were hers. She could go. The carriage had suffered no damage. There was still money in the chest within. Sure, she wouldn't have Gettie, but she had not lost Tommy. "And who says I don't choose to stay?"

A black brow rose and vanished beneath his unkempt hair. "My mother will return once she realises I'm not dead."

Nodding, she mimicked his gesture of running a hand against the scar, her nails slipping under the dark hair covering his chest. Her fingertips hummed whenever she touched his skin. The flesh against her fingers was warm and firm. "Sounds like you'll need someone to stick around and keep you from dying."

A smile lifted one corner of his lips. "And you would fight to keep me alive?" He cupped her cheek, his thumb tracing along her bottom lip. "The Citadel is full of men willing to give up their lives." His hand fell, taking his smile with it. "For all the good it did them."

Her fingers danced up his chest to curl over his shoulders. She gripped the bare flesh and drew him closer. "I would *kill* to keep you safe." The kingdom may need him alive long enough to sire an heir, but she needed more. And to never see him hurt again, to protect him, even when he didn't think he required it... she would give him her life no matter whether or not it would mean her death.

She told him what happened with the barbarian and the monstrous woman Lucias had called his mother after he'd passed out. How would she have coped without the compelling keeping her fear at bay? *Poorly*. But she would never admit such a thing to Lucias.

His smile returned, as soft as those deep brown eyes. "To think, all it took was for me to nearly die." His hand pressed on the small of her back, gently drawing her closer to him. Their foreheads touched. "You are aware of what will happen if you stay?"

Clara closed her eyes, certain her heart would pound its way out of her breast. He felt good against her. Strong even when weakened. Her cheeks burned at the thought, the heat running so deeply she wondered if they glowed.

"I warn you now, I won't be able to stop myself this time." His breath brushed her lips and her skin tingled. "I couldn't have you here with me and not—" His lips met hers. Soft and tender, yet with a promise of a greater intensity lurking in the background, wanting to be let loose, waiting for the right time to pounce. For the moment she yielded to it.

She clung to him, uncertain if her legs would hold her without his support. Clara took a shaking step back, Lucias following. Her heel tapped the wall at her back.

His body trembling ever so slightly against hers, he pinned her between him and the parapet. Lucias' hold on her waist fell, his palm slapping onto the stone behind her, the arm trembling as it held him upright. His other hand snaked up her side to her neck, his fingers entwining themselves in her hair.

He gently coaxed her head back, his mouth seeking out her throat and sliding down to her collarbone, his unshaven face hovering between tickling and scratching, before he returned to her lips with a hushed moan.

Clara braced herself against the stone, fighting to match his ferocity. Searching for something to keep her balance, she latched onto his head, uncaring her fingers slid into the crusted mass of his hair or of how he smelt faintly of dust and sweat. His lips were silken magic, although it felt as if he desired to take all the air from her lungs. And, may the Goddess protect her, he was succeeding there.

Lucias pulled away, his breath coming in the same heaving gasps as hers did. Their foreheads pressed together, he leant heavily on the wall, arching her back. "Marry me."

She stared up at him, clinging to his shoulders, her head still swimming. Her mouth moved without a sound. No one had said marriage might be an option. *Because the Great Lords didn't*. It'd been Lucias who had told her. What new game was he playing?

"I gave you the choice to stay or leave because I needed you to want *me*. Not the lord or for the sake of the kingdom, but because of the man." His lips curved and a sharp blast of mirth snorted out his nose. "A man who, from the moment you came barrelling into his chambers, fell completely and utterly in love with you." He sank both of his hands into her hair. "*You* with your glorious, stubborn little mind and a will I could snuff out in an instant, but tread so carefully around for fear of losing you forever." He brushed her cheek, freeing her face of her hair, his fingers chill against her flushed skin. "If you *are* to stay with me, and eventually bear my son, I'd rather it was as my wife."

Stunned by the barrage of his declaration, Clara struggled to find her voice. *He loves me*? Yes, he'd said so earlier. Although, she doubted he was aware of it. And here he was stating it again. Along with the offer of marriage. "But the Great Lords don't marry," she whispered. Not since the fourth one had slain his own wife. Lucias' own admission.

Lucias grinned. Cupping her chin, he tilted her head upwards towards his mouth. "This one does," he breathed against her lips. "I never wanted to settle for a mistress and, for you... I would tear apart the world at your whim, you only ever have to say the word and I'll do it." He stroked her cheek. "I'll do anything for you."

Clara stared deep into those dark eyes and saw what she

silently admitted had always been there. What she'd been too scared to admit lurked within herself. The one thing he'd reached for and all this time thinking he couldn't have it. *Love.*

A small part of her remained sceptical. It buzzed in the back of her mind, turning over the same thought. Would he still want her after he'd taken from her the last thing she possessed?

Pressing her cheek against his shoulder, she hugged him tight. "I'll marry you." Tear apart the world for her, would he? She'd rather it stayed intact. There was only one thing she wished from him. "But I go before the altar as a virgin."

Lucias went rigid in her arms and her heart gave a pained lurch. Then, he laughed. It was the most glorious sound she'd ever heard. He spun them about and leant back on the parapet to stare incredulously at her. "I did say *any* thing. I was not aware there were conditions on it." He pulled her closer. "Shame on you." His forefinger gently tapped the tip of her nose. "Do you think I would disregard my own kingdom's traditions so readily? If you wish to wait until after the wedding then we will do so." Grimacing, he rubbed the back of his neck. "Although it might prove difficult after a time."

"No doubt," she mumbled. The way he looked at her when he spoke had the heat in her cheeks flaring anew. At least she had custom on her side. *No, that's not quite true.* The kingdom had grown haphazardly over the centuries, absorbing everything it could from the surrounding lands through whatever means. It meant some of the kingdom's traditions clashed from one border to the other.

Like with the nomads around Endlight. There, the men shamelessly took their brides the night *before* they were joined in marriage. "I'd have thought you'd be angling for a nomadic wedding." Or whatever they called it. After so long, the tradition had probably spread to the city itself. Had not both the count and his son married their wives in the same fashion?

Lucias chuckled, a mischievous light dancing in his eyes. "Oh, we will be joined the nomadic way. After all, we shall be married at Endlight as soon as it is safe to travel."

Would they now? He promised she'd be a virgin on their wedding day then declared they'd be bound in the nomadic style? She jerked back, the small of her back bumping into his linked hands. If he was so eager to be joined in such a fashion, then why not do so with a nomadic woman? "And just what is wrong with marrying in Everdark?"

"You don't think we can merely nip down to the village and hand the priest a few coins, do you?" Lucias drew her back to him. "I'll be the first Great Lord in centuries to marry the mother of my child." He smirked and ducked his head. "Well, the future mother. The nobility will need to be in attendance. Such arrangements take time and I would not ask a woman who is close to giving birth to travel."

She frowned down at the arms encircling her. Giving birth? *A noblewoman at Endlight.* Did he mean Thad's wife? How far along was the woman? "You speak as if it'll take months."

"Many if we are, as I fear, about to face a war."

War. With those who ruled over the neighbouring realms. Surely they wouldn't dare to invade. *Lenora would.* So would the other kingdoms if they believed their nightmarish Dark Lord dead, the army scattered and the kingdom already ravaged from within. They'd see nothing wrong with marching in to conquer an already weakened land. "They'll be stopped at the border, won't they?" She'd sent messages. The men guarding the passages would be expecting the pair. If his mother didn't reach Ne'ermore, then no one would attempt an invasion. "It won't take months to convince them the kingdom is still armed, will it?"

"It may, it may not." The suggestive curve of his smile set her cheeks ablaze. "Are we having second thoughts towards waiting? You know, what with you being here for so long, few will be inclined to believe you stand before the altar untouched."

"We'll know." Was their awareness not all that mattered?

"Indeed we will," he murmured. "I hope you won't be so cruel as to deny me everything beforehand." His hands slid up her back, inching them closer together. "There are ways we can please each other without risking your virginity and I mean to teach you some of them on the eve of our wedding. But until then... To keep my sanity." A gentle nudge on her shoulders tipped her against his chest. "Don't refuse me the gift of your sweet lips."

Clara tilted her head up. He pressed her nearer still, crushing her body to him. She wrapped her hands behind his neck and closed the final gap between them.

She stood, barely. Her uprightness all rested on his strength as the intoxicating waves of his touch flooded her senses. No matter how hard she tried to keep her head clear, each beat of her heart brought a fresh swell.

Puffing, he let them both come up for air before reclaiming her lips and once again drowning her in such a wicked, exhilarating and terrifying longing for more of him.

How did he expect her to survive months of not having any more than this? These ways he promised to teach better be good ones or she may just allow him a lot more than a kiss before they were married.

THE END

ABOUT THE AUTHOR

Born and raised in New Zealand, Aldrea Alien lives on a small farm with her family, including a menagerie of animals, most of which are convinced they're just as human as the next person. Especially the cats.

She discovered a love of crafting other worlds at the age of twelve when she first conceived the idea of *The Rogue King*. Since that that fateful day, she hasn't found an ounce of peace from the characters plaguing her mind, all of them clamouring for her to tell their story first.

It's a lot of people for one head.

www.ingramcontent.com/pod-product-compliance
Lightning Source LLC
Chambersburg PA
CBHW021010120726
47905CB00009B/2938